His
Seduction

ALSO BY DIANA COSBY

His Captive
His Woman
His Conquest
His Destiny

His
Seduction

DIANA COSBY

KENSINGTON
Kensington Publishing Corp.
www.kensingtonbooks.com

KENSINGTON BOOKS are published by

Kensington Publishing Corp.
119 West 40th Street
New York, NY 10018

All Kensington titles, imprints, and distributed lines are available at special quantity discounts for bulk purchases for sales promotions, premiums, fundraising, educational, or institutional use. Special book excerpts or customized printings can also be created to fit specific needs. For details, write or phone the office of the Kensington special sales manager: Kensington Publishing Corp., 119 West 40th Street, New York, NY 10018, attn: Special Sales Department; phone 1-800-221-2647.

KENSINGTON and the k logo are Reg. U.S. Pat. & TM Off.

First electronic edition: August 2013

ISBN-13: 978-1-60183-170-5
ISBN-10: 1-60183-170-6

First print edition: August 2013

ISBN-13: 978-1-60183-247-4
ISBN-10: 1-60183-247-8

Printed in the United States of America

This book is dedicated to my grandmother,
an amazing person whose memory I will always cherish.
I will never forget our time together in the mountains of Vermont.
I miss you, Grandma. I love you so much.

ACKNOWLEDGMENTS

I would like to thank John F. Campbell for his historical insight in researching the Scottish War of Independence. In addition, I am thankful for the immense support from my husband, parents, family, and friends. My deepest wish is that everyone is as blessed when they pursue their dreams.

My sincere thanks and humble gratitude to my editors, Esi Sogah and Alicia Condon, my agent, Holly Root, and my critique partners, Shirley Rogerson, Michelle Hancock, and Mary Forbes. Your hard work has helped make the magic of Griffin and Rois's story come true. Huge thanks as well to Joe Hasson, for brainstorming *His Seduction* with me and allowing the magic of this story to breathe life. A special thanks to Sulay Hernandez for believing in me from the start.

And, thanks to my mom and dad, my children, Eric, Stephanie, and Chris, the Roving Lunatics (Mary Beth Shortt and Sandra Hughes), Kathy Geiger—president of my fan club, Nancy Bessler, my family and friends in Texas, and the Wild Writers for their friendship and continued amazing support!

—God Bless Our Troops—

Chapter One

Scotland, September 1297

"Slay the English bastards!" an outraged Scottish laird yelled to the rebels packed within the great room of Dunadd Castle. "Cast their entrails upon the fields of Berwick to rot!"

A clan chief at the front thrust his claymore into the smoky air. "Aye, 'twould be justice for the cruelty served upon our countrymen. Too long have we suffered beneath the English king's greed!"

Lord Griffin Westcott, Baron of Monceaux, halted at the entry amidst the curl of smoke belched from a large hearth near the opposite wall. Ignorant of his presence, leather-clad nobles continued their furious shouts, all directed toward the man whom Griffin served— King Edward.

Griffin's hand brushed the empty sheath where his dagger had rested; he had been relieved of its comfort by the guard before he was allowed to enter Dunadd Castle. His English heritage and his pledge to serve the king inspied little trust.

As the vicious clamor continued, Griffin's escort gave a curt nod. "I will announce you, my lord."

"My thanks." Few wanted him on Scottish soil, especially since they had begun planning for war against his king.

The guard stepped past Griffin, and cleared his throat. "Lord Monceaux, King Edward's advisor to the Scots, seeks entry."

Silence reverberated throughout the room like a blast of thunder. The Scots turned, their faces congealed in loathing.

Griffin eyed each man and met his scorn with a challenging glare.

Feet shuffled and claymores thumped in their sheaths as the

warriors parted to reveal their leaders, Sir Andrew de Moray and William Wallace, seated upon the dais.

Griffin stepped into the cast of dim torchlight. A room's length away, he nodded toward the rebel leaders.

Recognition flickered on both men's faces. De Moray stood with the slow, controlled movements of a leader and a man ingrained with military tactics gleaned from training with Swiss mercenaries.

"King Edward sent you," de Moray said, his voice hard. It wasn't a question.

"He has." From inside his tunic, Griffin withdrew the two documents he carried. "Sir Andrew, I carry a letter of safe passage from the king as well as a letter from your father."

De Moray frowned and slid a doubtful glance toward Wallace. "A letter from my father?"

Wallace raised a skeptical brow.

"Indeed," Griffin replied. "Both are urgent. 'Tis of the utmost importance that I speak with you immediately—in private."

"Nay believe the treachery spewed, Sir Andrew," spat a burly Scot with a wild black beard, his hand clasped upon the hilt of his claymore. "Your father wrote naught. Well 'tis known over the Highlands that he lies imprisoned within the Tower of London, cast there by the English bastard!"

Agreement rumbled throughout the chamber, but Griffin remained silent.

De Moray folded his arms across his massive chest. "Let Lord Monceaux state his business."

"Aye," William Wallace agreed as he shoved to his feet, "but here."

Be damned. The offer Griffin carried would do naught but bolster the warriors' anger, a fact Wallace must suspect. *Fine, then.* He nodded to de Moray. "King Edward promises to release your father if you will take his place within the Tower of London."

Furious shouts boomed.

De Moray raised his hand, and the room calmed. "And if I agree to your sovereign's offer, where will my father be released, and to whom?"

Griffin eyed him, aware a brilliant strategist like de Moray would deduce that the king's proposal would be designed to serve English needs. "Your father will fight with King Edward in Flanders."

"I see." De Moray's face betrayed naught. "And after the battle is over?"

"You will both be set free."

A cold smile edged the formidable leader's mouth. "And I am to accept Longshank's words as truth?"

At de Moray's use of the unflattering name given to the king due to his height, Griffin understood that the rebel leader had made his decision. "I but deliver a bargain offered."

"A bargain whose timing I find intriguing," Wallace stated. "An offer made when your king sends the Earl of Surrey north leading an immense contingent to seize Stirling Bridge."

It was a military secret Griffin himself had passed to de Moray and Wallace a few weeks ago. He remained silent, playing the game both he and the rebel leaders understood, their roles defined by need: Griffin's, to protect his secret identity as *Wulfe*, an English noble aiding the Scots to reclaim Scotland. The rebels', to lead their people and reclaim Scotland's freedom.

"My king's decisions are his own," Griffin said. "As I stated, I but deliver a bargain offered."

"A bargain offered," Lady Rois Drummond repeated as murmurs of malcontent whipped like a feral wind amongst the warriors. She glanced at her friend Sir Lochlann, who stood alongside her in the shadows at the back of the chamber. "'Tis rot. The English noble is in bed with the king and well aware that once Lord Andrew is placed inside the Tower, he will never be freed."

"Aye," Sir Lochlann replied, his body tense. "And, surrounded by his enemy, 'tis lucky Lord Monceaux is still breathing."

Rois took in the English baron. Brown hair secured at the back of his neck with a leather thong accented high cheekbones, and the hard curve of his jaw framed an unforgiving mouth. His stance was that of a warrior, of a man unafraid. She ignored the shot of awareness rippling across her skin. Much she'd heard about King Edward's advisor to the Scots, his loyalty, his cunning. A man who, if nae her enemy, would cause her gaze to linger upon him.

"What are you looking at, lass?" Lochlann whispered.

At the hint of jealousy, she shot her longtime friend a teasing glance. "I was thinking 'tis too bad he is of English blood. Fine he is to look at."

Lochlann's grey eyes darkened. "The man is nae one to trust. He spews naught but the English king's treachery."

Guilt touched her. She was wrong to tease her friend when she understood he wanted their relationship to be more. "Lochlann, I was but—"

"Pray you Lord Monceaux nae sees your father."

"Why?"

Lochlann leaned closer. "Several months past, your father re-pledged his fealty to the English king. Think you if Lord Monceaux sees the Earl of Brom, he will nae expose him as a traitor?"

Panic slid through her. Her da, like many Highlanders, had re-sworn to King Edward as a ruse to keep his land and evade war. "My father . . ."

"Will be hanged," Sir Lochlann finished.

She gasped. "We must keep Lord Monceaux away from him!"

"Then you had best pray King Edward's man steps nay closer to the dais."

Rois glanced to where her da sat at the front of the chamber before de Moray and Wallace, but twenty paces from the king's man, a man who could ensure her father's death.

"What can we do to stop the baron from moving any closer?" Rois whispered.

Lochlann shook his head. "Naught."

Naught? She refused to accept his claim. Since her mother's death, her father had sacrificed everything to raise her with a tender hand. When he thought her nae aware, she caught the sadness, the loneliness he tried to hide. Whatever it took, she would protect him.

"Bring me the writ." De Moray's voice boomed throughout the chamber.

Nay, Lord Monceaux must nae see her father! Rois rushed into the torchlight and pointed a pale finger at the baron. "He canna be trusted!"

Against the smoke and stench of anger, all eyes shifted to her.

Heart pounding, Rois took in the powerful lords, Scots who knew her, nobles who would believe her claim. She caught her da's frown and shook her head, thankful when he remained silent.

"And why is that, lass?" de Moray asked from his seat on the dais.

"Yes," Lord Monceaux added softly, his hooded gaze raking her from head to toe, "a fact I would be interested to hear as well."

The anger in the English baron's deep voice swept her, but his eyes,

God in heaven, their intensity seared her like a whip. What reason could she give to convince those within the chamber he was unworthy? Thoughts battered her mind, but she discarded each.

An idea ignited in her mind. Nay, she couldna. 'Twas outrageous? As if with her da's life at stake, she couldna take the risk.

With her heart pounding, she faced the Scots. "A month past, the baron took liberties with me. After," she hurried, refusing to meet Lord Monceaux's gaze, "he gave me a false promise he would return."

"God's teeth, lass," Lochlann muttered. "Are ye daft?"

Nay, desperate. Several warriors cast curious glances toward Lochlann, but she didn't acknowledge him. She refused to endanger her friend or her father. She would endure the consequences of her actions alone. Rois took another step forward and started to speak.

But her mind went blank.

Her father's face darkened with displeasure as he moved in her direction.

What was he doing! *Stay,* she mouthed, and motioned for him to remain where he stood.

With a frown, he paused.

Her body trembling with relief, she turned toward Lord Monceaux, his expression that of a man confident in his decisions, who scrutinized her as if prey. Heaven help her, what had she done? Could she make her father understand her actions? Would he ever forgive her? However much she longed to look at her father, she kept her gaze leveled on the intimidating warrior.

After a long moment, Lord Monceaux's mouth curved with a confident tilt. "You were saying? I believe something about why I cannot be trusted?"

At the soft challenge of his words, her irritation trampled caution. Fine, let the braggart talk his way out of this. "And, shamed I am to say, this man has left me with child."

Griffin stared at the woman in disbelief. Against the wash of torchlight, a tumble of chestnut hair embraced the sweep of her pale cheeks, and she had full lips that any man would desire. But it was her eyes that held him, eyes as green and enchanting as the fields of Scotland.

He stiffened. Her beauty mattered naught.

Griffin assessed the room, stunned by how the nobles eyed him with violence. Did they believe her ludicrous claim?

His anger grew. How dare the chit sabotage a situation already dire!

From her sultry burr, he knew she was a Scot and that she understood his presence within this enemy stronghold placed his life in danger. Did she want him dead? God's teeth, never had he seen this woman in his life!

The warriors closed around him, shaking their claymores, their teeth bared in the smoky light.

Bloody hell, if he didn't quell her lie now—

"He does nae deny it," one man yelled.

Griffin rounded on the Scot. "Wait!"

"Nay," a scar-faced laird growled, striding forward, "'tis long past time for waiting."

At the man's words, the woman shifted. Face pale, she took a step back.

God's teeth, she was not abandoning him in this mire. The woman would admit her lie! When she made to take another step back, Griffin caught her hand, aware of every Scot in the room watching and waiting for the slightest error, for any excuse to kill him. God's teeth! In all his years of service to the king, he had never been foiled by a woman.

Nor would he be now.

"My lady," Griffin said, his words strong, clear of doubt, and, through sheer will, void of anger. "'Tis my deepest regret you believe I have slighted you in any manner." He raised her hand, and was at once irritated by the sweep of awareness, by the softness that lured him.

Anger sparked in her eyes. She tugged to free her hand.

Griffin held firm, lifting her fingers and pressing a chaste kiss upon her knuckles. Nerves darkened her impossibly green eyes, eyes a man could drown in, eyes that would make him beg. Bedamned. After her outrageous claim, he should feel naught but contempt. But he wanted her, damnably so.

"If indeed I have left you with child," Griffin said, "'tis honor I offer you." Eyes narrowed, he scanned the room, meeting the impenetrable fury of each Scotsman's gaze. Satisfied, he turned to the stunning woman whose hand trembled within his. "Before your peers, I will take you for my wife."

Her face drained of color, a reaction he'd expected. Well he understood Scotland's custom of handfasting, that once a pledge was issued in public and agreed upon, they would indeed be wed. Feeling confident, Griffin waited for her to admit the truth.

The growing concern in her eyes assured him that she regretted her lie. 'Twould be but moments before she declared her false accusation to all, and he could return to de Moray's decision concerning King Edward's offer.

Silence battered the crowded chamber, thick with expectation.

Rois again tried to yank her hand free of Lord Monceaux's grip. He smiled down at her, but no warmth existed in his hazel eyes. Could she fault him for his resentment?

Aye, Lochlann had asked her if she was daft when she voiced her assertion. Well, now she sat in a fine mess. Proof her mind was indeed muddled.

Shame filled her. Of all of the mischief she'd stirred over the years, naught had reached this magnitude. Why had she insisted on attending the meeting? And what of her promise to her da to stay in the shadows unnoticed?

Her father.

Thank heaven the men crowding around her and Lord Monceaux were blocking him from sight.

"Enough," her father declared. "Let me through."

Nay! He couldn't make his presence known! Rois met the baron's smug expression. Pulse racing, she nodded. "Aye, I accept your offer of marriage."

The room exploded with shouts of outrage and disbelief.

Rois took advantage of the baron's complete shock and jerked her hand free, slipping into the throng of uproarious men. Under the shield of mayhem, she reached her father.

"Lass, what in God's name have you done?" Lord Brom demanded, his words all but smothered by the din.

"There is nae time for the telling now," Rois replied. Breathless, she towed her father toward the side door. "Hurry. Once we are away, I will explain everything. I swear it."

Her father's weathered face darkened further. "Aye. But only because the business I had here is done. And by God you will be explaining everything, that I promise you."

Relief swept through Rois as they stepped outside. Aye, she would explain, that would nae be a problem. Convincing her father to procure an annulment might be a wee different matter.

Chapter Two

Amidst the shouts of anger and stunned looks, Griffin scoured the great room for the woman who'd crafted this chaos. He found naught but the fierce Scottish nobles eyeing him with a mix of grim satisfaction and resentment. Blast it, had he asked to be married? If one day he were to take a wife, he'd expected to at least know the woman's name!

God's teeth, 'twas a mess.

A mess delivered to him in the form of a fine- looking woman. But her pale skin and intoxicating eyes would not sway him. Once he found her, she'd regret her lies.

"Silence!" Andrew de Moray's voice roared over the irate warriors. The chamber fell silent.

A muscle worked in his jaw as Griffin faced the imposing man on the dais. However much he wished to end this farce the woman had created, for his own pride, he could never expose he neither knew the woman's name nor had ever seen her before this day. Worse, how in bloody hell would he break the news of his marriage—to a Scot—to King Edward? Or, for that matter, to his sister and the MacGruder brothers?

The MacGruder brothers. He grimaced at the thought of the extended family gained after his sister Nichola's abduction by the Scottish rebel, Alexander MacGruder, had tumbled into a marriage. Then there were Alexander's older brother, Seathan MacGruder, Earl of Grey, and his younger brother, Duncan, and their adopted brother, Patrik—all married and in the thick of Scotland's fight for independence. As was Griffin. Indeed, they would find humor in his plight.

Except, by the time they learned of the matter, 'twould be after an annulment had been procured. Caught up in helping the rebels to reclaim their country's independence under the guise of *Wulfe*, he did not have a wife in his plans at this time, and certainly not this woman, who would regret whatever had driven her to the insanity of her false claim.

"The handfasting is over," de Moray stated. "I will speak with Lord Monceaux on the matter, but later. For now, there are issues of import we need to discuss."

"Aye," a Scot near the front shouted as he thrust his claymore into the air, "including telling King Edward to stuff his offer of free passage for you to the Tower of London up his arse!"

Cheers broke amongst the Scots, removing a layer of tension from the great room.

Andrew de Moray raised his hand. "Lord Monceaux."

The rousing yells faded and every eye focused on Griffin. He nodded to de Moray, playing the role the crowd expected from an English baron and King Edward's advisor to the Scots.

De Moray scanned the chamber of battle-seasoned Scots. From the firm set of the leader's jaw, Griffin suspected what his secret contact would say.

De Moray raised his claymore in the air. "Tell your king to go to Hades!"

Against the curse-filled jeers at the English king's expense, Griffin stowed the writ of safe passage inside his tunic. Once the room calmed, he nodded. "I will deliver the message to King Edward that you decline his offer."

Guffaws echoed throughout.

"Bloody coated his words are," a nearby laird yelled. "The English have nae the guts of the Scots."

A pox-faced man nodded, and another, his brow marred by rough jagged scars, shouted his agreement as the voices of the Scots again rose.

Andrew de Moray sheathed his blade. "Lord Monceaux, I will take the letter from my father." With confident steps, he strode from the dais. A pace before Griffin, he halted.

Griffin withdrew Sir Andrew's father's writ, and handed him the rolled parchment.

With a steady hand, de Moray unrolled the letter. As he read the request penned by his father's hand, the page trembled.

Griffin understood the gravity of de Moray's decision in declining his father's personal request. If the rebels lost the upcoming battle at Stirling Bridge, King Edward would sentence de Moray's father to remain within the Tower of London until his death.

The scrape of parchment filled the void as de Moray again rolled the letter. "Lord Monceaux, stable your horse for the night. Once this meeting has ended, we will speak in private. Then, a chamber will be provided for you and your wife."

His wife? God's teeth, de Moray didn't expect him to remain married? No, his friend but made the offer for their audience. Once alone, Sir Andrew would aid him in ending this ludicrous arrangement with the chit.

"My thanks," he replied.

De Moray turned and strode toward the dais. As he passed, the nobles shifted their attention to the front of the chamber, where Wallace awaited the other rebel leader's return as if the mayhem moments before had never happened.

No, by their guarded looks, each man remembered, Griffin mused, but whatever their reason, they had decided to not pursue it further, which made little sense. They knew her, of that he was certain. The nobles within this chamber were powerful men determined to win Scotland's freedom. Yet not one had interceded when the stunning woman had stepped forward with the ludicrous claims, nor when he'd made the offer to take her hand in marriage.

Why?

If nothing else, he was certain her father was not present at the meeting. Had he attended, surely he would have halted the fiasco. Frustrated, Griffin scanned the chamber. He caught sight of the red-haired warrior who'd reached for the woman when she'd first stepped from the shadows and challenged Griffin's credibility.

The man turned. Eyes hard and furious met his. Malevolence poured from his gaze as if a dam unleashed.

Griffin held the red-haired man's glare without apology. Her brother? Lover? He seemed vaguely familiar. Had they met before? Whoever this Scot was, the man would offer him a knife in his gullet before sharing any information of the woman's identity. From his reaction, the man was as displeased by her actions as Griffin.

And, by the angry gazes cast his way by the Scots around him, nor would he find answers about the woman from any in the crowd.

The woman?

No, for now, his wife.

With one last scan of the chamber, Griffin left the Scottish leaders to plan the last few details on how to halt the Earl of Surrey as he led his massive English army north to seize Stirling Castle. Later, Griffin would meet with de Moray and contemplate how to escape this wedded muddle.

"What were you thinking, lass?" Angus Drummond, the Earl of Brom, demanded. The wash of late afternoon light, littered with flickers of dust, framed her father as he glared down at her in the stable. "Calling the king's man out? Questioning his fidelity in a chamber full of formidable Scottish leaders?"

Rois rubbed the back of her neck beneath her father's censure, the soft nicker from her mare standing at her side offering little calm. "I explained—"

"Explained?" he blustered. "To protect me from being seen by King Edward's advisor to the Scots?" Amber eyes narrowed. "And you do that by wedding the English noble?"

"You do nae understand."

Aged lines settled deeper across her father's weathered brow. "Right you are on that, lass. From the first I should have stopped you. Foolishly, I hesitated."

"Da, as the Earl of Brom, you are a man Lord Monceaux would recognize. If you had spoken out and he had seen you, he would have disclosed your presence to the English king." She fought for calm, to quell the churn of emotions rushing within. "With your re-swearing fealty to King Edward but months before, think you he would nae brand you a traitor, or order you hanged before your people to serve as an example for any who dare betray him?"

He grimaced, but didna argue.

Because she spoke naught but the truth. They were at war, and he was an influential noble who had gained the admiration of many Highlanders, a man they followed without hesitation. King Edward would nae turn his eye from such blatant rebellion.

Rois clasped his hand, wishing he could understand her fear and her thanks for all he'd sacrificed to raise her these past eleven years since her mother's death. "I love you, Da, and canna lose you."

Tenderness edged the stern lines of his face. "Lass, even if

King Edward learned of my change of loyalties, many months will have passed—if, upon Lord Monceaux's return to Westminster Palace, he is even informed."

She released his hand. "What do you mean upon his return? Why would the king nae immediately be informed?"

"King Edward sailed for Flanders before the end of August."

He'd left the country? It couldn't be. Her stomach churned as she realized the ramifications. "Lord Monceaux said King Edward sent the letter of safe passage as well as the request from Sir Andrew's father."

"Both written before the king departed England."

She shook her head, nae wanting to believe it was true. "How do you know?" Rois asked, her words but a whisper.

Her father's gaze grew shuttered. He secured the saddle onto his mount.

"Da?"

He checked the cinch, glanced over. "It matters not. You should have remained in the shadows as promised."

"But Lochlann said—"

Anger flared upon his weathered face. "Sir Lochlann is a fool."

"He was concerned about you."

Her father led his steed to the entry. "Sir Lochlann is a man whose concerns are for naught but himself."

An argument they'd had many times over. Her father did nae understand. Lochlann was a man of ambitions, a man unafraid to work hard for his goals. His methods at times might be a wee bit rash, but didn't her own often cause a stir?

Like now.

After her mother's death, Lochlann had held her when she'd fallen apart, listened to her as she'd rambled with the hurt of loss. And with the passage of time, he'd lifted her spirits beneath the weight of grief. They'd become close friends. With his unselfishness when it came to her, how could it be otherwise?

"But that is nae the issue," her father continued. "If Sir Lochlann had concerns about me being in danger, 'twas me he should have warned."

"Da—"

"Enough." Her father shoved his foot into his stirrup, mounted, then looked down. "'Tis growing late. We will speak more once we arrive at Kincardan Castle."

"What of the marriage?" Amber eyes slanted toward the keep where Lord Monceaux remained, and her heart jumped.

Her father grimaced. "An issue I will take care of."

Relief rattled against her lingering nerves. "My thanks."

Her father's brow furrowed deeper.

Rois remained silent. He was angry. Could she blame him? It wasn't every day within a room filled with your fellow lords a father witnessed his daughter marrying the enemy.

"Mount up. The sun will soon set."

She stroked her mare's neck. "Go, I will nae be far behind."

"Rois—"

"Please, I need but a moment. I will nae linger."

"See that you do nae." With a curt nod, her father turned his mount, urged him into a canter. Hoofbeats clattered upon the cobbled entry as he exited Dunadd castle.

Desperate for time alone, Rois waved the stable lad away and checked the mare's hooves. How could her father dismiss the severe consequences had the baron caught sight of him? Or believe a man loyal to the English king would withhold such a fact from his liege lord? Nay, Lord Monceaux would have revealed her father's presence.

Lord Monceaux.

A man to whom, by Celtic law, she was wed. A man she should fear. Oddly, she found herself intrigued instead. Foolish to find herself attracted to a man professed to be her enemy.

Rois stared toward the gatehouse her father had ridden beneath moments before. Beyond the massive arch of stone, distant mountains lay illuminated by the soft golden rays of the setting sun, the roll of the land of her ancestors, which her people now fought to keep. A land that, if the rebels failed to win the upcoming battle, might very well be lost.

With a sigh, she picked up her mare's reins. Over the years she'd had her scrapes with trouble, and had she nae always explained her way out of every predicament, if sometimes with a touch of aid? A smile edged her lips. Granted, marriage might be a wee larger dilemma than shaving Gordon's cow on a dare. Or the time she slipped Hart's-horn in Aleyn's soup that for several days had left him paces from the privy. But days after, she'd admitted to mixing the herbs.

Now, her father had agreed to help her disentangle herself from the English baron. Da was a smart man, held formidable contacts. With his aid, a solution would come. 'Twould be reckless to delay and upset him further.

She wrapped the rein around her hand. What if her request for an annulment was rejected even with her father's help? Rois lay her forehead against the horse's muzzle. "If this fails, what am I to do?"

"Go back inside and tell the truth."

At the baron's deep English voice, Rois whirled, panic slamming through her.

Hands on his hips, Lord Monceaux stood at the stable entry, his muscled body taut, the setting sun framing a fierce scowl. Anger savaged his face as he took a slow step forward like a wolf stalking its prey.

Hands trembling, she edged to her mare's side. "Stay back."

"From my wife?" Mockery wrung his voice.

Her throat dry, she shook her head. "My regrets. I could think of no other way."

Hazel eyes narrowed. "No other way to do what?"

Heaven help her. She had to convince him to leave. Now! "You are free to go," Rois managed with amazing calm. "I willna hold you to your declaration."

A humorless laugh sifted from his mouth. "'Tis impossible when a roomful of Scots witnessed our handfasting. We are married, my lady." He stepped closer. "I will have answers of why you claimed such shameful lies and invited this mayhem. Then, I will find a way to rid myself of you."

Despite her common sense, his words hurt. She angled her chin. "I meant you no harm."

"Your actions this day offer a different proof."

"I . . ." She searched to find the right words. He did nae know her. And as he claimed, her shameful actions were all he could use to draw conclusions of her character. She studied the fierce man, taking in the hard slant of his jaw, the firm etch of his mouth.

How would that mouth feel against hers? Warmth slashed her cheeks. How could she think of such an intimacy? Was she mad? One did nae find someone determined to throttle you attractive.

Shaken, she struggled for control. Nay, from his honed body and fierce stance, this was a man of war, a man seasoned in battle, and a man who didn't back down from a challenge.

A fact she'd realized too late.

At her silence, his brows slammed together. "You can explain here, or I shall haul you back inside the great room and you can explain to everyone."

Her heart pounded as she searched for a way to avoid such a crisis. "I am sorry."

"God's teeth, you will be." He reached for her arm.

With expertise culled from years of riding, she leapt on her mare's back and kicked her forward. Without warning, instead of racing away, her horse whinnied and half-reared.

Rois held her seat—barely. Stunned, she glanced down to find the baron holding her mare's bridle. "Let her go!"

Cold determination sparked in his eyes. "As you wish."

Before she realized his intent, the powerful Englishman hauled her from the saddle, then slapped her mare on the rump. Her horse bolted.

Locked within his firm hold, Rois squirmed to break free as her horse galloped beneath the gatehouse. "Have you nay sense?"

"No," he said, his words tight, "that is your honor."

She tried again to break free; he held tight. "Release me."

More frustrated than he'd ever been in his life, and irritated by the attraction that hummed beneath the surface between them, Griffin glared at the chit. "So you can run, disappear, and I never find you?"

She remained silent, the guilt on her face confirming her intent.

"Who are you that you dare stand before Highland lords and spew such blatant lies?" At the flare of panic in her eyes, Griffin used the strategy of his size, and backed her up against the stable door. "The truth."

Instead of explaining, she turned away, her small pert nose lifting in a defiant tilt.

"Look at me."

Her gaze remained lowered.

Without hesitation, Griffin leaned his frame flush against hers, too aware of how the soft contours of her body fit snug against his.

Shocked green eyes locked on him, and she began to struggle.

Ignoring his awareness, and the incredibly erotic sensations igniting inside when her body shifted intimately against his, he lowered his head to but a breath away from her face.

"Your name."

She stilled. Her lower lip wobbled, then her tongue slicked over its lush fullness.

A shot of lust speared him. He gritted his teeth. *Focus on the woman, on the answers needed.* But this close, with her scent of woman and lavender surrounding him, her soft curves pressed snug against his growing hardness, he wrestled with his hold on sanity. Did she not realize what her moving against him made him feel? As he caught her covert glances toward him he realized yes, she did, which blasted helped naught.

Her breathing grew fractured.

Griffin tried not to notice, not to be drawn to the tender softness of her lips. Failed miserably.

"Lo-Lord Monceaux."

"Griffin," he whispered, "'tis my name."

Eyes as pure as the fields of Scotland lifted to his.

"Say it." For an unexplainable reason, he wanted to hear his name on her lips, the soft roll upon her tongue as if a delicacy tasted. Yes, he had gone over the bloody edge.

A flush darkened her cheeks with each second they lingered, as her scent wove around him, destroying his good intentions to stay away from her.

"Say it!"

In an act of pure rebellion, she closed her eyes. With her face caught in a mix of shadows and whispers of the fading light, she appeared as if she was a fairy sent to tease him, a seductress crafted for his every fantasy.

A fairy? The long ride and the chaos of the day invited such absurd thoughts.

Except shimmers of light played off her smooth skin as if beckoning, inviting him to touch. Griffin tried to ignore the softness of her breath against his mouth, the silkiness of her skin against his own, or wonder about the taste of her full lips against his. A mouth that drew him, made him want. God's teeth, 'twas madness to consider. 'Twas . . . his wife.

Bedamned. He claimed her lips, needing to discover her taste, to learn if her mouth was as silken as it looked, to know if it fulfilled every dream it promised. Trembling lips gave beneath his own as he took, savored, then angled her head to take the kiss deeper.

Her body stiffened against his, a split second before she pushed against him to break free.

Shamed by his actions, Griffin pulled back. The paleness of her face and the fear in her eyes destroyed any lingering desire. But her taste infused him, invited him back.

"Never would I harm you," he whispered.

"As if you expect me to believe you?"

"You can. Trust me." Was he insane? Except, for an unexplainable reason, he found this woman's opinion of him mattered. He wished he could owe his need for her to trust him to his oaths as a knight. But something about her moved him, which made not a whit of sense.

As he stared at her, her expression of confusion crumbled to wariness, a potent reminder of their situation.

On a curse, Griffin caught her hand, hauled her with him as he started toward the keep.

She gasped. "What are you doing?"

He shot a cold look over his shoulder. "Taking you back to the great room where this mayhem began. God's teeth, there I shall learn the truth!"

Chapter Three

Nay! Rois pried her fingers against Lord Monceaux's hold as he pulled her toward the keep. If he learned the truth, her debacle of a marriage would be for naught and her father's life would be forfeit.

Her fingers slipped free. She bolted.

"God's teeth!" Strong hands seized her waist, tugged her against his hard male body.

Frantic, she twisted in an attempt to break free. "I will scream!"

He spun her around. Furious eyes narrowed. "None will stop a husband his right."

"Bloody Sassenach!"

"'Tis not I who stirred this up. And, my lady," he said, frustration crushing his each word, "if your disdain reeks for the English, why in bloody hell would you marry one?"

Rois remained silent. Never must he learn her father's name and his true loyalty to Scotland.

"Fine then," the baron stated, "if you cannot provide me with answers, no doubt I will find them with Sir Andrew de Moray, William Wallace, or one of the many nobles inside."

Never would any of the Scots tell him. 'Twas bluster. 'Twas—

Before she could disparage his threat, Lord Monceaux lifted Rois and laid her on his shoulder. Heat slid up her cheeks, and she shoved against his back. "I am nae a sack of oats. Put me down!"

His muscled shoulder bounced against the flat of her stomach as he strode toward the keep. "Give me your word you will not try and run."

She gasped for breath. "You are insufferable!"

"No," he drawled, "I am your husband."

"If you put me down, I will nae run. As your wife, you can trust me."

Trust her? Far from amused by her false words, Griffin set her before him. From the glint in her eyes, she was concocting a new plan. One he would ensure failed.

"Fine then, walk at my side." He shot a warning look. "If you again try to run, you will find yourself again over my shoulder—this time, until we are inside the keep."

Her lips tightened, accenting the smoothness of her skin, the flush creeping up her cheeks, and her full mouth begging for a kiss.

Bedamned! He started across the bailey, keeping her close at his side. He wanted naught but this entire mess over.

Halfway across the worn earth, the hewn doors of the keep swung open. Nobles who had filled the great room poured out. Several warriors glared at Griffin as they moved past. Others shook their heads at the woman. And he swore he heard several whisper condolences.

By the time he reached the doorway with his new wife in tow, Griffin's mood rivaled that of an irate bear. Frustrated and ready to end this mayhem, he entered.

A guard positioned near the entry stepped forward. "Lord Monceaux, I have a message to give you."

A message? Unease rolled through him. He nodded.

"Lord Andrew asked that you be informed he and William Wallace are in private discussions with several lords and are nae to be interrupted."

Like a mace driven, a strong headache slammed Griffin's temples.

"But," the guard continued, "he left instructions that you and your wife are given a chamber at Dunadd Castle for the night. He sends his regards, and word that he will speak with you when you break your fast on the morrow."

On the morrow? Impossible. After delivering the missives this day, he was to meet with a secret contact that lived nearby. Not remain stuck here for the entire night wedded to a woman he'd never met. Not that she was hard to look at. If he'd been introduced to her under different circumstances, she would have caught his interest. But, in this debacle she'd left him no choice.

No. 'Twas he who'd acted out of character. Instead of confronting the false charge, stating that he'd never seen her, when he'd caught the sliver of fear in her eyes, he'd believed when cornered she'd admit her folly.

And for his decision, he paid a fool's price.

Annoyed he'd allowed a woman to rile his temper, Griffin scanned the great room in hopes of finding another noble aware of his covert aid to the rebels who would identify the woman at his side. Except for two clan chiefs in deep discussion in the far corner, one of whom shot Griffin a menacing look, all others had departed.

'Twould seem discovering who she was would have to wait. Griffin approached the guard. "Please take us to our chamber."

His wife cleared her throat. "But—"

"Do you wish to continue to walk," Griffin whispered in her ear, "or do I carry you?"

Face pale, she glanced toward the entry.

"You said I could trust you," he said beneath his breath.

Cool eyes skewed him. "I did, and I am a woman to honor it," she whispered back.

Griffin arched a brow. "We shall see."

As she shifted uneasily at his side, the guard shot the woman a worried look.

No doubt the guard knew her. As he was viewed as their enemy, neither would the man tell him her name. "Lead the way," Griffin ordered, in hopes his firm tone provoked the Scot. If his *wife* wouldn't tell him who she was, maybe the guard would slip up and expose a critical detail of her identity en route to their chamber.

Instead, tight-lipped, the Scot gestured for them to follow. The remnants of cooked meat and herbs from the evening meal scented the air as he guided them past the blazing hearth toward the turret.

Griffin's unwanted wife cast him a worried glance.

As she should. 'Twas not him who started this mess, but by God 'twas him who would finish it.

At the second floor, the Scot led them down the corridor. The spacious hallway reminded him of the MacGruders' home, but the similarities ended there. The few adornments reflected naught of the grandeur or uniqueness of the many works of art in Lochshire Castle.

A Scottish castle his sister, Nichola, an Englishwoman born and raised, now called her home. A fact easy to understand considering the warmth and acceptance shown her by the MacGruders, unlike his own home in England—Rothfield Castle, inherited upon his parents' death—which held naught but cold memories. A truth that kept his visits to the ancestral fortress short, and his time away long.

Neither had this day's events changed anything. With his service to King Edward, combined with his double life as *Wulfe*, little room existed in his life for a woman or wife, much less love.

Love? No, that he would never find. Neither would he look. Too often women were drawn to him for his status and wealth. Long ago he'd abandoned the notion of finding a woman who loved him for himself.

At the second entry, the guard halted and opened the door. "My lord." Rois recognized her friend's concern as her own nerves threatened to break her fragile control.

Griffin tugged her inside, shoved the door closed.

Alone.

With her husband.

Hazel eyes studied her with smoldering fury. Anger she'd roused. The English lord's control told her much of the man, another reason he remained in King Edward's employ.

"You know him," Lord Monceaux said as he glanced toward the door.

Rois hesitated. "He is a friend."

"One who worries about you."

"It is what friends do." She glanced toward where his hand held hers. "You may release me."

He quirked a challenging brow. "May I?"

Another wash of heat rose up her cheeks. "Please."

The baron held firm.

She swallowed hard. He but toyed with her, a dangerous game she'd begun. Except, 'twas was no game, but a necessity to save her father's life.

Awareness tingled through her as the Englishman lifted her fingers, studied where a scratch marred the back of one hand, then turned her palm over. He slid his thumb across a hint of calluses earned from working with the horses, and frowned.

"You are nobility."

She stilled. "How do you know?"

"Your acceptance in a room filled with commanding Scottish lords."

"I might be a woman sent from the kitchens with ale or wine."

"You could, but are not." He traced a finger across a scrape. "You are allowed to work?"

"Unlike the delicate noblewomen of England, I refuse to live within pampered constraints."

He raised an intrigued brow. "Who are you?"

The determined edge to his voice smothered the wash of civility. Fine, she preferred directness as well. "A woman who is desperate."

"Explain." At her silence, his thumb stroked the delicate skin of her wrist with soft intent. "We have the entire night. I shall glean the truth, however necessary." He scanned the room, his gaze pausing at the bed before shooting her a meaningful stare.

Heat and chills slid through her. She'd overheard whispers of romps, mutters from women who cursed their husband's touch. Except, cornered in this chamber with a man she'd never met before this night, for an unknown reason, Rois sensed he'd nae hurt her. Or regardless of the veiled threat, take what she would nae willingly give.

Why wasn't she afraid? More so, terrified of his warrior's stance, his powerful muscles, and his ruthless intelligence? Mayhap 'twas his eyes. Or, mayhap, as angry as he'd been at first, he had nae touched her with violence or threatened her harm.

Memories of his kiss in the stable swept her mind, the heat, the thoroughness of his mouth's touch. Never before had a man's kiss ignited awareness within her until her entire body burned with the wanting. But Griffin's had.

A man now her husband. A man she'd foolishly wed. A man who wielded his mind with the deftness of a sword.

And, a man who worked for King Edward.

Shaken by her unbidden desire, she looked away. Aye, the man was dangerous. However free from harm, alone in this chamber with this virile warrior, she was far from safe.

Gentle fingers caught her chin, turned her face until their eyes met. "Your name." At her silence, he lowered his head a degree.

Her breath caught.

"Tell me."

Her heart pounded as his male scent wrapped around her, tempting her, luring her to tell him, to accept what he offered and so much more.

"I canna."

He brushed his mouth over hers with sultry promise. "I will know your name." He skimmed his hand along her jaw, then over the hollow of her neck. "And your every curve. Intimately."

Her entire body trembled. Rois closed her eyes, tried to convince herself 'twas a dream. Except, the warmth of his fingers against the rapid pulse at her throat assured her this was far from a slumber's fantasy.

At his touch, her thick chestnut lashes flickered opened. Green eyes riveted on Griffin, the nerves within clouded by desire. His body trembled with need. God's teeth, he'd believed if the woman thought he'd seduce her, she would tell him her name, and the reason she'd falsely attacked his character. Never had he expected to see his own hunger reflected in her eyes.

A cool September breeze sifted through the arched window, tossing wisps of her chestnut hair against her cheeks, drawing his gaze to her lips. The memory of her potent taste hummed through his mind. Another gust tugged on her gown, outlined her full curves with clarity that a blind man could see.

His body burned and his mind spun with images of them naked, of him sliding deep within her warmth. From the corner of his eye he caught sight of the bed.

"Nay!"

At the panic in her voice he released her hand, but kept her body trapped against his. "We have all night," he said, drawing out his words. "I will have my answers. The choice of how we spend the time is up to you."

Cool eyes leveled on him.

He almost laughed. Did she believe him ignorant of her desire, of the way her pulse raced beneath his touch? She wanted him, but her pride or stubbornness refused her to admit such. The same obstinacies guiding her refusal to admit her identity.

At her continued silence, Griffin sighed. "I see you have made your choice."

A frown edged her brow. "Choice?"

He slid his thumb across her full lower lip. "Of how we will spend the hours until dawn."

She jerked away.

Tired of her games, ready to end this farce, Griffin grazed the curve of her neck with his mouth. "Yes, enjoying each other's company is a much better way to collect our thoughts."

"Do nae."

The tremble of her voice had him pausing. "Your name then."

She looked away, but not before he caught her hesitation. Soon she would tell him. Both knew it. He nuzzled her chin and caught her slender waist, drew her full against him, the softness of her body heaven itself.

She gasped.

"I think 'tis time we were introduced. Well past," he added, ignoring the bite of sarcasm, "since for some reason you decided to toss my life into chaos."

Her body shuddered. "I never meant to involve you, 'twas only that I needed to protect . . ."

"Who?"

Her gaze darted away. "Myself."

"From what? Or," Griffin drawled, "from whom?"

"Please, I do nae wish to involve you."

Griffin gave a rough laugh. "My lady, claiming you carry my child is far from the way to ensure our paths remain untwined."

A sigh, slow and filled with distress, fell from her lips. She nodded. "You are right."

"Tell me who you are."

"I canna."

"No," he said, "you choose not to."

Guilt swept her face, but she remained silent.

Did she think him so easily dissuaded? She would soon learn otherwise. "We will set aside this discussion for now."

Green eyes widened with relief. "Truly?"

"Aye." He claimed her lips softly, slowly, savoring her taste. Her hands came up against his chest; he caught them. Breaking the kiss, he drew her fingers to his mouth. As he nibbled upon each, he shot her a meaningful glance.

"Lord Monceaux—"

"Mmmm." He turned her hand over and kissed her palm. "'Tis much better than words wasted, is it not?"

She tried to jerk free.

He held.

Desperation filled her eyes as they darted toward the entry, then back to him.

In but moments, she would reveal everything.

Her breath hitched. "I tire of your games."

He skimmed his hand along the length of her back. "I assure you, when I find myself wed to a stranger, I do not find the situation entertaining. However, until you wish to end it"—he swept her into his arms—"we will find a modicum of satisfaction."

She struggled within his hold, her curvaceous body igniting unwanted erotic images.

Bedamned. Never had a woman affected him as she, but his desire for the chit would not dictate his actions. This night he would have the information he sought. And, if she decided to give herself to him, neither would he deny what they obviously both wished.

"Unhand me!"

"With pleasure." He strode toward the bed and placed her upon the coverlet. Holding her gaze, he laid his body atop hers, shifting his weight to his elbows.

Her throat worked as she swallowed hard, her nerves easy to read. "My lord, I—"

"Griffin. Say my name. I am your husband, am I not?"

Her lower lip trembled. "A-aye."

"It seems we have two things in common."

"Two?" she whispered.

"Our state of marriage. And our desire."

"I do nae want you."

Be it tiredness or exhaustion of the day's lengthy travel, her blatant refusal of what a fool could easily deduct left him on edge. "I think," he said, his each word slow, with intent, "that you want me, my lady, very much." He caught her mouth in a demanding kiss, assured but a taste of her would ease his needs, sate his sanity to where he could focus on his goal. Instead, with each passing moment, the sweetness of her lips urged him to savor.

"Griffin."

His name upon her lips, half desperate, half needy, pleased him. "Admit you want me."

"I . . ."

Well aware of how to please a woman, he gentled his kiss. More than one way existed to win a battle. So, he kept his moves easy, his touch gentle, determined to break down her barriers.

Her stiff movements eased. As she relaxed against him, she began kissing him back. As in the stable, need engulfed him.

Griffin restrained himself, barely, allowing her to set the pace, wanting her to foolishly believe herself in charge. But as moments passed and her kisses grew hotter, his masterful plan faded to slashes of need. With his body hard as a rock, all he wanted was to strip her naked and drive deep inside her.

Her moan dissolved another layer of his control, destroying his every good intent. From the expertise of how her body moved against his, his reservations about her virginity fell away.

Pleased by this unexpected boon, Griffin pressed his body intimately against hers. Her moans fueled him, the desperate return of his kisses more so as he deftly slipped open her gown.

The softness of her breast spilled into his palm and he had to taste. On a groan, he shifted lower, swirled his tongue around her hardened tip.

"Griffin," she whispered on a half gasp. "Please—" A moan ended her words, and she arched beneath his touch.

God's teeth, she was sensitive. Wanting to watch her fall apart, he used his hands to tease, to linger, to expose her flesh and caress her most intimate place. As she arched up, he slid his fingers within her slick folds.

She gasped, twisted against his touch.

"Let yourself go." Wanting her over the edge, her screams of release filling the room as he took her this first time, he swirled his tongue around the sensitive tips of her breasts and used his fingers to push her higher until she was wild beneath him.

On a fractured breath, her body arched, tensed. She cried out, her climax incredibly beautiful. With a soft moan, she collapsed upon the bed, sweat glistening on her skin.

He had to have her—now. His mind a blur of need and heat, Griffin reached to open his trews.

A rap echoed on the door.

He ignored the sound, and jerked the next tie free.

Another knock, this time harder.

"Be gone!" Griffin yelled.

The woman below him stiffened and her eyes flew open.

"Ignore it," he urged her. With a curse on his tongue, he glared at the door. "I said—"

"'Tis of the utmost importance, my lord," a deep Scottish voice boomed from the other side. "Sir Andrew requests your immediate presence."

God's teeth! Griffin laid his head against the woman's breast, her scent, heat, blissful insanity. Anyone else and he would tell them to bugger themselves. Was it not his blasted wedding night?

The woman shifted beneath him.

His body throbbed. He pressed a kiss upon the curve of her breast. "I will not be long."

"Move off me," she gasped.

Griffin lifted his head. She watched him, her expression dazed, her eyes a mix of pleasure and shame. He took in her full breasts, slick with the sheen of sweat, their tips taut.

Red swept over her face. Hands trembling, she jerked up the bodice of her gown like an innocent.

An innocent?

No. She was . . . A sinking in his gut intensified as he recalled the way she'd responded to his caresses. Eagerly, yes, but also with a new wonder. No, it could not be. He fought for calm, assured himself he was wrong.

"Tell me you are not a virgin."

Her blush deepened.

Griffin closed his eyes, muttered a curse. He'd all but bedded the lass. Thankfully her maidenhead was still intact. "Who bloody taught you to kiss like that?"

"My lord," the Scot called from the other side of the door. "'Tis urgent!"

On an uneven breath, he lifted the woman's chin. "I promise you this. We will finish upon my return." Griffin released her and shoved off the bed, straightened his garb. "I am coming." He shot his wife a cool look.

Beneath his censure, she sat up, her fingers shaking as she hid her temptations from his view. After he was confident she was as decent as a new bride could be, given the situation, Griffin strode to the door. He jerked it open.

The knight on the threshold nodded. "Sir Andrew awaits you in his private chamber.

"Watch over"—bloody hell, he realized he still didn't know her name—"Lady Monceaux. Until my return, no one is to come in, or out."

The Scot stepped to the side. "Aye, my lord."

With a last warning look toward the rumpled woman in heat-inducing disarray, Griffin strode off.

Her heart pounding, Rois scrambled from the bed. She shot a glance to where her friend, Piers, waited in the doorway. Shamefully, her body tingled at the things Griffin had done. Heaven help her, this marriage she had concocted 'twas a shameful mess.

"Hurry," Piers called.

"Aye." With a last tug to secure her gown's ties, Rois ignored the lingering hum of her body and rushed to the doorway.

Her friend cast her a worried look before they turned and hurried down the turret.

Thankfully he asked no questions about her haphazard state. Her mind replayed how Griffin had touched her, teased her until she'd lost control. Nay, she couldn't think of the intimacies allowed now.

In the turret, with her husband nowhere in sight, she rounded the corner, then drew to a halt.

Torchlight illuminated Lochlann where he waited at the foot of the steps. A scowl deepened his face as he took in her tousled state. "Come."

"It is nae what it seems." Why did she feel the need to explain? Nay, her own guilt at allowing the Englishman's touch, of wanting more, incited her words. "Grif— Lord Monceaux caught me in the stables trying to flee." Her friend's hard look eased. In part the truth, but she would tell him naught more. Like she enjoyed the fact that she was attracted to the enemy or had found pleasure at the way he'd touched her.

"There is little time to discuss the matter now." Lochlann motioned her forward, then hurried out a side door.

Rois exited, glanced up, thankful thick clouds shielded the meager attempts at moonlight. In the shadows, they rushed toward the gatehouse, the whisper of their shoes upon earth and grass in time with her frantic breaths. "How did you know where I was?"

As they neared the formidable arch of curved stone, Lochlann spared her a meaningful glance. "Sir Piers informed me where the English baron had taken you."

At the mention of Griffin, shame filled her once more. "I didna accompany the baron willingly."

Lochlann arched a doubtful brow, then gestured toward the nearby corridor. "Hurry. We must be far away before your husband"—he bit the word out— "discovers de Moray and Wallace have left."

"My cousin Andrew didna request Lord Monceaux's presence?"

He shook his head.

Griffin would be furious. Then she understood. "You planned this?"

Satisfaction curved her friend's mouth. "Did you think I would leave you to rot with the English bastard?"

"Nay." Neither was this the time to admit she'd found Griffin far from cruel. Rois hurried after Lochlann, grateful he led her past the gate to two saddled horses tethered within the shadows. She swung upon her mare as he mounted his steed. "Where are we going?"

"To Kincardan Castle, to see your father."

"What of Lord Monceaux? Surely he will search for me."

Lochlann gave a cold laugh. "He will try."

Panic swept her. 'Twas her actions that had placed Griffin in this situation. "What have you done?"

"Ensured he will nae follow this night."

The finality in his voice sent a shiver through her. "You will nae harm him."

"Nay, though a sound thrashing is what the bastard deserves." Lochlann whirled his horse and kicked him into a gallop.

With a glimpse toward the keep where Griffin would soon discover their chamber empty and realize he'd been duped, Rois nudged her mare into a gallop to follow Lochlann into the night.

Chapter Four

Griffin stared at the guard in disbelief. "Andrew de Moray has departed Dunadd Castle?"

The knight standing before the doorway cleared his throat. "Aye, Lord Monceaux."

"He left no message for me as to why my presence was requested?"

"Nay, my lord."

Anger seeped through Griffin topped with a healthy dose of chagrin. He'd been duped, tricked into leaving his wife alone. His wife!

"And Wallace?" he asked, damnably aware of the blasted answer.

"Gone with him, my lord. He said they would nae return until the morn."

The morn! He eyed the guard, discerning naught but confusion on his face. The guard wasn't in league with this trickery, but well he knew who was. "My thanks." Griffin departed. Alone in the turret, he bolted up the tower stairs. Leather slapped upon stone, echoing his gullibility.

Why hadn't he suspected such deception from the first? But with his body raging its demands, the woman's moans of release scrambling his logic, he'd reacted, accepted the guard's message as truth.

And now he paid the humiliating price.

At the second floor, he glared down the corridor.

The entry to his chamber stood unguarded.

Flashes of the concerned looks the guard had given the woman as he'd escorted her and Griffin to their chamber came to mind. Of course, the man whom he'd ordered to guard his wife was her friend.

His wife. Blast it. A fine laugh they'd had as they fled. Griffin stormed down the hallway and into the bedchamber.

Empty.

The tousled sheets, and her scent of woman and lavender lingered, signs mocking her earlier presence.

He rubbed his brow, the headache of hours before returning with a vengeance. God's teeth, in mere hours one wisp of a woman managed to infiltrate his life and create absolute chaos—a feat which many a man had never come close to achieving, and for their efforts had died.

Disgusted that he, who navigated the most complex issues, with this one woman had failed miserably, he stalked to the door. He'd find her. It would be a meeting she would sorely regret.

At the entry, Griffin halted. And what Scot below would help him, a man they considered their enemy? With de Moray and Wallace away, he would find no friend in Dunadd Castle.

But the Scots knew the woman. Regardless of her wedded state, they would hide her if she asked. Had their plan to aid her this night not proved such? The last thing he needed was to go about announcing his wife had slipped away without him even knowing her name.

Exhaustion from the day's travel blurred his thoughts. Wherever de Moray and Wallace had gone, the rebel leaders would not return before the morn. Until then, he'd complete the next assignment for which he'd ridden here—meeting with another secret rebel contact living but a brisk ride away.

Outside the arched window he caught the sweep of blackness, a cold emptiness holding naught but the affirmation of night. The breeze tumbling through the carved stone held the scent of the distant loch and the harvested fields beyond.

A hint of winter tainted the air, and with it the promise of a land ravaged by brutal cold. A somber time, more so with the approach of the upcoming battle. Would troops led by de Moray and Wallace to defend Stirling Castle from the English be enough to keep the stronghold in Scottish hands? He swallowed hard. For Scotland's freedom, he prayed so.

A low rumble of voices echoed from the corridor.

What in Hades? Griffin peered down the torch-lit corridor. Illuminated by the yellowed light, a crowd of men, who from their wobbly gait were well into their cups, sloshed down the confines.

"There he is, lads!" a red-haired, scraggly bearded man yelled.

Hoots and hollers rang out.

"Come to celebrate we have!" A rough-looking man who reminded him of a poorly dressed dwarf lifted his tankard. "Here's to your hand-fasting to the lass and the bedding."

Crude suggestions rang out. Drunken laughter boomed with each one.

With a grunt of disgust, Griffin stepped inside the chamber, slammed the door, and barred it shut. From their inebriated intent, 'twould seem they weren't involved in his wife's escape, only in celebrating his marriage. Or, was this, too, another part of the well-planned ruse?

With a shake of his head, he leaned against the sturdy door. The fanfare outside was traditional after a couple wed. 'Twas the woman who'd tied his brain in knots. He glared at the tumbled sheets where he'd almost claimed her.

A virgin.

He closed his eyes, and her gentle curves, her taste stormed his mind with body-burning clarity.

'Twas a blasted curse! He strode to the window. Torchlight smeared the bailey in lashes of broken yellow and outlined the guards as they made their rounds upon the wall walk. Beyond the castle walls campfires flickered where thousands of de Moray and Wallace's followers waited, ready for the battle against the English.

And somewhere out there, or mayhap within Dunadd Castle, hid his wife.

Griffin scowled at the hewn walls of the immense fortress. She was here, but he would not find her this night. If he opened the door, the drunkards would shove inside. Her absence would raise naught but questions, questions for which he had no answers.

'Twould seem his meeting with his secret contact would be delayed until the morn. With a grunt of disgust, he strode to the bed and glared at the rumpled bedding. He lay down, jerked the coverlet over him, and closed his eyes. He willed time to pass, but her faint scent teased him along with the images of her naked and moaning in his arms from her release.

By God, he would sleep this night if it was the last thing he ever did. He shifted to his side, the crackle from the hearth playing cadence to the rumbles of the men outside.

"Pass the ale!" a deep voice boomed.

Curse it! Griffin opened his eyes. On the pillow a breath away, a strand of chestnut hair shimmered in the wash of firelight. He lifted the silken wisp. No, he'd not be alone. Her lock of hair would be in blasted accompaniment.

A fine wedding night indeed.

With the strand clenched in his fist, Griffin closed his eyes, determined to find relief, even if for a few hours. He welcomed the fog of sleep, the bliss of feeling nothing.

Warmth pulsed at his chest.

God's teeth, what now? He peered at where the halved Magnesite he wore around his neck rested upon his chest.

The gemstone glowed.

No, he neither saw nor felt the warmth. 'Twas his mind scrambled from this day's chaos. But as he studied the gem, its light brightened.

Surrounded by candlelight in Kincardan Castle's solar, Rois worked to catch her breath from the brisk ride home, her body still trembling from the night's chill.

"Answer me," her father demanded.

"How can you question why am I nae with my husband?" she asked in disbelief.

A scowl upon his face, Lochlann stepped forward. "Lord Brom—"

Her father slid Lochlann a cool look. "Silence." He faced Rois. "You are married, are you nae?"

She gasped. "But—"

"Are you nae, lass?" her father pressed.

Panic welled inside Rois. Was her da changing his mind? Did he want her to remain married to the Englishman? "Aye, but you said before you left the stables you would help me."

Her father's fierce gaze shifted to Lochlann. "Leave us."

Her friend turned to her. "Rois, do you want me to stay?"

Her heart ached at Lochlann daring to defy her father. He would remain, true friend that he was. But she'd created this mess, one she would somehow straighten out.

"'Tis for the best that Da and I speak alone," she said. "Please."

She refused to allow Lochlann to involve himself further. Rois touched his forearm gently. "Go."

A muscle twitched in his jaw, then Lochlann stalked to the door.

Red mottled her father's weathered face. "Brazen he is to show such disrespect. I shall—"

Rois stepped before him. "Da, please. Let him go."

Shrewd eyes narrowed as they followed her friend out of sight, then settled upon her. "Sir Lochlann is above himself and needs to be taught a lesson."

"He is upset."

"Upset?" Her father grunted. "He is an upstart who interferes where he does nae belong."

"Da, this is nae about Lochlann."

Her father nodded. "That it is nae."

Expectant silence hung in the air.

Rois wrung her hands. "You canna expect me to return to a man who is our enemy."

"A fact you should have considered before you trapped him into marriage."

"He didna have to agree."

An aged brow shot up. "King Edward's man cornered in a chamber filled with angry Scots? A man whose honor lay at risk? Nay, I think his decision was wisely made. Had he of nae offered you marriage, with the warriors in the chamber prepared for battle against his king and their tempers high, Lord Monceaux would now lay dead."

Guilt deflated her anger and she dropped her hands to her sides. "Wrong I was to have charged the baron with such a deed, but as I explained, it was the only thing I could think of to distract him from seeing you."

At her father's silence, unease rippled through her. A crazy thought wedged into her mind. Nay, she was wrong.

Wasn't she?

"Da, you do nae expect me to remain married to the Englishman?"

His jaw tightened, and amber eyes rimmed with frustration darkened. "I should escort you back this very moment."

Heart pounding, Rois watched his face, his every expression, for a sign he would follow through. "But you will nae, will you?"

"Wrong it is for you to stay apart from the man you wed. But, the morrow and riding to Dunadd Castle to set things straight will come soon enough." He nodded. "Go to sleep, lass."

Confident her father would help annul her marriage to the Englishman, relief swept through her. Her father had but scared her, a fitting punishment for the caliber of her deed.

"I love you, Da." Tears choked her words, those of love, of a girl grown to womanhood during turbulent times.

He grimaced, yet naught but love framed his countenance. "As I you. You are all I have left of your mother."

Aching for his loneliness, she laid her head against his chest. "I know you miss her."

"I do." He wrapped his arms around her in a tender hug, the sadness on his face seasoned by time. He was a man who had struggled alone to raise the daughter he loved. "I will always miss her. But these troubled times allow little luxury for memories. Our thoughts must be on winning Scotland's freedom."

A tremor slid through her as she stepped back, wishing she could stop time. "A date is set then for the troops to depart for Stirling Bridge?"

"Aye, in two days. We canna allow the English to reach Stirling Castle."

"I know." A danger faced by her father who stood against the English, as every Scot. She gave one more hug to the man who'd raised her, a man she'd do whatever necessary to protect. Except, she could nae shield him from battle. Only pray.

He reached out, tousled her hair, and smiled. "On with you now and try to rest." He dropped his hand to his side, and his smile faded. "I love you, Rois. Whatever happens after this night, always remember that."

Tears welled in her throat at his soft words. He worried about her, about the dangers of the impending battle. What would happen if he didna return? Nay, he would come back. More, he would stand with the other Scots, victorious.

Shaken, she headed to her chamber. Inside, she shut the door and pressed her hand against the sturdy wood. An ache built in her chest. So many men lay camped in the nearby fields, men she had grown up with, men she called friends. Rois made the sign of the cross and said, "Please, God, keep them safe."

With a heavy heart, she looked around her chamber, taking in the small gifts given to her by her father throughout the years. She walked over to the table and lifted the bejeweled comb he'd surprised her with upon her ten and second year. She slid the pad of her finger against the crafted ivory, the ridges of teeth a soft tickle against her skin. Her smile of remembrance faltered. Many years had passed since, and so had the innocence of her youth.

Innocence?

Warmth slid through her at thoughts of Griffin's touch, the intimacy, of how he'd made her body feel. Never before had she experienced anything but a kiss with a man. But he'd made her skin tingle, her body ache with . . .

Ashamed, she closed her eyes. How could she think of him or the things she'd allowed him to do?

On a shaky breath, she opened her eyes and took in her room, that of a child. A room where she now stood as a woman, and one who'd known the caress of a man.

God forbid if Lochlann found out.

Her fingers trembled as she replaced the comb. Exhausted and overwhelmed by the myriad of thoughts, she quietly changed, then crossed her chamber. The softness of her bed was welcoming, but far from alleviated the worries of the morrow. So much was changing. This day had proven, in moments, one's entire world could be tossed upside down. For her, a temporary issue her father would see repaired. She wished only she could dismiss as quickly her worries for her father's safety in the battle ahead.

At a distant yell, Griffin withdrew his dagger beside his head and shoved to his feet. Naked, he blinked, fought the haze of sleep, and struggled for cognizance.

Embers smoldered in the hearth exposing a chamber adorned with simple furnishings; a bed and a small stand cluttered with a plate of half-eaten bread, cheese, and an empty goblet of wine.

No threat in sight. He lowered his weapon. Where was he?

A man yelled from the bailey.

With a frown, he strode to the carved window. The first hints of day exposed the dying fires scattered about and the thousands of men encamped around them.

Memories of yesterday rushed him.

De Moray's refusal.

His debacle of a marriage.

His wedding night spent alone.

Rubbing his face, Griffin took in his bedding scattered about. Not from overuse, but as if thrown about while caught up in a dream. A dream?

No, a nightmare.

His marriage was real, not a delusion from which he could awaken. And standing here was not settling the issues of his unwanted wife, his upcoming meeting with de Moray, or that with his secret contact.

A rough snore sounded from the corridor.

The images of the drunken Scots celebrating his sham of a marriage last eve etched his mind. He grimaced. They'd passed out.

A muscle worked in his jaw as he splashed water onto his face and dried his hands. He tossed the rumpled bedding onto the mattress, dressed.

Through the window a somber blanket of clouds smothered the sun, casting ominous hues of purples and grey upon the earth. The somber colors as if an omen foretelling of emptiness, coldness, and death.

Griffin shook off his unease and focused on the men outside the castle as they tended to their horses, sharpened their blades, or practiced with their swords.

The warriors were on edge, and rightly so. They'd received word that the Earl of Surrey was leading thousands of seasoned English troops north. When the Scots stood their ground at Stirling Bridge, many untrained and holding naught but the weapon in their hand, they would face their opponent greatly outnumbered.

Many would claim the rebels faced sure death, a slaughter in the making. Except they underestimated the courage and the heart of the Scots.

Against incredible odds, Griffin had faith, believed de Moray and Wallace would find a way to outmaneuver the English. They knew the land, how to motivate their men, and with de Moray having trained with the Swiss mercenaries, he held the skill to exploit every opportunity and lead the rebels to victory.

The Scots had not asked for war. King Edward's greed after the Scottish King Alexander III's death was the catalyst for this upheaval.

Now, confident that mere pockets of resistance remained in Scotland, clad within his arrogance, he'd sailed to Flanders and to yet another battle, leaving the Earl of Surrey to cleanse Scotland of the remaining unrest.

Little did the king or his minions understand the Scots' determination, nor that true credit for such a well-planned uprising against the English belonged to the Bishop Wishart. King Edward embraced suspicions of the bishop's loyalty but, against the church and without solid evidence, he could bring no charge.

By the time King Edward returned from Flanders, the fate of this day would be long past. Griffin prayed that given the size of the English force, the planned strategies that he'd pass to de Moray would give the rebels an edge.

God help Scotland if the rebels, standing their ground against the English at Stirling Bridge, failed.

With a heavy heart, he strode to the door. A slight scrape sounded as he removed the wooden bar and edged it open.

Soft snores mixed amongst an errant guttural grunt echoed from the corridor.

Had he expected any man able to crawl to his feet this early after their drink-fed night? With a grimace, he set the bolt aside, opened the door wider.

A man slumped half inside, his red beard laden with an indefinable nasty glaze. With a mutter, he shifted, grumbled, and then let loose a hearty snore.

Griffin shook his head in disgust. The entry and the corridor were littered with casualties of too much drink, some with their bodies contorted into awkward angles, while others lay sprawled with their mouths oozing drool. At least someone had enjoyed the last few hours. He shook his head. Given the reason for their celebration, he would have chosen to spend the night on this side of the door as well.

And belaboring the point changed naught.

With careful steps, Griffin picked his way through the casualties reeking with soured ale and odors he'd rather not identify, thankful when he reached the turret.

He started down the curved steps. With each, the murmur of voices in the great hall increased along with the scent of fresh-baked bread and roasting meat.

A deep hearty laugh sounded near the exit. "Did you see the baron's face when the lass accused him of leaving her as well as carrying his babe?"

Three paces from the bottom step, Griffin halted. Blood pounding, he waited, willed the man to reveal the name of the woman he'd married.

"Stunned he was," a second man agreed. "And rightly so. I doubt before yesterday past, the lass ever laid eyes on Lord Monceaux."

Chapter Five

Hands curled into fists, Griffin fought the surge of anger. These two Scots knew she'd lied? Knew yesterday he'd never set eyes on the woman before? A sinking in his gut assured him that more than these two men knew the truth—likely everyone in the chamber.

Anger pumped through his veins, a raw, scorching slide that burned through his hard-won calm. His body trembled with the urge to confront the men, to demand why they'd allowed this farce of a marriage.

No, if asked, neither would tell him.

They knew not that he was *Wulfe*, the English noble who worked in secret to aid the rebels. To them he was King Edward's man, the enemy, which again raised the question of why no one had halted his marriage. However frustrating the situation, he must tread with care. Something was greatly amiss for the powerful men at the meeting yesterday to have allowed such an ill-fated event.

"Lady Rois has made a muck of it this time," the first man said, his burr deep.

Lady Rois. Her name at last! And as he'd suspected, she was of nobility.

"Lady Rois," he breathed, savoring the rush of victory in learning this critical fact. He frowned. His secret contact had a daughter named Rois, but never would he have allowed her such foolery. For years he'd met with Lord Brom, who was a man with a clear mind and a firm hand. Though he'd never met his daughter, no doubt she was as rational and clear-sighted as Angus. Besides, Rois was a name common enough. That she was of nobility would make her easy to find.

His mood lighter, Griffin dismissed the name befitting the feisty woman, a woman who if he allowed would linger in his mind. Now, to learn her surname and clan, then he would track her down.

"Do you think her father will save her this time?" the second Scot asked.

"'Tis dealings with the church he will have to do," the first Scot replied. "But, he is an influential lord with many a connection. And aye, methinks he will save the willful lass."

Willful? Griffin scoffed. The woman didn't need to be saved, but held accountable. Not that he would be landed with that task of teaching her responsibility. Her father could keep it. 'Twas a motley-minded fool that allowed his daughter free rein, and according to the warriors' account, a foolish path she often trod.

Neither did the men's confirmation her father was powerful yield surprise—since Rois had been allowed entry into yesterday's war meeting.

Where had her father been yesterday? Not in the chamber to witness his daughter handfasted to his enemy. Even a lackwit would have stepped forward and halted the insane event. Or would he? Unease churned in his gut. With the woman a handful, had he remained silent out of relief at having found someone on whom to foist the responsibility for his daughter?

But who was her father? To end this unwanted union, they would have to meet. And, unless the man was known to him, it would be far from a pleasant affair. As if any occasion since his catastrophe of a meeting with Rois could be deemed affable.

Guilt edged through him. Yes, it could. Last eve he'd found pleasure in her body, her taste, and in the way she'd responded to his touch.

A virgin.

With the way she'd responded to his caresses, he'd assumed she'd had lovers before. A foolish assumption. Except, caught off guard and his body burning hot, he'd followed his instincts.

Instincts? No, desires. He had wanted her every alluring inch. Griffin muttered a curse. And when was the last time he gave in to lust? Not since he was a lad of ten and six.

"Aye, but did you see the baron's face when she agreed?" the first man said, breaking into Griffin's musings. "I wonder what the Sassenach would have thought if he had known that everyone in the chamber had suspicions he had nae seen Rois before?"

Laughter, hearty and whole, rang out. "Aye, furious he would be."

Furious? No, furious was too kind a word. The entire time he'd stood surrounded by the Scots, held beneath the warriors' threatening glares, they'd believed the woman had never seen him before. And when she'd spoken of carrying his babe, they'd thought that a mistruth as well.

Yet, all had remained silent.

Amused at his quandary.

Entertained as they'd witnessed a hated Englishman make a complete arse of himself by his offer of marriage to a stranger. Not one blasted man had stepped forward and halted her foolery.

Which returned him to the question of *why*?

Had his offer left them stunned? Had each man believed that however impetuous in the past, Lady Rois would never agree to this lunacy?

Regardless, 'twas too late to change the outcome. From the men's discussion, her father was a man who held connections with the church, and could intervene to end this marriage. Nor would he be learning the noble's name standing here. On a deep exhale, Griffin took the last few steps and entered the great room.

The gazes of the men inside riveted on him. The chamber grew silent. Tension hung in the air, thick and potent like a storm brewing.

"Is Lady Rois abed?" a nearby Scot with his claymore secured at his back asked.

Laughter sprinkled about.

Jaw tight, Griffin met his gaze. Did they know he'd slept alone on his wedding night as well? God's teeth, at this point, he'd believe anything.

"Lord Monceaux," Andrew de Moray called.

At his friend's voice from the front of the great room, relief swept Griffin.

De Moray motioned to an empty chair at his side. "Sit beside me as we break our fast."

Aye, but he needed a friendly face. Well aware of the distrustful glances of many of the surrounding warriors, he wove his way through the rough mix. As he neared the dais he caught a glint of humor in de Moray and Wallace's eyes. Unease sliced through Griffin. His friends could not approve of this abominable situation. So why had neither intervened at the woman's ridiculous challenge?

Once seated, a platter of meat, porridge, and bread was placed before him. A serving woman filled his nearby goblet. "My thanks." Griffin waited until the woman had left, then he met the gaze of his friend, thankful they were seated out of earshot from the hostile crowd. "Blast it, one would think I had three eyes and four ears."

De Moray chuckled.

Griffin shot him a hard look. "'Tis far from a laughing matter."

"'Tis but a touch of levity as we prepare for battle."

Aye, the days ahead weighed heavy in Scotland's bid for freedom. Griffin took a drink of wine, set the goblet down. "If I had not wedded the lass, I would share your humor."

His friend's smile widened. "I think you and Rois will make a fine pair."

Griffin choked as he tried to swallow the wine. Coughing, he worked the chunk of bread down. "Fine pair? You both knew I had never seen the woman before." He pressed his hands on the table, a wedge of anger slipping past. "Why did neither of you stop her?"

His friend wiped his hands and tossed the towel aside. "'Twas nae my place."

"Nor mine," Wallace added.

"Not your place?" Griffin asked, sarcasm dripping from his each word. "And whose was it then?"

"The lass's father," Wallace replied.

Griffin sat back in disbelief. "Her father was in the room?"

With a nod, de Moray chewed his bread leisurely as if they were discussing a mundane topic such as the weather of the day.

"Then why," Griffin said, struggling to accept the shocking news, "did *he* not stop her?"

"'Tis a question you need to be asking him." De Moray lifted his goblet in a mock toast. "With his silence, I am thinking he approved the match."

Griffin's mind rolled through the faces within the great room. "I know but a few Scottish lords with a daughter in the chamber. More so, none who would have allowed such misbehavior from their daughter."

"'Twould seem," Wallace said, "you didna see the lord who sat at the front of the chamber. He mentioned late last eve when we spoke that you were to meet with him this day."

It couldn't be. Throat dry, Griffin worked to accept what de Moray had revealed. "Angus Drummond, Earl of Brom, is Rois's father?"

A lopsided smile grew on de Moray's mouth. "Aye."

"He said nothing," Griffin rasped, needing to say the words, to find a token of sanity in this chaos. "Lord Brom must have heard when his daughter accused me of taking liberties—of getting her with child."

"Aye," de Moray replied, "which is what leads me to believe he approved of the match."

"God's teeth." Griffin picked up his wine, drained it. He'd married Angus Drummond's daughter! Sweat clung to his brow. Thank God King Edward was in Flanders. It would be weeks, mayhap months, before news reached him of Lord Brom, one of the king's most trusted Scots, renouncing his oath and having sworn his fealty to Scotland. Or, of Griffin's marriage to a traitor's daughter.

De Moray arched a brow. "You are fine with the marriage then?" He took a long drink of his wine. "Happy I am to hear it. She is my cousin, and well I expect you to treat her."

Rois was de Moray's cousin? Griffin managed not to spew the wine. Fingers trembling, he set the goblet on the table. Should he be shocked by the latest twist in this mire of events? Another reason no one had halted their marriage. With her father and de Moray in the chamber, none would question their judgment, nor allow their own anger at the handfasting to interfere.

"Griffin?" de Moray asked.

"I must speak with Angus immediately," Griffin replied.

Wallace laughed. "One would be thinking you would still be abed with your wife."

If Wallace or de Moray knew that his wife had escaped, never would he live it down. "There is much to do before I return to England."

De Moray sobered. "Aye."

Relieved the topic of Rois was set aside, Griffin turned his thoughts to a more serious matter. "Sir Andrew, when King Edward learns you refused his offer to replace your father in the tower, he will be furious."

"Aye." De Moray's eyes narrowed. "Dimwitted he is if he believes me foolish enough to walk into the Tower of London. He thinks to lure me by sending his seal upon a letter for my safe passage and my father's plea." He grunted. "King Edward cares little about my father supporting him in battle."

"Indeed," Griffin agreed. "He has received word of your success in sweeping through the Highlands, and now moving troops south. He wants you stopped."

De Moray wadded the cloth before him, tossed it aside. "He can rot in Hades."

"An opinion I share." Griffin held de Moray's gaze. "But eventually he will learn of your refusal to replace your father."

"And because of it, my father will remain in the Tower of London." De Moray rubbed his face, shadows haunting every crease. "I very likely have sentenced my father to his death."

"No," Griffin said, his words firm. "Any guilt lies upon King Edward. Since his wife's death, he cares not who suffers due to his decisions, or who he kills."

"Aye," Wallace agreed. "All the bastard cares about is power, to claim yet another country."

His lips a thin line, de Moray thrummed his fingers upon the goblet. "Even if I had agreed, think you he would have nae ensured an accident during battle to guarantee my father's death? Or, ensured that I never would be allowed to leave the tower alive?"

Griffin nodded. "With each passing year King Edward grows colder, and if possible, angrier."

"More so," Wallace agreed, "as his son is far from the heir he wishes to pass the crown."

King Edward's rants on his son's incompetence echoed in Griffin's mind. "Edward II will never be the leader his father is."

De Moray's eyes met Griffin's. "But King Edward's mood or his son's affairs are nae our immediate concern. That would be Stirling Bridge."

Griffin nodded. "Aye. The reason I have come."

De Moray stiffened. "You have more information?"

"I have."

Wallace nodded, rose. "Come, let us talk in private."

In silence, Griffin followed the men, aware that once they'd finished, he would face another tense meeting, that with Lord Brom.

Rois stepped into the solar and paused. Her father sat upon his carved stool near the hearth inspecting his sword before securing it within its sheath. Images of him over the years as he'd greeted her each morning swamped her, his smile, the twinkle in his eyes, his warm laugh.

This morning he prepared for war.

She swallowed hard, fought the swarm of emotions as she closed the door. "When do you leave?"

At the roughness of her words, he looked up, the frown furrowed in his brow exposing his worry.

Tears burning her eyes, she remained by the entry. If she went to him now, hugged him, she would break down. He needed her strong. That she would give him.

Her father set his weapon aside. "On the morrow."

Fear rippled through her. "I thought 'twould be a few days yet."

"Things have changed."

She clenched her hands at her sides. "I shall keep you in my prayers."

Tenderness cut through the worry upon his weathered face. He walked over. "As I you." He hesitated. "If I do nae return—"

"You will."

"Lass. There are no guarantees in battle, more so when reports are that King Edward has sent north the Earl of Surrey, who leads thousands of troops."

She started to speak, but he interrupted, "Nay. You will hear me out."

Fear wound through her with a numbing coil. Hear him out?

"It is time you have a man to protect you, one who will be there if for some reason I do nae return."

Her heart slammed in her chest. "Da—"

"'Tis nae the time to allow emotions to guide us, Rois. Our choices must be made through wisdom, and through the necessity of reality."

Reality? "Of what do you speak?" The upcoming battle her father faced incited horrific images of swords slicing flesh from bone, warriors' faces raw with agony as they crumpled to the ground, and their screams of pain.

"The baron."

Eyes widening, she gasped. "You canna expect me to remain wed to King Edward's man?"

His mouth tightened. "'Twas the man you chose for your husband."

"It was—"

"Your decision"—he gave a firm nod—"and one I shall honor."

"Last night you said you would take care of the marriage!"

Determined lines creased his weathered face. "And so I will."

She fought to control the panic racing through her. "By allowing me to remain wed to the enemy?"

"Rois—"

A hard rap sounded on the door.

Face grim, her father nodded. "'Tis the baron."

"How do you know?"

"A guard informed me of his approach moments ago. I bade him to escort Lord Monceaux here upon his arrival."

And her da had nae warned her. Nay, he'd wanted her ignorant and planned this meeting without her consent. How could he after she'd married the enemy to save him?

Heart aching, she understood. He was afraid he would nae return from the battle at Stirling Bridge, and believed that finding someone to protect her would help keep her safe.

Her throat tightened as she fought back tears. How could she be angry when his decisions toward her were made out of love? Except, did he truly believe her safe with the Baron of Monceaux?

There must be something he hadn't told her. Had he received insight from one of the many informants he met with in private? Considering he despised the English with his every breath, only one reason would make him foist her in the enemy's arms—he believed the rebels would lose.

A firm rap again sounded upon the door.

Nausea swept Rois as she fought to clear her head, to accept his belief in Scotland's demise.

"Enter." Her father's voice echoed as if from far away.

The door creaked softly as it swung open.

"Lord Brom, Lady Rois."

Lord Monceaux's deep baritone shuddered within the room.

In slow motion she turned toward the man she'd wed, and the man whom her father entrusted with her care. The man both well understood was their enemy.

Her nightmare had begun.

Chapter Six

At Lord Brom's bid to enter, Griffin strode inside and halted. Framed between two large swords on either side of a majestic mantle, Lady Rois stood beside her father. Face pale, she laced her fingers together before her. Her expression was one he recognized, a look he'd seen yesterday when she'd confronted him in the great hall—fear.

As from the first, her fey-like beauty stunned him, drew him like no woman had ever before. After touching and tasting her last eve, images of her naked and responding to his lovemaking ignited in his mind. His body started to harden, and he willed the erotic thoughts away. God's teeth, he need not think about the things he'd done, or what he'd almost taken.

A virgin.

An innocent, who, if not for the interruption by the Scottish knight, he would have bedded. Not that his marital vows didn't bestow upon him such a right, but had he taken her, he would have destroyed any hope to reclaim his freedom. In hindsight, the humiliation of a wedding night spent alone seemed a paltry price.

"Lord Brom," Griffin said, formality necessary in his daughter's presence. Never must Rois learn her father was a contact in his work as *Wulfe*, or of their secret meetings to help gain Scotland's freedom.

Eyes somber, Angus strode forward, clasped Griffin's hand. "Lord Monceaux."

"I regret to come at such troubled times, my lord, but"—Griffin glanced at Rois, then back to the Scottish lord—"'tis best we speak alone."

"Alone?" Angus asked.

"Yes, my lord," Griffin replied. "To . . . discuss the unfortunate tangle of events of the day past and how to proceed."

Thick charcoal brows dropped into a frown. "Unfortunate tangle of events?"

God's teeth, did Lord Brom not understand that he wished to spare Rois the embarrassment of speaking so openly of an annulment? Though the men had grown close through contact over the years, the dialogue between him and Angus would be difficult enough.

Angus nodded for him to continue.

So be it. "I wished to spare your daughter any discomfort in my discussing an annulment."

Aged eyes narrowed. "'Tis unnecessary."

Unnecessary? No, disengaging his life from this troublesome woman was a definite necessity. "Lord Brom, I understand your concerns for your daughter. While you are off to fight, I will keep her safe."

The deep lines of worry on his brow eased.

"Da, this can wait—"

Angus shot his daughter a warning look. "We will discuss this now. 'Twas your actions yesterday that brought about this meeting."

Griffin nodded.

"I explained my reasons." Rois glared at him. "I need nae *his* protection!"

"Fear not, my lady," Griffin said. "Our time together will be but days. Once your father departs for battle, I will escort you to a nearby nunnery. There, you will await his return."

Hues of red splashed upon her cheeks. "You will take me nowhere!"

"Aye he willna," Lord Brom stated. "Lord Monceaux, as your wife, Rois will remain with you, her protection and welfare your duty."

A foreboding settled within Griffin's gut. Why was Angus pressing the issue? The ramifications of Rois at his side were simple—in addition to placing her in danger, each day she remained with him increased the risk of her learning of his secret identity. Neither consequence he wished to contemplate.

Griffin cleared his throat and leveled a hard look at Angus. "My lord, think you 'tis wise for your daughter to remain with me given the circumstances?"

Rois's gaze shifted from Griffin to her father. "What circumstances?"

"None that will change my mind," Lord Brom replied, his voice firm. "Lord Monceaux, you requested my daughter's hand before witnesses, and she accepted. By Highland law, you are wed."

Requested? The woman had challenged him with ludicrous accusations in a chamber of men who believed him the enemy.

"My lord," Griffin said, amazed at the control in his voice, "With Rois sleeping at Kincardan Castle last eve, and I at Dunadd Castle, we never spent the night as man and wife. Our marriage is but words spoken. An annulment will hold few challenges."

Lord Brom crossed his arms. "You are telling me that after you and Rois handfasted, you both did nae spend time in the bridal chamber alone?"

Griffin's throat worked as images of Rois naked and trembling from her release infused his mind. "For a brief while, my lord, but—"

"But?" Angus boomed.

Heat streaked Rois's cheeks, and she looked down.

"'Tis my daughter's honor that you will be keeping!"

Blast it! Griffin rubbed his brow. Hadn't he assured Angus he would protect Rois while the Scot was away at battle? "My lord, your daughter is an innocent, her honor intact."

"And what say you, lass?" her father demanded.

Her fingers tense, she lifted her eyes to meet her father. "'Tis as he claims."

The embarrassment in her voice troubled Griffin. For an unexplained reason, he found himself wishing to spare her further upset. "Regardless of her poor choices yesterday, 'twill take but a connection within the church to end this union." A powerful connection they both knew and worked with, Bishop Wishart.

"I disagree," Lord Brom replied. "Your time alone with Rois has compromised my daughter's reputation. You handfasted before our people, a vow I expect you to keep."

Griffin stared in disbelief. Lord Brom expected he and Rois to stay married? The rebel leader was a man of wit, a man of profound intellect, except 'twould seem when it came to his daughter. Panic slid through Griffin as he searched for a reason that would return him to the sanity of his unwed state. Thick moments passed as the intelligence that had served him throughout the years, the cunning that'd assured him a position with King Edward, fled.

Griffin shifted. "I—"

Angus raised his hand. "You are wed. A union I find myself pleased to see."

At the gravity of Lord Brom's expression, the worry churning within his wizened eyes, Griffin understood why Angus had remained silent when he'd offered to handfast with Rois—he sought protection for his daughter. Protection Griffin had once sought for his sister, Nichola, after the tragic loss of their parents. A loss due to his irresponsibility.

Bedamned.

He shoved aside the dark memories of his past. This moment was not about the reckless decisions of his youth, but about a father concerned, a man who he would trust with his own life. Angus prepared to ride off to war and worried for his daughter. What father would not, more so a man who had lost his wife and raised a child alone?

However much Griffin understood her father's concern, neither would Rois and her impetuous decisions beleaguer him.

"Da, please rethink your decision—"

Angus rounded on his daughter. "You cornered Lord Monceaux, questioned his honor without provocation."

Panic widened her eyes. "Nay. It was nae my intent. 'Twas to—"

"Were you forced to handfast?" Angus interrupted.

She lowered her head. "Nay, but I explained my reason to you, Father."

Lord Brom's face remained impassive.

"I would like to hear her rationale," Griffin muttered. Observing father and daughter together, it was clear where Rois inherited her stubbornness.

"The lass intervened," Angus stated, "because she considers you a threat to me."

"A threat?" Griffin asked.

"Aye—"

"Da, do nae tell—"

"Lass," Angus said. He focused on Griffin. "She believes that if you saw me at the rebel meeting, you would report my shift of fealty to King Edward."

Griffin nodded. This explained everything. Terrified that, with the news, King Edward would order her father hanged, Rois had confronted Griffin with an untruth to keep the man who'd raised her, the father she loved, alive.

Her need to protect her father was one Griffin understood, and a decision he respected. He remembered the death of his parents, and the guilt that they wouldn't have been traveling had he not been imprisoned.

Face pale, Rois cleared her throat, pulling him from his thoughts. "He is King Edward's advisor to the Scots. Da, do you nae understand that Lord Monceaux's knowing you have withdrawn your fealty to King Edward is a sentence to death?"

Griffin stepped forward. God's teeth, why had Angus allowed her to remain? "Fear not, my lady, I will not report your father's presence at the rebel meeting, nor his change of loyalties."

Green eyes sliced him with disbelief. "Do you think I am a dimwit and believe you speak with sincerity? Once you stand before your king, you will reveal everything."

Blasted stubborn. "I will reveal naught."

She angled her chin. "Do nae presume I am easily swayed by your practiced words."

The woman would bedevil the calmest of men. "My lady, I give you my word."

"By God," Angus blustered, "This discussion is done. Rois Drummond, 'tis long past time you wed."

A tremor shuddered through Rois's body. "How can you entrust me to our enemy?"

Her father remained silent.

Da intended her to remain wed to the Englishman? How could her father entertain such a scandalous alliance?

An idea so stunning, so shocking slipped through Rois's mind. She wanted to dismiss it, but no other reason existed—mayhap Da knew Lord Monceaux!

Hope exploded against her fear. Lower lip trembling, she took in the formidable man, his dark scowl fierce, and his eyes blazing with anger. Her heart sank. A foolish thought. Never had her father mentioned meeting King Edward's advisor to the Scots. So, how could her father consider leaving her in Lord Monceaux's care?

"Da." Desperation wove through her whisper. "You canna leave me with this man."

Eyes filled with love and worry held hers. "My child, this day I depart for battle. The Scots face enormous odds at Stirling Bridge against de Warren's troops. 'Twill ease my mind knowing you are safeguarded."

Safeguarded? No, sentenced. With her da's mind made up, for whatever his reason, at this moment he was blind to her dilemma.

"You will return. I refuse to believe otherwise." Her voice broke. Rois jerked free, nae wanting her father to see her tears.

Soft steps echoed as Lord Monceaux walked forward. "My lady."

She whirled. "Do nae touch me, ever!" Her fear for her father found a foothold. "And if you tell your king of Da, I will kill you, I swear it."

Her father's mouth tightened. "Rois!"

"Let me, Lord Brom," Lord Monceaux said with quiet calm.

"Let you?" she said, furious the baron could be so in control when her entire life lay shattered around her. "How dare you tell me or my father anything?"

Her father nodded. "'Tis his right as your husband."

"A temporary fate," she replied.

"Lass, always will you be my daughter," her da said, his voice rough with emotion. "But with your words spoken yesterday at Dunadd Castle, you are now Lady Monceaux. That I willna change."

Rois floundered for a reply.

"Worry not, Lord Brom. I will keep your daughter safe. If necessary, with my life."

Were they both insane? Rois shook her head. "'Tis lunacy."

The Englishman's face hardened. "If you want your father protected," Lord Monceaux warned, his words hard with authority, "you will remain with me—a bed you made."

Her heart pounded. She shot a glance at her father. "Da?"

"Lord Monceaux, I am retreating to my private chamber. Once you finish speaking with your wife, please have a servant bring you to my quarters. There are a few issues I would like to discuss with you in private."

Her father was leaving them alone?

"My thanks, Lord Brom."

A wizened face she so loved softened. "I love you, Rois. Never forget that." With a gentle smile, he departed.

The soft click of the door echoed like a crack of thunder.

Alone.

With the enemy.

Trembling, Rois stepped back. "Leave me." At her soft command, his jaw tightened.

"We will come to an agreement first."

"Go to Hades." His soft laugh grated on her temper. "I find nothing amusing about the situation."

His smile fell away. "I assure you, my lady, neither do I. But for now, 'tis what fate, or rather *you*, have created."

"'Twas not I who proposed marriage."

"No," he replied, his words soft with a hint of anger, "but 'twas you who claimed I left you with a babe."

"I thought you a threat to my father—a belief that hasna changed."

"And what part did the red-haired Scot who stood near you play?" Lord Monceaux asked. "He looked none too pleased by your false claim."

Sir Lochlann. "He is a friend."

A muscle worked in the baron's jaw. "A friend?"

Sir Lochlann wanted more than friendship, an aspiration she didna share. A fact she'd nae tell this Englishman.

At her silence, he nodded. "While we are wed, you will meet with no man without me or proper escort present."

"How dare you dictate my actions!"

"I dare much." Hazel eyes darkened with warning. "Until our union is disengaged, you will heed my commands."

"I will nae spend my time with you."

"You will. Nor will you cause me grief—your father's life depends on it."

"A threat?"

"An assurance."

"Bastard."

"At times."

"And others?" she flung out, her words reckless with fear.

"A trusted friend." God's teeth, why had he said that? Never would he and Rois be friends. Once Angus returned, he would convince the man of the folly of allowing his and Rois's marriage to continue. But he would keep watch over Rois in the meantime, and for the sake of his sanity, he would negotiate a fragile peace.

Griffin nodded. "Please, use my name."

Green eyes he could drown in watched him with distrust, but he also caught the fear. There was so much she didn't understand, nor ever could.

"Why should I?" she asked.

He drew in a slow breath, reminded himself of all of the reasons it was best to find common ground. "'Tis my name."

"You know little about me."

Tired of her assumptions that had landed them both in this bloody mess, he caught her wrist. "On this you are wrong. From our time last eve, I know parts of you very well." Beneath his thumb, her pulse sped up. Good, let her be nervous. Never would he harm her, but he'd not tell her that. "I have given my word to your father to protect you until his return."

"Why did you agree to watch over me?"

The soft incredulity surprised him. He expected another blast of anger, but not confusion, or a sincere desire to understand. "Because I am a man of honor."

"And?"

He'd thought her a creature of emotion, a touch spoiled, both perhaps true, but he'd missed the sharp intellect. With Angus as her father, he should have suspected as much.

"I admire Lord Brom."

Surprise shifted to wariness. "He is your enemy, a man who is helping to plan a siege against English troops you support."

Careful with your reply. "Have you never admired someone with whom you disagreed?"

"Mayhap." She hesitated. "Why do you admire my father?"

Numerous reasons came to mind as he recalled the years he'd known Lord Brom. A man not afraid to stand his ground, or hold a tender heart beneath the fierce mask he wore. A man whose heart still ached with loneliness years after his wife's passing.

Over the years Angus had become to him like a father, a man he'd admired for raising a daughter alone. Due to the sensitive nature of the contact between him and Lord Brom, Rois had never seen him. Never had he imagined one day that the Scottish lord would be the father of his wife. Life was filled with odd twists.

"I admire your father because he is a man of principle, a man who one can always turn to for rationale when it seems to elude others." Except with Rois. Information he wished he'd known earlier.

"He is." Lips pressed together, she studied him for a long moment. "For King Edward's man, you seem to know my father well."

Tread carefully. "'Tis my job to be informed."

"Of the enemy."

"Of the situation."

She arched a skeptical brow. "And what are your plans for *our* situation?"

At her nervous drawl, he relaxed. "I agreed to protect you while Lord Brom is away," Griffin clarified. "Upon your father's return to Kincardan Castle, I will convince him that with our countries at odds, our union is a poor idea."

She laughed, a soft sound that shot straight to his gut. "A poor idea—an understatement. Tell me, how will you achieve this when my father has made up his mind? Da is nae a man easily swayed."

Comfortable with this easy banter, Griffin nodded. "One of my strengths is negotiation."

"You may know my father from your research, but I have lived with him for eight and ten years."

"I have confidence in my abilities, my lady."

She shot him a cool glance. "Add arrogant to the list."

"The list?" he asked, curious.

"Of your annoying traits."

A debate, if he allowed, could continue. "My lady, we must leave."

She stilled. Her face washed of color. "I am remaining here."

He sighed. "Your cousin offered us a chamber in Dunadd Castle."

Rois hesitated. "You spoke with Andrew about us?"

"I did."

She slid her tongue over her lower lip in a nervous glide. Griffin assured himself he didn't notice the moisture glistening upon her lips, a mouth he'd had the pleasure to taste. "Until our marriage is dissolved, there is little choice."

Panic flickered in her eyes. "I canna stay in the same chamber with you."

Griffin slowly inhaled, then released the calming breath. "Think you your father will allow you to remain here?"

"If I stay with you, how can we claim we nae have . . ."

"Consummated the marriage?"

A flush swept her cheeks. "Aye."

"Worry not, I will do my part."

"Rest assured," she stated, "you are the last person I would ever want to touch me."

Ego bruised, Griffin stepped closer. "Trust me, my lady, if I wanted you, you would be welcoming me."

Challenge flashed in her eyes. "Never would I want an Englishman."

"Proven by your release last eve?"

Her hand shot out.

He caught her wrist a whisper from his face. "Play not with what you do not understand. You are a maiden, an innocent, and know nothing of what I speak. Last night's lovemaking was but a taste of the pleasures to be found."

The bravado in her eyes faded, exposing the nerves she fought to hide. She looked away.

"Rois." She didn't look at him.

Her body trembled.

Moved by something so simple, he found himself needing to assure her. "I will keep you safe."

"Aye."

The belief in her words left him humbled. "Rois, why did you accept my touch when I am a man you despise?"

She turned to him then, her look still wary, but he saw confusion as well. And if he looked closer, he saw something fragile, something he yearned to keep safe. Shaken by the emotions she stirred, he let her go.

"Griffin?"

His name upon her tongue slid over him like finely woven silk, and his body hardened. Irritated that he wanted her like the air he breathed, he stepped back. "I am going to speak with your father."

Her face cooled and any hint of warmth was erased from her voice. "I will nae go with you."

"My lady, you will not be given a choice." With a warning look, Griffin spun on his heel and departed.

Chapter Seven

The cool morning air battered Griffin as he guided his mount over a decaying tree trunk littered with moss. Rocks clattered and leaves holding hints of color swirled beneath the flash of hooves. He savored the rush of wind, the tang of fall rich in the breeze, a time when the earth rested to renew with the spring.

Breaks in the trees exposed the familiar outline of the Highlands, the cast of rock as formidable as the Scots who prepared to fight. The home of Andrew de Moray, who, alongside William Wallace, would lead the Scottish rebels to battle in but days with the English against fierce odds.

God help them.

An image of Rois asleep flickered through his mind, of how he'd crept out of their chamber at Dunadd Castle after she'd fallen asleep. He'd not told her of his meeting with the Earl of Surrey this morn, nor would he. When she'd awoken and found him gone, was she relieved? Or, anxious for her father's safety, did she give his absence little thought and rush to Kincardan Castle to be with her father these last precious hours before he rode away to battle?

As Griffin neared the base of the mountain, the two rebel leaders rode from a copse of trees to meet him. His mount whinnied as he drew him to a halt. He nodded to de Moray as he reined in his steed before him, then to Wallace at his side.

"Lord Monceaux," de Moray said. "What news do you bring?"

"We knew King Edward planned to send a large contingent," Griffin said, his words somber, "but 'tis far worse than we anticipated. The Earl of Surrey and Hugh de Cressingham ride toward Stirling Castle with an army of around fifty thousand."

"Blast it," Wallace muttered. "We have ten thousand men in our ranks at best."

"There is more." Griffin took in the grim expression on each man's face, damning the news he would impart. "They travel with heavy cavalry and Welsh archers."

De Moray cursed. "As with his razing of Berwick, Longshanks believes his sheer numbers can destroy the last of our rebellion. But in this he will fail."

Determination carved Wallace's face. "Aye. We are far from weak-kneed lackeys who cower and run at the first sign of a fight. This is our land, and by God, we will stop King Edward's forces before they reach Stirling Castle."

"Are there any changes to the original troop battle layouts we discussed?" Griffin asked. With so many untrained rebels in their ranks, he doubted that winning against the seasoned English warriors could be achieved.

"Nay." De Moray fisted his reins. "We will position our men along the hills of the bridge across the Forth, north of Stirling Castle. 'Twill give us the best advantage to attack."

Griffin rubbed his jaw. "Think you the Earl of Surrey is foolish enough to order his men to cross the bridge?"

Wallace grunted. "With the boggy land, 'tis the quickest route across."

"It is," Griffin said, far from convinced, "but they could ride to a ford a short distance away where knights can cross in great numbers."

"'Tis indeed an option which, if I led my men, I would consider," de Moray agreed. "And one we must prepare for."

"Aye, that we will," Wallace agreed. "Neither can we forget Hugh de Cressingham rides at the earl's side and is holding the coin. However influential, he's naught but a self-serving fool, one who embraces his power as much as his next meal."

Griffin smiled, as did his friends. "One would think a man of illegitimate birth would understand the struggles of the poor, use his ascension to become treasurer of the English administration in Scotland to build a bond between the English and the Scots. Instead, on both sides he has cultivated naught but dissent."

Wallace nodded. "Indeed, the Scots call him the *Treacherer*, and the English the *Son of Death*."

"He is a nasty lot," de Moray agreed. "'Tis surprised I am he still breathes with so many despising him."

"Bloody luck," Wallace said.

"Mayhap at Stirling Bridge," de Moray said, "we will see his luck and his reign of terror end."

Silence settled around them, a void thick with questions. Griffin caught glimpses of the rough-clad men hidden in the trees. How could they not worry? De Moray and Wallace led but a handful of ill-trained warriors against tens of thousands of seasoned English soldiers.

Lord Brom, riding with additional troops, appeared on the horizon. Had Rois spoken with her father before he'd departed? He prayed so.

Mirth sparkled in de Moray's eyes. "You seem deep in thought. From your grimace, methinks you ponder if, upon his return, Lord Brom will let you out of the marriage?"

Griffin grimaced. "He will see reason."

Wallace chuckled. "If asked, I agree with Angus that the true challenge will be in Rois allowing you to protect her while her father is away. She is nae a lass who cowers to a man, but is a proud, determined woman who holds her own. A trait gained upon her mother's death."

Griffin remained silent. With Angus and Wallace close friends since their youth, he'd expect Angus to share his concern with Wallace.

"Aye, 'twill be a shame to miss you attempting to bend my cousin to your will." Lord Andrew smiled. "I think 'tis safer to ride into battle." He glanced around and his expression sobered. "'Tis time to leave. Take care, my friend."

"Godspeed to you both," Griffin said.

"My thanks," de Moray replied. "I wish you luck. To deal with my cousin, you will need that and more."

Wallace chuckled. "Aye."

De Moray whirled his horse and cantered toward where his men camped within the forest, Wallace riding at his side.

Luck? Griffin frowned at his friends as they rode toward their men awaiting them, and dismissed de Moray's comments about Lord Brom. He would protect Rois, regardless of whether she was willing. As for the annulment, once her father returned, he would see the insanity of not allowing Griffin to begin proceedings. For now, his prayers would be with the Scots. With the overwhelming odds they faced, they would need each and every one. With a heavy heart, he urged his mount to a canter and headed toward Kincardan Castle.

"Da?" Rois called from the great room of Kincardan Castle.

As Griffin suspected, she'd returned to her home. At the fragile hope in her voice, sadness weighted him. She believed her father had forgotten something and, however briefly, had returned.

He stepped inside the great room, and his breath left him in a rush. Like a wayward fairy, Rois stood near the hearth, her chestnut hair wild and unbound, her ruby gown caressing her slender curves.

Green eyes fell upon him, and her smile faded. "When I awoke without you in the chamber at Dunadd Castle, I thought you had left."

He ignored the coolness of her comment, and desired to step closer, to touch her. "I had an errand that needed my attention."

She remained silent.

He walked to her, and she stiffened, her eyes wary. He held her gaze, let the crackle of burning wood fill the void. "You know me naught, a fact over the next few days that will change."

"With my father away, there is no need for us to remain together. I will be safe here. Kincardan Castle is well armed—"

"And with most of its knights away—" Griffin interrupted.

"Women can wield arms."

"They can, but I will take precautions to keep you safe until your father returns."

"Precautions?" She edged her tongue over her lip in a nervous slide. "You believe the Scots will lose and the English will storm this castle?"

"I believe the battle will be vicious, and many a man will die—on both sides." He said nothing further about the upcoming clash or his beliefs. 'Twas hard enough not riding alongside the Scots in their fight for freedom. Nor would he feed her worry further. How ironic that the wedding, however unwanted, had led to a timely reason why he couldn't aid the English.

Rois stroked her finger along the side of her gown, glanced up. "My father will return."

Nerves cradled her voice, the same he held for the safety of the Scots. "I pray he will."

Her alluring face settled into a wary frown. "You would pray for your enemy's safety?"

Intelligence sparked within her green eyes, intellect which lured him. The last thing he wanted to be with her was captivated. Her full curves and innocence drew him enough, but with each moment he spent in her presence, he wanted her more.

"Rois," he said, his words soft, a cadence he used to disarm, "our time together is not a battle."

"Considering your heritage and loyalty, how can it be otherwise?"

"The days ahead can pass with peace or distrust. The choice is yours."

Rois studied the Englishman, confused by his candor. Or, did he offer her a false ploy? She'd heard of Lord Monceaux's ability to negotiate peace in a tense situation. A strength Griffin had obviously employed to convince her da to entrust her care to him while away.

He gestured to the door. "Let us go."

Her breath caught. He'd promised to keep her safe, but she'd assumed he'd meant in Scotland. "I refuse to travel to England."

A muscle worked in his jaw. "We will ride to a hiding place within a day's ride."

A hiding place within a day's ride? Her pulse raced. "Where?"

"A cave hidden by a patch of thick brush alongside a large mountain."

A shiver swept through her. How could he know about Dunagn, the rebel hideout? Had her father told him? Nay, Da would never expose the secret mountain hideaway to the enemy. She knew of Sir Cressingham, the English treasurer's, tortuous methods to gain information for the English. Had he employed his grisly methods upon a Scot to discover such a significant rebel hideaway?

Regardless of how Griffin had acquired the information, she needed to warn the Scots the hideout was known to the English and no longer safe. She must slip away from Lord Monceaux and spread the word.

"I canna go with you." Rois walked to the hearth, far from warmed by the sweep of flames. Listen to her, she sounded like a shrew. She glanced over her shoulder. "Forgive me, 'tis nae that I am ungrateful for your offer of protection or doubt your abilities, but, 'tis simple. Neither of us wishes to be together."

Hazel eyes narrowed. "You will accompany me. How you travel is up to you."

Memories of his carrying her in the bailey over his shoulder came to mind. The arrogance of this man would make a toad's blood boil. "Are you threatening me? 'Tis nae English soil you stand upon, but Scottish, *my* homeland. If you think my servants will allow you to haul me out, a fine lesson you will be learning."

He crossed his arms against his muscled chest. "I am your husband; none will stop me."

"My father—"

"Has passed orders to the servants forbidding them to interfere."

Hurt swamped her. Would her father request such?

"Rois," he said, his words tender, "Throughout my life, never have I treated a woman harshly. Nor will I begin now."

She would ride out with him with her dignity intact, but if he thought she'd remain with him until her father's return, he'd soon learn otherwise.

"I will leave with you." And when the opportunity arose, she would slip away.

"Good, 'twill make it easier for us both." He caught her hand and led her from the keep.

Servants outside continued their work, but Rois caught their covert glances, their curiosity as she followed Griffin toward the stable. However, they didn't hurry to aid her, or use the sticks with which they turned the wash upon him. Was it true? Had her father indeed warned anyone to nae help her if she wished to leave the baron? However much she wanted to dismiss it, 'twould seem the truth.

Inside the stable, a large steed stood readied and a small leather bag lay secured behind the saddle.

She gasped. "My garb?"

"Your father had a servant pack what you would need."

Tears burned her eyes. How could her father be so blind?

Lord Monceaux urged her forward.

Her each step as if weighted with stone, she walked toward the horse. Her time with this English noble would be brief. Once she escaped and after she'd spread the warning about the rebel hideout being exposed, she would remain far from home until her da came back.

If he returned.

Emotion choked her. Nay, she refused to believe he wouldn't return. Rois shoved aside the terrifying thoughts and focused on now. She had friends with whom she could stay, knew people who would help pass word that Dunagn was known to the English.

Lord Monceaux helped her mount, then swung up behind her.

"Why do I nae have my own steed?" Rois asked.

"To ensure you do not escape."

She stared straight ahead as they cantered through the bailey, ignored the people around her and focused on the roll of mountains ahead, the land barren of color except for the aged whisky tumbles of brown and battered grass and decaying scrapes of green.

Against the clack of hooves, the morning breeze carried with it the smell of change, and a hint of winter chill.

Her breath shuddered out as she scanned the break of dawn into which her father had ridden to join the other Scots, his weapons readied, his face proud. A burst of cool wind drew her from her heavy thoughts. Above, clouds clung low upon the rock and earth like an ill omen. She shivered.

"You are cold?"

Griffin's voice swept her, the rough deepness a potent reminder of the formidable man she must escape. She shook her head.

"Tell me if you are. If we make good time, we will arrive before sunset."

As they rode, his mount began to climb the steep weather-buffeted land. Wisps of white swirled around them, chilled fingers of clouds severing her view of Kincardan Castle.

Within the haze of white, Rois identified weathered landmarks, the rough land blotched with fading patches of green in an ode to the oncoming winter, a time when the scent of peat wafted in the kitchen along with stews laden with meat and herbs, and the rich aroma of bread. She'd always loved the months held captive by the snow-laden land, the time spent with her father, and his stories of the past warming her heart.

Griffin's mount snorted, and she struggled for calm. Would her father return? Would the rebels win?

Enough!

To ponder circumstances she could nae change would but undermine her already strained control. She refused to give in to doubt, or forget the reason she must escape. If indeed Griffin knew of the hideout, she must warn the others.

Hours later a murky outline of jutting rocks came into view before her; the entry to the hideout.

She swallowed hard. He indeed knew the whereabouts of Dunagn, had nae once wavered as they'd ridden. In this cloud-soaked land, only a man familiar with the terrain could have found the rebel hideout.

Or known that it sat empty.

What other rebel secrets did the Englishman know? How much about the rebels had he gleaned or shared with his murderous king? Emotion burned her throat. Damn him, and those who would betray the rebels' cause.

The scrape of brush had her focusing on where the baron shoved aside the thatch of brush, a mangle at first glance that would encourage most to ride past. He removed another branch to expose the entry.

Tears burned her eyes. The Scots lay outnumbered against King Edward's armed force, and here was this Englishman who knew of rebel secrets that could erode the delicate hold they had upon winning their freedom.

However much she wished to be free of him, to warn the others of Dunagn's exposure, she would remain a wee bit longer and learn what other rebel secrets he knew.

Had Lord Monceaux nae asked for peace between them? Well, that she would give. And if he believed she'd make a truce with the enemy, then 'twas his error to regret.

Chapter Eight

At the cave's mouth, Griffin leaned forward in his saddle and tossed aside the last of the branches shielding the entry.

Golden streams of sunset struggled against the creep of night, exposing dust motes caught inside the cavern in a playful dance. A place to take refuge and get his thoughts in order.

As if the next few days cloistered with Rois would offer a sliver of peace? With a woman as beautiful and stubborn as she was, their time alone would be a test of his will.

He dismounted, his grip on his horse firm. Griffin glanced toward the woman who had dismantled his carefully constructed life, far from fooled by her feigned display of ignoring him. Well he'd learned to not underestimate her. The intelligence lurking within her mind was as potent as the emotions roiling in her heart, the reason her father and others loved her.

Rois sat astride his mount, her body straight, her gaze unflinching, and her tightened jaw exposing a hint of nerves. Indeed, she would be on edge. Her father rode off to war without a guarantee of return while she hid with an English lord she knew little about, or believed she could trust. A mire she'd made, and yet . . . her reasons were those he could admire.

What would it be like to have a woman love you with such completeness that she'd risk everything to protect you? A familiar ache of loneliness trickled through him. Senseless musings. With his life embroiled between his guise of serving King Edward and his true loyalty given to the Scots under the identity of *Wulfe*, no time existed to entertain the thoughts of a woman in his life.

Or love.

The weight of his blade sat heavy in its sheath, prodding him to join the rebels marching toward Stirling Bridge. As if he held such a choice?

Except for a few Scots who knew his secret identity, the rebels would view him as their enemy. Neither could he raise his blade with the English, wield it against those whose plight he sought to rectify.

Bedamned this entire situation. Bedamned that he would remain safe while his Scottish in-laws and friends battled for their lives against the English.

"Griffin?"

At the uncertainty in Rois's voice, he set aside his mulling and scanned the familiar curve of land, the blackness of night smothering the last hues of sunset with steadfast intent. He was here and considering everything, 'twas for the best. Not that he had to like it.

"The days will pass quickly," he stated.

"Will they?"

Through her bravado, he caught the edge of doubt, her strong features almost fragile. Her father's explanation that her mother's death when Rois was a child had caused her to grow up too soon echoed in Griffin's mind, and he softened further.

"No harm will come to you while you are with me." He found his words mattered, wished she would believe him, believe in him.

She eyed him, wary. "Because of your vow to my father."

If he could only tell her the truth of his loyalty, but he wanted her to know he understood the sensitive woman she was. "Yes, because of your father. But also because you care about the fate of others when many a person in this war-torn land has become bitter with hardness. That is a testament to how unique you truly are."

"Fine words, my lord."

Tired from the last few days of travel, he remained silent and guided his mount inside. The scent of time and quiet infused the cavern's air, the clop of his mount's hooves somber. Near the back wall, Griffin halted his steed. He stepped to his mount's side to help Rois dismount.

With expertise she swung down. The moment her foot touched the timeworn dirt, she stepped several paces back.

He exhaled. The tension between them was not what he would wish. What was he thinking? Wishes were for the innocent, for those not scarred by life. Mayhap 'twas better that between them lay distrust.

At a darkened indent, he secured his mount, fed him the stored hay, and turned. She hadn't moved.

"Rois?"

Silence.

Within the shadows playing upon her face he caught the nerves. God, she was beautiful. Memories of her taste, of his hands skimming along her supple curves, filled his mind. The image of her beneath him ignited.

"We are safe here. I will make a fire to ward off the chill." On a hard swallow he strode to the stacked dry tinder left for such a purpose. *Keep your mind on the task.* He angled his flint, struck hard with his dagger. Sparks sprayed the dry wood in a brilliant tumble.

At the curl of smoke, he gently blew on the flame. Dried grass crackled, sputtered with hues of orange and blue. In a steady slide, he fed bits of wood to the fire until it built to a steady glow.

Pleased, Griffin sat back and found Rois unpacking bread, cheese, and wine. Had she decided that a truce could be found?

She glanced back, her chestnut hair rich against the burst of flames, her face embraced by the fire's glow.

Too aware of her, he stood. "I will make a pallet." With his body aching for her, the last thing he needed to be thinking of was bed.

"'Tis unnecessary."

At the nervousness in her words, he faced her. "I am making two separate areas for us to sleep."

Her face remained impassive. "My thanks."

Though she thought herself immune to him, the way she responded to his touch last night proved otherwise. As if thinking about the intimacy between them helped anything.

Disgusted with his weakness when it came to her, he busied himself preparing where they would sleep. After, he strode to where she'd poured them each a cup of wine. He lifted the goblet and downed it in one swallow.

Eyes veiled, she watched him, her hands slowly rubbing her arms against the cold.

On a muttered curse, he refilled his cup, wishing for several bottles to empty. Griffin lowered the half-filled goblet. No, with her he needed his every wit.

He nodded. "Please, sit."

After a long moment, she knelt beside the flames.

Griffin joined her. He reached over and picked up the wedge of cheese and slab of bread, split both, handed Rois her share.

The crackle of flames punctured the silence as they ate. A gust swept inside, the scent of smoke pungent against the cool September air.

"'Twill be cold this night," he said.

She kept her gaze averted. "'Tis fall in Scotland."

"At least," Griffin said, keeping his tone soft, "there is nae snow."

"But it will come."

He exhaled. "Rois," he said, "I am but trying to make time pass in an affable manner."

Her fingers around her wedge of cheese tightened. "Time will pass, regardless of what either of us wishes."

"It will, but the tension between us is something we can dictate."

"Dictate?" Cool eyes met him. "'Tis an expected word choice from an Englishman."

"I did not ask to be handfasted to you," he said, anger trickling into his voice.

In the glow of firelight, guilt swept her face. "Nay," she said, her words soft, "that error was mine." She looked away.

Her abrupt admission had caught him off guard. "Rois?"

The concern in Griffin's voice touched Rois. Heaven help her, if he knew the yearnings his presence invoked, if he realized he made her care for him, he could hurt her.

"You are right." The whisper of her voice faded as she faced him. "We have but days together. Anger will only make each difficult."

Intrigued eyes assessed her, the intelligence within assuring her he missed little.

Why had she believed that by spending a bit more time with him, she could learn his secrets? Days together offered little time to earn more than a token of his trust. And with her feelings toward Griffin growing, 'twould risk personal disaster to remain. At the first opportunity, she must escape.

Through the opening of the cavern, she scanned the gloaming sky, a hint of stars within the darkening heavens. Well she knew how to protect herself, live off the land if necessary. Once he slept, she would leave. First, she needed him to lower his guard.

"You are from a large family?" At his silence, she cleared her throat. "Never mind. I should nae have asked."

"A sister," he replied. "Nichola."

From the warmth of his tone, one he loved. Many a time she'd wished for a sibling, someone to talk to when winter surrounded her for months on end.

"The way you hold yourself, your confidence, I would have taken you to have brothers." Rois took a bite, swallowed. "She lives with you in England?"

"No."

She tore off another bit of bread. "She is married, then?"

Griffin ate a piece of cheese, swallowed. "Yes."

"Your sister lives in England, near you?"

"No."

At his hesitation, she studied him. "If nae in England, then where?"

His jaw tightened.

Her question had upset him, but why? Careful nae to expose her interest, she pretended interest in eating, then shot him a teasing smile. "Is where you sister lives such a mystery?"

He shrugged. "Scotland."

Scotland?

"You are frowning," Griffin said.

"Why would I be pleased?" Rois replied. "My father rides off to war against England, and I learn your sister's English husband has been granted Scottish land seized by your king's army."

He lowered his cup of wine, leveled his gaze on her. "My sister's husband acquired nothing."

What trick did he play? "You stated she lives in Scotland with her husband. Is that nae how an English noble would claim Scottish land?"

With slow precision, Griffin set his goblet aside. "You assume she married a man of nobility."

Rois hesitated. There was something she was missing. Curious, she nodded. "With your rank and position with the king, I would think you would allow no other."

"My sister married a man she loved. As her husband is a Scot, she resides in his homeland, as one would expect."

"A Scot!"

At the incredulity in her voice, satisfaction filled Griffin. He'd surprised her, not that he'd meant to tell her anything about his personal life. But given his request to try to make time pass in an affable manner, if sharing a bit about his family would help, so be it.

"Yes. Nichola's husband was born and bred in the Highlands."

Questions flickered in her eyes. Her shock matched his own when he'd learned his sister had fallen in love with the Scot.

"How?" A flush rose up her cheeks. "Do nae answer. 'Tis nae of my affair."

"'Tis not," he agreed.

"But you will tell me?" she prodded with a gentle smile, her passion to know—that same passion which often resulted in ill-gotten decisions—rich within her words.

Charmed, he weighed the ramifications of divulging more about Nichola, and decided it offered little threat. "Her rebel husband abducted my sister for ransom."

Her eyes widened. "She married her abductor? It makes little make sense."

Griffin smiled then, her surprise well worth the disclosure. "I agree. But my sister is not a woman to follow a path given." He sobered. Due to the trauma of her youth. Instead of growing up in a home with parents who loved her, his poor judgment had delivered her a life of having to run their household while he was away on dangerous missions, an arduous life for a child of eight summers to shoulder, more so after the tragic loss of their parents.

"You accept her marriage to a Scot?"

He hesitated. He'd give her the truth. "At first I was furious, but I love my sister and would do anything for her. After I came to know him, watched them together, I saw they truly loved each other." He studied her a long moment. "To find love in this difficult time is a rare gift."

"It is," she replied, her words cautious. "Does your king approve of her marriage?"

Griffin stared out the cave's entrance. "King Edward's agenda is filled with trying to quell the Scottish uprisings and war against Flanders. Little time remains to concern him with my sister or her decisions."

Her eyes widened in disbelief. "You kept it from him?"

The woman was too perceptive. Griffin faced her. "At times, life's complications offer choices far from clear. Nor can decisions be easily made."

Rois thought of her father, his false loyalty given to the English king, and wondered if Nichola's husband had done the same? Emotion built inside her. How close was her da to Stirling Castle?

"You are quiet," Griffin said.

She shrugged. "I am thinking."

He studied her for a long moment. "About?"

Her fears for her father she would keep to herself. "Your sister, she is wed to a noble?"

A smile edged his mouth. "I did not say he was a noble."

Stunned, she stared at him. "Nae of noble birth?"

"He is a knight."

"Why would . . . Your father allowed such a match?"

His smile faded. "My father is dead."

Her heart ached, well aware of the grief that came with the death of a beloved parent. "I am sorry for your loss."

"My thanks." He set aside his uneaten food. "Many years have passed since."

"How did he die?" Rois asked.

He rubbed his jaw. "Trying to save a fool."

The roughness of his voice alerted her there was more he kept hidden, much more, but she'd far from established enough trust between them for him to confide such personal details. "What did your mother have to say of your sister's marriage?"

"She died with my father."

At his whispered words, pain scraped her soul. "My mother, too, died when I was young." Rois stared into the fire. "Her death, the emptiness it left inside me, is something that I live with daily." Griffin closed his eyes, then opened them, his pain stealing her breath.

"In life each of us faces tragedy," he said in a rough whisper. "How we react and whether we choose to move forward defines us."

"It does." From the melancholy in his tone, she sensed he spoke of more than his horrendous loss. God forbid, what had he experienced to carve such devastation in his life? Rois didn't want to care for Griffin more than she already did. Neither was she coldhearted. He had suffered, terribly so. She'd lost her mother, yet still had her father. He had neither. "I am pleased your sister has found happiness."

His entire body relaxed. "As am I."

Silence echoed between them, but she caught hints of darkness in his eyes, shadows of struggle from his past.

Beneath her quiet gaze he leaned forward and stacked several larger pieces of wood on the burning pile. "This should last throughout the night."

He was closing the topic, but she found herself wanting to know more. His pain and his ability to overcome adversity while yet attaining a position of trust to one of the most powerful men in the world intrigued her.

"Do you see your sister often?"

He stilled. "Why?"

His cool tone piqued her interest further. "I grew up without siblings. One would think if you are close, regardless of her husband's loyalty, you would visit."

Griffin set the piece of wood in his hand aside. "I see her on occasion."

Rois raised a brow.

"We are close."

Warmth touched her heart. "I am glad." And found her words held truth.

He brushed the heel of his boot through the dirt on the cave's floor, glanced up at her. "Though you have the penchant to rile a person, 'twould seem you have many people loyal to you."

People? Nay, however vague the reference, by the edge in his voice, he spoke of one—Lochlann. Why? He could nae be jealous. Or, could he? A thrill ran through her at the thought.

"I am blessed that many people care about me," she replied.

Griffin mashed the sand flat with the toe of his boot. "Are you?"

"If you have a question, ask me," she said, her words crisp. "Enough dancing around the issue."

"Fine, then. I speak of the warrior who tried to stop our handfasting."

Rois hesitated. "'Tis simple. He thought to defend my honor."

"Did he? Or were his reasons more personal?"

"You know nothing about him," she challenged.

"He loves you."

She brushed several strands of hair from her face. "He is a friend."

Griffin grunted. "Is that all he is?"

Panic shot through her, and Rois shoved to her feet. "I owe you no explanation."

Like a panther, he uncoiled himself and rose. His slow, controlled movements were those of a warrior, of a man used to having his way. She understood why King Edward had chosen this man, for his thoroughness and for his lethality when engaged in a mission. And at the moment, his mission was her.

"Until our marriage is annulled," he said with quiet precision, "you are my wife and your actions will be above reproach."

"You care naught about me."

Shrewd eyes watched her. "I have made my expectations clear." He leaned his muscled body toward her slender frame. "You would be a fool to test me. Our time together will be minimal. Upon your father's return, the annulment will be quickly achieved."

A hope she clung to as well. However much he made her feel, naught good would come from further discussions. She needed him to believe she'd accepted his terms, naught more.

Distant voices echoed from outside.

The slide of steel echoed upon leather as Griffin drew his sword and he shoved to his feet. He kicked out the fire. Whisper quiet, with hints of starlight illuminating the night, he crept to the entry.

Long moments passed.

Griffin glanced back, gestured for her to move deeper within the cave and remain silent.

A faint voice heavy with a rich burr echoed in the night.

The men were Scottish. She stepped closer.

A hiss slid between his teeth. "Stay there."

"I may know them."

"And," he replied, his words crisp, "you may not."

Rois halted, close enough to hear whoever passed nearby. As the voices grew faint, she sagged back. They were Scots. By their direction, they were en route to join de Moray and Wallace. Proof the English hadn't pushed this far north.

Damn King Edward, his greed, his need for complete control. She should be out there preparing to fight alongside her da, nae forced to remain with an Englishman who served the English scum.

She stared past Griffin to where stars continued to grow brighter in the night, the trees in the distance outlined by iridescent swaths and shadows. Enough light to travel by. When she slipped out once Griffin fell asleep, she would travel to where her clan and others prepared for battle. She could wield a sword, would fight to the death if it brought her country freedom.

"They have passed."

At Griffin's quiet words, she started.

Against the flickers of starlight, a frown settled across his brow. He motioned her back.

In silence she complied, anxious for the time with a man who was her temporary husband to end. But she wouldn't travel alone. Once she slipped out, she could catch up to the Scots who'd passed and travel with them. Anxious to rejoin her father, she wrapped herself in a solitary pallet. As for the information about Griffin's knowledge of Dunagn, she would pass that information to her da. Why hadn't she thought of that before?

"Are you nae going to rest?" she called.

At the cave's mouth, he scanned the surroundings. "I will keep watch to ensure they do not return."

"You think they saw the campfire?"

"No, but neither will I take the risk."

"So far north of the border," Rois said, "if the warriors noted any sign of a fire, they would assume it was made by a rebel."

He stretched his back. "Mayhap you are right."

Guilt sifted through her that she would deceive him this night. 'Twas her own doing that had led to this entire mess. He'd acted with naught but honor.

A gust of wind swirled through the cavern.

"Griffin?"

"Yes?"

"I appreciate your caring about what happens to me."

A long silence filled the night. "Go on and try and sleep."

Rois settled in her pallet. 'Twas too late to change her actions, but soon she would be out of his life. Shifting to her side, she drew up the blanket and feigned sleep.

Groggy, Griffin opened his eyes. What had woken him? Dagger in hand, he shoved to his feet. He glanced toward Rois. In the meager hint of starlight, he caught a hint of her outline. Relieved she was safe, he crept to the entry.

Stars coated the sky, embracing the low-hanging moon. A cool breeze swept past rich with the smell of earth and the tangle of leaves. He made out the slope of land, the wash of hills in the distance.

Rubbing his eyes, he worked past the last remnants of sleep and again scanned the area. What had disturbed his sleep? Except for the shudder of barren branches against another strong gust, naught seemed out of place.

Griffin frowned, surprised he'd slept so long. By the position of the moon, the new day was encroaching. Soon, the first hints of grey would crease the sky. No sense in returning to his pallet now. He rarely slept through the night. That he'd almost done so proved his state of exhaustion.

He glanced toward the bedroll where Rois slept. Whatever had caused him to awaken hadn't stirred her.

A wave of tiredness rolled through him. After one last search of the moon-washed land, confident no one was about, he walked to his pallet.

The kick of the wind swirled around him as he sank upon his blanket, the cold bite but a wisp of what winter would deliver. He glanced at the blackened embers. However much he wished to rebuild the fire for the warmth, with others about, he refused to take the risk.

He looked to where Rois's form lay bundled beneath her cover. Images of her naked came to mind. No, he did not need to think of her. With an exhale, he lay down and closed his eyes, listened to the bursts of wind, his even breaths, anything to not think of her.

Another gust of wind swept through the trees. The few leaves clinging with feeble hope clattered against the bony branches, a pathetic sound against this unending season of change.

With each breath, his mind tumbled into a soft haze. Images of Rois stormed his mind, the flicker of her eyes, defiant, then softening as he'd begun to make love to her. His body hardened.

On a muttered curse, he sat up and rubbed his face. And how many days would he remain in this cave with a woman he wanted with his every breath? Yes, he would leave her alone, the penalty to make love with her too high.

He grimaced at her dark outline. Considering his thoughts, 'twas best if he could not see her. He lay back again and closed his eyes. Unbidden, he caught himself listening for her slight sigh that he'd come to expect every so often as she'd slept.

The tumble of wind and leaves filled the quiet.

With a frown, he listened for her soft breaths.

Nothing.

Unease ripped through him, and he sat up. Surely Rois wouldn't be so foolish as to try and leave.

Still, each time he'd awoken in the night, he'd heard her shifting around. Out of sheer exhaustion mayhap she'd fallen into a deep sleep. Or, perhaps her blanket had fallen over her head, smothering any sound.

Even if she wanted to leave, where could she go? If she headed for her home . . .

The Scots who'd passed close by last eve.

No, she was too smart to try something so dangerous. She missed her father and worried for him, but she would not risk traveling to fight by his side.

Praying he was wrong, he moved to where she lay. Griffin pressed his hand against her blanket.

The firm mound clunked under his touch.

Clunked?

He tore away the covering, touched the bulky shadows.

Wood.

Bedamned! Fear tearing through him, he shoved to his feet and rushed to the entry. The eerie shadow of clouds amidst starlight braided the land in a magical wash. No, there was naught magical about this night.

His horse! With a curse he made to the back of the cave.

A soft nicker greeted him.

She'd left his horse, which meant she traveled on foot. And if he was right, she hurried to catch up to the Scottish knights, men who, if strangers, might harm her—or worse.

A shudder ran through him as he quickly saddled his mount. God forbid if she found the warriors before he intercepted her.

Chapter Nine

Under the first hues of the turbulent dawn, Rois shoved aside the limb of another tree as she slipped through the forest. Loose stone gave beneath her feet. The rich scent of earth and dew filled her each breath.

"On with it," she muttered, ignoring her exhaustion and reaching up to catch the next branch, shoving her toe into a solid foothold. She must catch up to the Scots who'd passed near the cave where she and Griffin had taken shelter. Several times throughout the long hours, she'd caught the faint murmur of voices ahead. With the denseness of the forest slowing their pace, it had to be them, but she would nae be foolish enough with the possible threat of Englishmen near to call out.

The cool morning breeze whipped strands of hair around her face. Rois wiped them away, took a deep breath, and continued up the steep incline.

A deep voice thick with a burr echoed from ahead.

The Scots!

Relief pumping through her, Rois ignored the sharp leaf-barren limbs tugging at her garb.

Rocks slid beneath her feet with each step. Sweat clung to her brow. As she crept higher, she caught the wisps of dawn smothered beneath the churn of thick, ominous clouds. A storm was moving in. The unsettled weather was minor compared to Griffin's outrage when he discovered her gone. Had he awoken? Or did he still sleep, ignorant of her escape?

Even if he searched for her, 'twas too late. After she explained her circumstances to the Scots, they would take her with them to Stirling Bridge.

Boisterous laughter echoed from ahead.

Nerves shot through her, and she released her grasp on the next sturdy limb up the steep incline. What was she doing? This was nae the time for doubts. How many strangers had she met over the years?

Met, aye, but with her father at her side, a man known and respected.

Nay, she'd made her decision. 'Twas exhaustion that instilled her concerns. She reached for the next branch.

Ahead, someone cursed.

Rois let go. In the black of night her plan to join the small band of Scots had seemed rational. As she'd journeyed she'd envisioned their warm welcome and protection. With the men but paces away, their language as foul as a bear-mauled badger, merits of the idea faded. Mayhap she should find her own way to join her da?

A burst of laughter sounded ahead.

Odds stood the men were honorable, their language of warriors, men unaware of her presence. Yet, if they were honorable, why did they nae travel with Wallace or Andrew? Or, had duties delayed their travel?

Nay, she refused to take the risk. Rois half-walked, half-slid down the incline. She'd find her way to the battlefield alone. Many a time she'd ridden through the forest along this same path.

Her da would be furious at her coming, but once she'd arrived, it would be too late for him to send her back. She touched the dagger secured at her waist. With the Scots outnumbered, another fighter would be welcome. Mayhap—

A hand smothered her scream as she was hauled against a very male, very muscled body. She tore at the fingers, twisted against the firm hold to break free.

"Quiet!" Griffin hissed in her ear.

Heart pounding, she nodded.

"I heard something," a nearby warrior said.

"I did as well," a second man replied, his burr deep with suspicion.

"Johan, Rogier, circle wide," the first man ordered. "Whoever is out there, we will find them."

"Aye," a deep voice boomed. "If 'tis the bloody English 'tis my blade he will feel."

"Indeed," the first man agreed.

Griffin wanted to throttle Rois. Did she not realize the danger she'd placed herself in? He took quiet steps back and drew her behind a thicket. "We must leave before they see us," he whispered. "If they discover us, we are dead."

Rois nodded.

Surprised by her quick acquiescence, he frowned. "Do you know them?"

"Nay," she whispered.

He inhaled a deep calming breath. "You were going to saunter up to strangers?"

She turned toward him, frustration in her eyes, but he quietly interrupted, "No, there is no time to talk sense to you. Bloody foolhardy!" Griffin ignored her struggles as he tied a cloth around her mouth, tugged her with him, and backtracked into the bog.

The roll of clouds enveloped the struggle of daylight, the muted light as welcome as the grass silencing their steps.

Calls of the warriors expanding their search echoed nearby.

Griffin grimaced. Before long they would stumble over the broken ground where he and Rois had crossed, then follow their trail. After her actions yesterday past, why had he not expected her to flee? Had he truly believed her content to await her father's return?

A mistake he'd not make again—if they lived.

Neither would he allow Rois out of his sight. She might believe the rebels would aid her, but he had his doubts. These men headed for battle, a clash that could very well leave them dead.

"Over there!" a deep voice called.

Blast it! Griffin pushed Rois ahead of him. "I have secured my horse a ways ahead. Run!" She bolted forward, and he followed in her wake.

"I see him!" another voice boomed. "Through the thicket."

Brush crashed.

Griffin ran faster. They'd spotted only him. If they could put more distance between them, he could hide Rois and lead the men away. At the bottom of the slope, with Rois several paces ahead of him and lost within the thicket, he glanced back.

Three Scots. Two several leagues back, but another to the left closing fast.

He sprinted after Rois.

"Halt!" the man with the deep burr called.

Bedamned! Rocks and grass tore free as Griffin half-ran, half-slid down the dirt and leaf-strewn slope.

"Christ's blood, 'tis an Englishman!" Outrage echoed in the Scot's voice.

Fear glazed Rois's eyes as she glanced back.

"Go!" Griffin ordered.

Her footsteps pounded upon the pungent weave of decaying leaves.

Almost there. Within the dense cover of fir ahead, they could hide until the men abandoned their search and turned toward Stirling. The scrape of branches had him glancing back. The nearest warrior stood several paces away!

"Halt!" the Scot boomed.

Rois whirled.

Blast it! Griffin jerked her gag free. "Keep going. Do not turn back."

"I willna leave you here alone," she rushed out. "'Tis my foolishness that endangered us both."

However impressed by her admission, at her taking responsibility for her actions, now was not the time to argue.

"Run," he said, "I will catch up!"

She shook her head.

Limbs snapped, this time closer.

God's teeth, 'twas too late now for her to run. Whatever the cost, he must keep her safe. "Whatever I say agree," Griffin whispered. "Understand!"

"Aye."

Sword raised, Griffin faced the rebel. "I have no quarrel with you."

The stocky Scot halted several paces away, a dagger firm in his grip, his claymore secured in his sheath on his back. He eyed Rois, and appreciation warmed his gaze.

Griffin silently cursed.

The Scot's gaze shifted to him. "Who is the lass?"

Distant footsteps grew louder.

But moments remained to escape. Griffin gave her hand a squeeze. "My wife."

The Scot grunted with disbelief. "By her garb, the lass is a Scot." He sheathed his dagger and withdrew his claymore. "What say you, lass, are you indeed wed to the Sassenach?"

Her hand trembled in Griffin's. "'Tis true."

"You lie, but I understand," the Scot replied, "'tis self-preservation. Do nae worry, lass, about the bastard's threats."

"He has threatened me naught." Fear rattled her voice.

"Nay?" the Scot asked, "Then why are you with an Englishman when our country is at war?"

Shielding Rois, Griffin slowly stepped forward.

The Scot's eyes narrowed. "I believe your presence is forced."

"Rois, run!" He caught his attacker's hand, but the Scot rammed him. Griffin slammed to the earth, his breath hissing out in a rush.

"Bloody bastard," the warrior spat as he dove atop Griffin. His free hand shot out.

Pain shattered Griffin's head. Vision blurry, he made out the Scot again raising his fist. He jammed his boot against the warrior's gut, kicked.

The Scot fell back.

Griffin dove, pinning the knight to the ground. One of the man's comrades called out from nearby. He drove his fist into the man's face.

Eyes rolling into his head, the warrior slumped back.

On a groan, fighting to focus, Griffin pushed to his feet. He touched his jaw where he'd taken a fist, pulled away. Blood smeared his fingers. After a glance toward the direction where the man's friends approached, he turned and ran.

At the crest of the hill, he spotted Rois crouched amongst the brush. As he neared, she stood.

She reached to touch the gash on his jaw.

Griffin caught her hand and pulled her with him toward where he'd hidden his horse. "Go!"

"You are hurt." Her words rattled between breaths as she ran at his side.

"It matters not."

"I am sorry."

"No time to talk now," Griffin stated.

But there would be, Rois silently finished. The cut on the side of his brow would need stitches. And his eye had already started to swell.

A soft rain began as they sprinted into the thick of the forest. The ground rich with soggy moss thankfully muted their steps. With a curse, he made a sharp turn.

"Where are we going?" she asked.

"To my horse, but he is still too far away. Until the men leave, we must hide."

Around the next bend an enormous fallen tree lay nearby. A tangle of vines strangled the weathered bark in a hideous display.

Griffin tugged her to the weave of roots exposing a large hollowed-out trunk, stepped back. "Inside."

The rich tang of decaying wood filled the air as she stared at the cobwebs adorning the darkened entry. Memories of being trapped as a child in a cavern flooded her.

Pulse racing, Rois stepped back. "I canna go in there. There could be—"

He shoved her inside, followed. "Crawl. Now!"

Rois fought for calm as she inched forward, the mulch of tree rot and dirt clinging to her fingers like a macabre nightmare. She swallowed hard, climbed deeper.

Sodden footsteps hit the ground nearby.

Griffin reached out for a limb cluttered with dying leaves, propped it against the exterior of the opening, then shifted his body to block the meager light.

Blackness encased her, a smothering darkness that threatened her fragile hold on her composure. Thick moments passed, inciting the terror of her youth, the nightmares that as a child often scared her awake. Eyes adjusting to the bleak setting, she began to make out details.

Through the breaks around Griffin and the entwined brush, the vague outline of the forest came into view. Splotches of rain increased to a downpour, the lash of water brutal as gusts beat against the trunk with merciless violence.

The suck of a boot sinking in mud echoed nearby. "Where the bloody hell did they go?"

Another man cursed. "They are nearby."

"Aye," the Scot shouted against the whip of wind. "Go north. I will circle round and meet you on the other side of the ben."

"What of Rogier?"

A grunt. "He should have awakened by the time we finish with the English bastard."

"And the woman?"

Crude laughter echoed. "Once I have had my fill, you can have her."

Rois swallowed against the bile rising in her throat. Griffin reached back, took her hand, and gave a gentle squeeze. Tears misted her eyes. She'd believed the Scots would nae harm her. Thank God she'd hesitated; more, that Griffin had saved her. If the men had caught them . . .

She shuddered at the horrific thoughts. Overwhelmed by the events of the past two days, and the deep-seated fear she never would see her da again, tears rolled down her cheeks. She slowly began to rock, the ball of terror inside growing.

"Rois?"

Griffin's soft whisper stoked her guilt. "I was a fool to believe the men safe."

In the dismal gloom with the thunder of rain pounding against the hollowed-out trunk like a drum, he turned, drew her against his chest. His pulse, strong and steady, calmed her.

"You saw the Scots as but countrymen, those who shared your beliefs, your values." He pushed away several strands of hair from her cheek. "If only 'twas so easy. 'Tis war, the fear, the terror ahead can twist the thoughts of many a man, including those normally guided by honor."

When Griffin should be angry, frustrated by her impulsiveness, he offered support. Moved, she lay within his protective hold. Damn him for making her care for him more. He was the enemy, a man who had threatened to expose her father to the English king, a man who asked nae for the mire she'd dragged him in.

And, he was her husband.

She swallowed hard. Heaven help her, but she'd made a muck of it.

The rain pounded in time to the steady beat of his heart. Rois shifted, unnerved by her complete sense of contentment. "Now what?"

"We wait a little longer, then retrieve my horse and return to the hideout. We will remain there until your father's return."

Her father. She rubbed the dull ache building in her brow. Had the battle begun? Were the Scots fighting at this moment? Was her father en route home? Or dead? She shuddered.

"You are cold?"

"Nay."

"Rois, look at me."

She kept her head against his chest.

In the murky light, he lifted her face, his breath soft upon her cheek. His mouth pressed against hers, his kiss a soft reassurance.

Griffin lifted his head, his breathing uneven. "I will protect you."

"Nay," she replied, needing truth. "You will try."

He nodded. "If need be, with my life."

"So dramatic." She fought to keep her words light, but with her emotions fragile, they crumpled into a rough whisper.

"Dramatic?" He shook his head, the shadows against his face somber. "No, a promise. You know me not. Yet, I ask that you give me your trust."

A denial rose to her lips, then she hesitated. "You saved me because you gave your word to my da to protect me, did you nae?"

Long seconds passed. "I did."

His agreement left her empty, aching inside. She was a half-wit to want him, to believe there'd ever be more.

Silence fell between them, broken by the thrum of rain, the sweet scent of dampened earth and decaying tree filling her each breath. She took in the man who, if allowed the time, might break her heart.

Nay, surely she confused her feelings of gratitude for more because he'd rescued her. "My thanks for saving me."

Quiet echoed around them.

"Griffin?"

He released her and stared at the wind twisting the leaf-sodden limbs shuddering against their shelter. "You have thanked me. There is naught more to say."

Guilt edged through her. "I have offended you."

A rough laugh fell from his mouth. "No, clarified my thoughts."

At the angst in his voice, hope ignited. Could he be coming to care for her as well?

"What do you mean?"

Her soft inquiry poured through Griffin in a disarming slide. Never could he explain that the threat to her life, more than his promise to keep her safe to Lord Brom, had guided his actions. It was her, the feelings she inspired. The past had taught him that when one tossed emotions into the mix, it muddled clear views, trampled upon common sense.

With her body but a touch away, exhaustion and worry caused his mind to wander—a dangerous act. He refused to allow her to become important in his life.

"We will wait a little more," Griffin said, his voice blunt, "then we will depart."

"I see."

He doubted she did. If indeed she was aware of how she affected him, he didn't need confirmation. Their time together would be challenging enough without her knowing how much he wanted her. Memories of how close he'd come to consummating their marriage haunted him. God's teeth, with her body a breath away, the soft scent of woman filling his every breath, 'twas difficult enough to refrain from touching her.

"Griffin?"

He turned and inched toward the opening. "'Tis time we left."

"You said we were going to wait a while longer."

He stilled. What was he bloody doing? He didn't lose his focus— except 'twould seem with Rois.

"You are upset with me, as you should be," she said.

"Your leaving was foolish."

Silence.

"Was it not?" he pressed, clinging to anger. Anger was safe, as it clouded his thoughts of making love to her.

"I need to be with my father."

He scowled. "Do you think he would have wished your presence on the battlefield?"

The muted light illuminated the determination upon her face. "Many women have fought beside their clansmen in the past."

Was the lass mind-ticked? "Battle is no place for a woman."

"And 'tis for a man?"

He clenched his hand into a fist, then slowly unfurled his fingers. The lass would test the stoutest man. "From youth," he explained, ire tainting his voice, "men train to wield their swords."

"You speak of a man's physical strength. What of their hearts, what of their battered souls as they witness a friend's blood spilled upon the earth?" Her lower lip trembled. "Tell me, can you prepare for that?"

Memories bludgeoned him of the good and honorable men he'd known, the many men who'd lost their lives beneath the sword, men he'd buried. "No," he whispered, his voice rough, "no one can prepare for that. Neither is battle a fate I would wish you to see." He took her hand. "War is not filled with the glory the bards recite. Battle is wrought with the confrontation of blades, of lives severed and blood staining the earth until 'tis a river of grief. With the cost of life each battle brings, no one truly wins."

Against the feeble rays of light, tears glistened in her eyes. "Many a man I have stitched together after battle. Too many others have I watched die. Well I know the price of war, but who says 'tis men who must sacrifice their lives, men who must raise their blades to defend a country they love? Tell me," she demanded. "If the men are dead, think you nae 'tis the women who must protect their homes, and raise their swords to defend their land?"

The passion in her words moved him, her fierce loyalty more so. He caressed his fingers along the curve of her cheek. "'Tis the way of our life."

"So say men."

"Rois—"

"My opinion matters not, I know."

"It does," he replied, "but 'tis too late to change the beliefs of our people."

She stared at him for a long moment. "'Tis too late only if we decide so."

What could he say? Never before had he considered otherwise, but she was right. Lives were guided by beliefs. Though muscle wielded a deadly blade, 'twas the mind that did the planning and made the decisions on the battlefield.

The pummel of rain rapped upon the sodden wood with a steady thrum. With the Scottish rogues in search of them, he should feel on edge, but he found his thoughts more on Rois, how with each day spent with her, he wanted more.

A mistake to even ponder such.

He tugged her hand. "Let us go. The men should have moved on. If indeed they are still in the vicinity, the rain will shield us from their view and wash away our tracks."

She nodded.

With haste, he led her through the weave of trees, and prayed the Scots had not discovered where he'd hid his mount.

Hours later with the sun setting heavy in the clearing sky, Griffin halted his steed before the cave they'd hidden in the previous night. After moving the shield of brush hiding the entry, he led her inside, then replaced the branches.

He turned. Rois stood paces away, trembling. He silently cursed, but he'd not make the same mistake. "'Tis too dangerous to make a fire."

"Aye."

The wind blustered outside, hard with the edge of cold, the shadows of night smothering the last remnants of day. "'Twill be dark soon, a good night's rest will serve us both well."

Rois rubbed her arms. "I must care for your gash."

As they'd raced through the forest, he'd forgotten the cut he'd received during the fight. Griffin touched his brow, pulled away to find blood caked on his fingers. He winced at the tenderness of the swollen skin.

"The swelling will go down in a day or so."

Her guilt-fed words had him glancing up. He shrugged. "I have lived through far worse."

"Mayhap, but I will treat your wound."

"Will you?" He'd meant to tease her, to lighten the mood, but somehow the moment shifted to something intimate. After this day, with his frustration at Rois's escape and saving her from the Scottish rogues, he should be immune to her. Except with each passing moment, he wanted her more. Beneath his gaze, her blush deepened.

Clearing her throat, she glanced toward the supplies he'd piled near his mount. "Are there herbs as well?"

"Yes." 'Twas best to let her treat him and be done with it. The hours ahead would prove to be challenging indeed. After removing the items she'd need from his saddle pouch, he sat. Rois expertly cleaned and treated the area with water, then patted the wound dry. "I need to sew a couple of stitches."

He nodded.

"The bleeding has stopped and the wound will heal, but it will leave a scar."

"'Twill not be my first."

Indeed, Rois mused. Thin, aged scars graced his jaw and a long line marred the side of his neck. Scars of a man who'd lived, scars of a man who was unafraid to fight for what he believed in.

"Aye, you have more," she agreed, "but this one is my doing."

The hard set of his face eased. "How could you know the Scots were an untrustworthy lot?"

"Do nae give me an excuse. I should have considered my actions instead of acting on my emotions."

"As when you challenged me on the day we wed?"

At the edge in his voice, she held his gaze. A truth she'd earned. "A fact I deeply regret."

"Do you?"

"Aye."

He exhaled, a long, frustrated sound. "I know."

If his words had held condemnation, that she could have accepted. But his understanding and gentleness left her humbled.

Under different circumstances, she would seek to deepen the draw between them. But she could nae change reality. His country and hers were at war. Her father as well as many others she loved battled against his king. Any hint of what might exist between them was forbidden.

"Acting on my emotions is an error I seem to repeat over and again," she admitted, needing him to understand.

He crossed his arms. "If you know of your weakness, why do you not address it?"

She stared at him a long moment. "Do you think I have nae tried?"

"Mayhap your last *effort* will aid you to try harder in the future." In the fading light, he retrieved the blankets and made a single pallet.

Uneasiness crept through her. "Where is your bed?"

"We are sleeping together. The last time I left you alone, you escaped while I slept."

The nonchalance in his words had her taking a step back. "I canna."

He glanced up, his mouth grim.

Rois cleared her throat and rubbed her forearm. "We are to procure an annulment."

"Our sharing of blankets will not make you less chaste."

"But—"

"Rois, we will do naught but sleep."

Pulse racing, she stepped back. "Do you think I have nae learned my lesson?"

"I believe so, neither will I take the risk."

Arrogance, pure and simple. She angled her chin. "And what if, once you are asleep, I slip from our covers without you noticing?"

A grim smile touched his face. "'Twill not happen."

"Your being a light sleeper will nae keep me from leaving."

"I agree."

She hesitated. "You agree?"

Instead of answering, Griffin shoved to his feet, walked to his mount, and withdrew a short cord.

Her heart pounded. "What do you think you are doing?"

"What I should have done from the first." Before she could bolt, he caught her arm.

"Let me go!"

"I will, once Lord Brom has returned."

She twisted her wrist in an attempt to break free. "You canna expect to keep me bound 'til he arrives?"

"I never said I was going to."

"Then what are you doing with the rope?"

"Tying our ankles together for the night." Griffin started to lean over.

"Wait!"

He straightened, shot her a hard look. "Rois, we both are tired and need sleep."

She couldn't be tied to him all night! "Are you addled?"

"With you," he agreed with a grimace, "on many an occasion."

The braggart. "This is naught to jest about."

He leaned over, secured the rope, and bound their ankles in a snug knot. Griffin gave the rope a tug. "No, but a safer option."

At the roughness of his voice, she took in his face as he straightened. In the last shards of light, she caught a trace of desire in his eyes.

Memories of how he'd touched her left her body aching. Her eyes shifted to his mouth, and she wanted his lips on hers. "Griffin," she whispered, "I think our sharing a bed is a poor decision."

His look was one of pain and pure male appreciation. "I agree, which, regrettably, changes naught."

Chapter Ten

Against the flickers of waning light, Griffin halted beside the pallet he and Rois would share. He loathed securing his and Rois's ankles together, but after the events last night, he couldn't trust that she would remain with him in the cave.

Rois cleared her throat. "I need to change into dry clothes."

A fact, with his emotions in mayhem, he'd overlooked. "I will remove the rope—temporarily. Try and run, and next time I will not give you the privacy to change."

"I know my limitations when it comes to you," she said, her voice cool.

He grunted. "That I sincerely doubt." With a few quick tugs, he removed the binding. After a warning glare, he strode to the back of the cave, where he'd hidden a satchel. He withdrew a gown for her and dry garb for himself, then walked over and handed Rois her clothes. "I will wait near the entry until you are through."

She accepted her gown. "My thanks."

Griffin walked to the cave's opening. He leaned against the cool, smooth stone and stared at the last few rays of the setting sun shimmering in the sky.

The distant splat of damp clothes hitting the ground echoed behind him.

Images of Rois naked slid through his mind. He fought the temptation to steal a look, but seeing her tempting body would help naught. Already he was too aware of her, his almost having made love to her in Dunadd Castle leaving an all too clear memory of her luscious curves and intoxicating taste.

"I— I am finished."

Griffin took a steading breath. "Turn around."

Without hesitation she complied.

He walked over. Once he'd secured the last tie on his garb, he stood. "Rois."

She turned.

He lifted the rope. "Come."

Anger burned in her eyes. "I am nae allowing you to tie me willingly."

A wash of tiredness swept through him. "A fact you have made excessively clear."

Head held high, she crossed the distance, placed her ankle against his. "Be done with it."

"We will be bound for but hours. 'Tis not as if I am banishing you to the Otherworld."

Eyes wide, she scanned the cave. "'Tis nae good to jest of the fey, or of the home where they live."

Griffin thought of his sister's family, the MacGruders, Scottish rebels who believed in tales of the fey, the wee folk a common belief in the lives of many a Scot. He touched the halved Magnesite hanging from a chain around his neck, and thought of the MacGruder brothers' grandmother who'd gifted the gemstone to him many years ago. An amazing woman whose insight had touched him deeply.

He smiled as he thought of the brothers' belief that their grandmother's chamber held magic. That the halved stone she'd given to each of her grandsons was a talisman to predict a future mate. Though each MacGruder wife had obtained her matching half of the stone her husband wore around his neck, Griffin dismissed the belief as whimsy. Regardless, the brothers believed the tale of the stones' ability to draw a man's mate.

"Why are you smiling?" Rois asked.

"Distant memories." He explained no more. They need not build a relationship on any level. With care he helped her lay beside him. "Our bodies' heat will keep us warm."

"I was fine with the blankets I had last eve," she said.

"You would tell me that regardless if you were wet to the bone and your teeth chattered all night."

Aye, she would. With a sigh Rois settled at his side, the tug of rope a potent reminder of her situation. "Do you think all brides are treated with such restriction?"

Griffin shifted his back to her. "Only those who try and flee."

She didn't want to be charmed by his good-natured teasing. Why couldn't he be cold and brutal instead of a man who, in addition to having quick wit, she was learning held great compassion? Her father would never have allowed her to marry a ruthless man. But, still, he'd allowed her to marry their enemy.

Her father. Rois's thoughts sobered. Please let him be on his way to Kincardan Castle. She refused to think of other dismal possibilities.

Rois shifted her thoughts back to the reasons her father would allow her to wed Lord Monceaux. Several came to mind, but only one made sense—Da knew him. With her father a powerful noble, 'twas easy to believe he'd met the baron during high-level meetings discussing King Edward's demands or the Scots' unrest. And with each encounter, her father had grown to respect Griffin regardless of his fealty, had sensed that in a time of desperation, Lord Monceaux was a man he could trust.

But with her life?

Unsettled, nae wanting to find further reasons that erased the tension between them, or think of his kiss in the hollowed log that'd touched her deeply, she shifted as far away from him as possible.

"Go to sleep," he grumbled.

Why did his voice, rough with exhaustion, have to sound so appealing? "Do you snore?"

"No."

"Talk in your sleep?"

He exhaled. "Rois?"

"Aye?"

"I neither snore nor talk in my sleep. Rois, you will be safe."

"I know that."

"I know you worry for your father. As do I. Know I pray he returns safe."

Humbled by his concern, by his thoughtfulness, she nodded, with her emotions so fragile, nae trusting herself to speak. As she lay in silence, the creep of cold slid over her. With a grimace, she inched toward him.

"I am moving closer only for warmth," she clarified.

He grunted. Moments later his soft, steady breaths filled the night.

"Griffin?"

The slightest of snores echoed from his mouth.

Asleep. For the best. He need nae discern she'd moved against him because in addition to warmth, she found comfort at the nearness. She was afraid. How could she nae be? Her father was at war, a battle that defined Scotland's future. Neither had she recovered from her confrontation with the Scots earlier in the day.

At the howl of wind edged with an icy chill, she pressed her body fully against his. If only for the next few hours, she could pretend he was someone who cared for her, would hold her forever if the need arose.

The patter of rain tapped against the ground.

Sadness swept her, and Rois stared out into the night, catching wisps of the stars between the clouds racing across the blackened sky. With tears blurring her vision, she prayed. *Please God, when the fighting is over, let my father live.*

A distant neigh echoed through Griffin's sleep-tumbled mind. Someone was outside! He started to stand; a rope pulled at his leg.

A woman's sleepy groan came from his side.

What in . . . He muttered a curse. He'd bound Rois to him last eve. Griffin untied the rope, then hurried to the cave's entrance. An icy wind whipped against his face as he scanned the curve of hill and earth below.

Sunlight glinted across the morning sky and fog clung with greedy hands obscuring the land, with naught but wisps of treetops below rising above the misty churn.

Fragmented clops of hooves against the rain-laden earth echoed from the southwest.

He searched the thick weave of mist.

The murky outline of a horse and rider came into view.

Faded.

Moments later the rider reappeared.

Whoever it was, they came from the direction where De Moray and Wallace had taken their troops to confront the English at Stirling Bridge.

He rubbed his brow, frowned. Was the battle over?

Had the Scots won?

Griffin glanced inside the cave. Rois lay beneath the covers asleep. As tired as he was from rescuing her yesterday, he'd awoken several times during the night to find her pressed against him in sweet temptation.

His body stirred at the thought. He grimaced. 'Twould seem his protecting her offered its own brand of punishment.

The thrum of hooves grew closer.

Griffin turned.

As the rider passed below, he leaned forward in his saddle, his hand on the whip urging his mount faster.

Whatever had occurred, he must know. Griffin rushed over and shook her shoulder. "Rois, wake up."

A grumble slipped from her mouth. Her tousled hair and sleep-thickened lips caught the golden rays of dawn and emitted their own sensual appeal.

"Rois," he said, irritated at his weakness when it came to her. "'Tis no time for sleep."

Her heavy lids flickered open. Green eyes glazed with sleep stared at him, then widened. She sat. "What is wrong?"

"A Scot, possibly from de Moray's ranks, just rode past toward Kincardan Castle."

She gasped. "Word from the battle?"

"Mayhap."

Rois stumbled to her feet. "We must return. I need to know if he comes with news of Da."

Griffin agreed. Had the rebels lost? Were the English marching toward the stronghold? Did this man ride to warn the Scots to flee deeper into the Highlands? Once he'd saddled his mount, he lifted Rois, then swung up behind her.

In silence they rode, the swirl of fog dense in places making the travel treacherous. He cursed every stream they crossed, each hill they crested to find another beyond.

Hours later, the thick stone walls of Kincardan Castle rose before them, the hard-edged crenellations imposing, the quarried stone hewn by man to protect as well as intimidate.

Rois shivered.

Griffin drew her closer against him. "I know you are cold. We will be there soon."

"I am nae cold," she replied, her words unsure, "'Tis that I feel . . ."

"Uneasy?"

She glanced back, frowned. "How did you know?"

Griffin guided his mount toward the imposing fortress. "I feel it as well."

An uneasiness that'd haunted him twice before in his life, and both had delivered enormous consequences. The first time, the day of his parents' tragic death. The second, the day of his sister's abduction.

With a prayer on his lips, he guided his lathered mount beneath the arch of stone of the gatehouse, the clatter of hooves in the dank confines foreboding. Inside the bailey, he drew his steed to a halt.

Ominous clouds loomed above as a crowd of women and children milled inside. Amidst the throng, a lone rider sat upon his horse. Beneath the dirt and blood, sadness marred his face.

"Sir Lochlann," Rois whispered.

Griffin's angst grew. Why had Lochlann returned alone? If the Earl of Surrey's troops had crossed Stirling Bridge, with the English far outnumbering the Scots, de Moray and Wallace would have little time to send anyone to warn their families to flee.

Heart in his throat, Griffin kicked his mount forward. As they reached the edge of the crowd, Sir Lochlann turned toward them. Fury flared in his eyes.

"God no," Rois gasped. "Something terrible has happened."

"We will soon know," Griffin replied. The Scot's anger was no doubt inflamed from seeing Rois seated before Griffin. Not that he entertained thoughts of keeping Rois as his wife. The woman was beyond trouble. She had a stubborn streak through her that'd make a badger take note. But her eyes, God in heaven, her eyes exposed her every thought, her sensitivity, caring, and passion.

Griffin set aside his musings. He needed to focus on the news the rebel brought.

The crowd fell away as Lochlann nudged his mount to Griffin and Rois. Two paces away, the Scot drew his steed to a halt. Worry-clouded eyes rested upon Rois.

"Is it Da?" Fear shook her voice, and Griffin wrapped his arm around her waist, gave a gentle squeeze.

Lochlann nodded. "'Tis why I returned," he rasped. "Your father is alive, but the wound . . . Christ's eyes, 'tis brutal."

Rois's body began to shake. "Will he live?"

The Scot swallowed hard, cursed. "We are unsure."

"Nay!"

Whispers of Lord Brom's condition rolled through the crowd, and several women began weeping.

Tightness wrung Griffin's chest as he drew Rois against him. He loved Angus like a father, prayed that he would live. "Your father is a strong man, Rois."

Tear-filled eyes met his. "But just a man all the same." She turned. "Lochlann, what are his injuries?"

"Lord Brom has a large gash on his side, another in his head, and," Lochlann explained, his words strained, "we removed an arrow from his shoulder."

Rois wiped tears away from her cheeks. "Where is he? I— I must go to him."

"Nay," Lochlann replied, "Your father bids for you to stay away. 'Tis too dangerous."

Griffin agreed. Rois needed to remain where she was safe. "And what of the battle?"

"The battle at Stirling Bridge is over," the Scot boomed, pride filling his voice. "Once the English bastards had a taste of our blades, they ran like dogs with their tails between their legs."

Cheers rose from the crowd as the people around them turned to hug each other.

De Moray and Wallace's forces had turned back John de Warenne and Hugh de Cressingham's troops? Incredible. "The Scots were vastly outnumbered," Griffin said through the happy yells, fighting to wrap his thoughts around the magnitude of this victory, the wonderful impossibility.

"Aye," Sir Lochlann agreed, "a detail made clear by de Moray as he spoke with us on the morning of the battle. But the Sassenach tried to cross Stirling Bridge."

Tears rolling down her cheeks, Rois shook her head. "Such a choice makes no sense."

As the crowd talked excitedly around them, Griffin shook his head. "It does not. The bridge is wide enough for only two men to cross at once. Warenne's battle skills are far too superior for him to make such a poor tactical decision."

Sir Lochlann grunted. "The poor decision is owed to the English treasurer. Cressingham values money more than the lives of men. His shouts of discontent at Warenne, of his desire to hurry on with the battle so he could leave, echoed across the river."

"Still," Griffin said as he mulled what Cressingham should have understood, "if they had sent the troops to the ford a short distance away, they could have crossed numerous horsemen abreast with ease." What he and the Scottish leaders had previously discussed.

"Aye, on that we agree." Sir Lochlann grimaced. "In the end, for the poor decisions made, King Edward's men paid the price. As did the Treacherer."

Treacherer. Griffin grimaced. A name given to Cressingham by the Scots. His abusive ways earned him no friends amongst the English. Instead, his self-serving actions had gained him the title of the Son of Death.

"What happened to Cressingham?" Rois asked.

At her question, several people nearby quieted, their attention on Sir Lochlann.

"Flayed him, they did." Lochlann grunted. "The bastard will nae be ordering any more Scots cut down."

Gasps echoed from the women, and Rois's face grew deathly white.

"That Cressingham is dead is enough," Griffin warned.

Red streaked the Scot's cheeks, and he nodded to Rois. "Aye, 'tis nae a description fitting a lass's ears."

Mayhap not a lass's ears, but Griffin understood exactly who the description had been for—him. However jealous, however much Sir Lochlann hated Griffin, for the Scot to upset Rois further was unforgivable.

"It matters nae," Rois said, her voice trembling, "I must see my father."

"Nay, Lord Brom's request was clear," Sir Lochlann stated. "He wishes you nowhere near the battlefield."

She stiffened. "My father may be dying. You will take me or heaven help me, I will ride there myself."

"'Tis no place for a lass," Sir Lochlann growled. "Though the battle was swift, the carnage 'tis a sight that makes a seasoned warrior cringe."

Rois scowled. "Well I know the price of war, and the cost."

"Rois," her friend said, "as Lord Monceaux cautioned, though the English fled, to be outside the castle walls is far from safe. And, more worries we have." He paused, shot Griffin a hard look before turning back to Rois. "'Tis your cousin."

"Andrew?"

"Aye," Lochlann said. "He is severely injured."

Griffin stilled. God's teeth. Wallace knew the basics of how to wage a fight, but the crucial strategy backing the rebels was de Moray's. Expertise gained from his time in Europe, the tactics achieved by his training with the Swiss mercenaries.

"How badly?" Griffin asked.

Hatred flashed in Lochlann's eyes. "'Twould seem we will both know when we reach him. Sir Wallace bade me bring you to the encampment to take de Moray to Cumbuskenneth Abbey."

"De Moray requested the Englishman's presence?" a Scot nearby asked with skepticism.

Lochlann's mouth tightened. "Aye."

Whispers of disbelief raced through the crowd.

Yet another reason the Scot was furious. Griffin would never reveal he could be trusted by the rebels, or of his close bond with both Wallace and de Moray.

Her face pale with shock, Rois shook her head. "I canna lose them both."

"We must leave immediately," Griffin said, far from looking forward to traveling with the Scot, a man who would kill him without hesitation.

"Aye. Except"—Sir Lochlann frowned—"Sir Wallace made it clear that Rois was to travel with you, but her father wants her kept away from the battlefield as much as possible."

A muscle worked in Griffin's jaw. "'Tis bloody unsafe."

"At the risk of earning Wallace's displeasure, I questioned the wisdom of Rois leaving as well. Neither do I agree on having an Englishman anywhere near de Moray," the Scot stated, his voice crisp, "but he refused to discuss the reason behind either decision."

And with good reason, Griffin mused. To request an English lord who held a high position within the king's court to escort one of the Scots' most powerful leaders was a decision that would raise many a rebel's ire. But the Scots trusted Wallace, understood he did nothing without good reason. God forbid if Wallace's request reached King Edward's ears.

Still, why would Wallace want Rois in accompaniment? To say something was amiss put it mildly. Like the rebels, Griffin would do as Wallace asked.

"To remind you," Sir Lochlann said, breaking into his thoughts, "I will ride with you and Rois as well."

As if he'd forgotten? The Scot's presence would make for a tedious trip. The Scot hated him for having wed Rois, for the wedding being allowed to stand, and for Griffin being asked to take de Moray to Cumbuskenneth Abbey. Each day, Griffin's displeasure with Sir Lochlann increased as well. 'Twould seem they shared a common bond.

"And," Sir Lochlann glanced at Rois, "to keep your cousin safe, they moved him a distance from the battlefield."

"How far is he from my father?" Rois asked.

"Several leagues," Sir Lochlann replied.

Griffin cursed. "'Tis still too near the battlefield."

"Aye," the Scot agreed. "But the decision was nae mine."

"I care little who made the decision," Rois said. "I wish to see my cousin, but I *will* see my father first. I am nae a weak-kneed woman who needs protection."

Tenderness and concern creased Sir Lochlann's face. "Christ's eyes, Rois, I would nae keep you away from your father. But 'tis nae my choice."

To Griffin, the sincerity in the Scot's voice rang false. Lochlann may wish to take Rois to her father, but he doubted true concern lay behind his reason.

"Once we pack enough food to travel, we will leave immediately. As for our destination," Lochlann said, his gaze on Rois, "we will follow Wallace's request and your father's." The Scot dismounted, strode to the keep.

As he watched the Scot walk away, Griffin grimaced. Rois might believe Sir Lochlann a man to depend on, one she called friend, but Griffin was far from convinced. He would keep a watch for the notions Sir Lochlann would surely try to put in Rois's head. Blast that Wallace had asked Rois to ride with them.

Or . . . had he?

Wallace's request for Griffin to escort de Moray to Cumbuskenneth Abbey rang true, more so by the Scot's anger. But had his friend indeed requested Rois's presence as well?

The more Griffin pondered the questions, the greater his disquiet. Though he had no proof, one thing he believed without a doubt . . .

Sir Lochlann was a liar.

Chapter Eleven

Rois drew her cape closer, the whip of wind chilling where she, Griffin, and Lochlann had made camp. An ache built in her chest as she scanned the fragmented land, hard sweeps ravaged by winter, valleys smoothed by the passage of time. She cursed the fading day, inhibiting their ability to continue to travel. What of her father? Was he struggling to live? Or, was he already . . .

She closed her eyes, fought to control her emotions. On a deep breath she lifted her lids, studied the wash of land blurred through her tears. Frustrated, terrified for her father's life, she brushed the tears away. Da lived. She savored the belief in her mind; it was much needed assurance to her battered soul.

Flickers of dying sunlight rippled across the sky, the rays like waning fingers of orange. Along the horizon, a glow built within the heavens, a subtle shimmer that embraced the land as if magic cast.

Magic?

Nay, naught but worry existed this day, the weight of her thoughts far from those inspired by the fey. All she wished for at this moment was to know that her father lived.

Rocks clattered nearby.

Rois turned.

From around a tall boulder, Lochlann made his way toward her, his thick red hair tied at the nape of his neck. He reached the flat boulder where she sat, and halted. "Dinna ye mind if I sit with ye?"

She gave him a smile, comforted by his concern, his familiar face welcome during this turbulent time. "Nay, 'twould please me."

"And me." He glanced toward where Griffin tended the horses, scowled.

"None of that now," she said.

Lochlann grunted. "The bloody Sassenach should nae be charged with escorting de Moray to Cumbuskenneth Abbey. Odd, I find it, for Wallace to be making such a request."

A disquiet Rois shared, but as her father had said many times, war oftentimes made strange bedfellows. Whatever guided Wallace in asking Griffin to escort her cousin to the abbey, he did so with good reason.

"I believe Wallace's request is more a strategic move," she said.

Lochlann settled beside her, rubbed his thighs. "You have an idea of the why, then?"

She picked up a weather-smoothed stone, rolled it in her palm. "Nay, but having met Wallace several times in my life and given his keen mind, neither can I believe he has made the decision in error." He shrugged, but she caught the tension in his shoulders. "Lochlann?"

He faced the dwindling rays.

"You are upset," she said. "More so than because of Wallace's request."

His jaw tightened as he turned to face her, grey eyes hard with shadows and anger. "You should nae be with the Englishman."

Rois set the stone aside. "Lord Monceaux and I handfasted."

"Bedamned, Rois, the marriage was a farce."

"'Twas my fault. And now my father's wish. But," she said, her voice but a whisper, "temporary."

"Is it?"

Stunned by his accusation, she stared at her childhood friend, with whom throughout the years she'd shared many a secret. "Aye, why would you think our union anything but?" Even as she asked, a part of her found regret that indeed the marriage would end, and in weeks if nae days Griffin would ride away and she would never see him again. Absurd thoughts indeed when he was her enemy.

And he was . . . Wasn't he?

"Rois?"

Unsettled by her thoughts, she stood, the shimmer of the sun's rays illuminating the land as it faded, just like her dreams of love or happily ever after.

"'Tis growing late," she said. "'Twill be a long day of travel on the morrow."

Lochlann stood, towered over her, the wisps of light embracing his hard expression. "You have feelings for the Englishman."

"It is nae what you think."

"Nay?" He cursed. "Has he touched you?"

She narrowed her eyes. "I am a woman wed. I will nae be discussing what Griffin and I do in private."

"You were handfasted in an act to protect your father, an act that I curse myself for allowing."

Guilt swept her, the memories of how Griffin had touched her, how she wanted more. "Lochlann, you didna—"

"This entire misfortune is because of me. Never should I have told you of the Englishman's threat to your father. I should have found a way to convince Lord Brom to leave before the baron noticed him seated at the front of the chamber."

"It matters nae," Rois replied. "The deed is done."

Lochlann took her hand, laid it over his heart. "A deed that will soon be undone. Of that I swear."

At his intimate gesture, she tried to pull away; he held tight. Panic swept her. "Release me."

"I will nae let you go. I love you, Rois. Have since you were a wee lass and shot down my stick fortress with your slingshot."

Laughter and sadness melded in her throat at the image of the blustery indignant lad. "Lochlann, we are nay longer children."

His eyes searching hers, he stroked her face with the pad of his thumb. "Aye. You are a woman well grown, a woman whom I love and have always loved."

Alarmed by his intensity, Rois again tried to withdraw her hand. For a moment he held, then released her. She stepped back. "Lochlann, I am married. 'Tis unseemly to speak of such."

His nostrils flared. "I will nae give up on you, lass."

Regret touched her. She was too aware of Lochlann's deep emotions toward her, of the many years he'd wanted her, and how she'd turned him away. Though she loved him as a friend, as much as she'd tried to care more for him on an intimate level, never would her desire for him be more.

She shook her head. "I—"

"Rois." Behind her, ice etched Griffin's voice.

She whirled. Her husband stood several paces away. The grey cast of the advancing night warred with the shimmers of the new moon against the fury carved on his face.

Hand clasping his dagger, Lochlann stepped forward.

Bedamned her friend for provoking Griffin. Rois stepped between the two men. "Has a runner come?"

A runner? Griffin muttered a curse. As if his wife alone with another man professing his love was not reason enough for his intervention? Rois belonged to him.

Until their annulment.

Griffin awaited the sweep of relief of his impending freedom, of the day when he could ride away without the weight of a woman who promised naught but complications. Instead, a sense of emptiness left his heart with a subtle ache.

His heart? Laughable. He could not have deep feelings for Rois. He'd known her but days.

Yet the emptiness remained.

Frustrated, he forced his thoughts to his realization of moments before. When he'd first seen Lochlann in the great room at Dunadd Castle, he'd thought the Scot looked familiar. Amidst the chaos, he'd dismissed the memory as quick. But as he'd rounded the corner, the anger in Sir Lochlann's voice had invoked an image of a Scot in an inn abusing the woman two years past. The bastard would never touch Rois!

"Stay away from my wife," Griffin warned. "Touch her, look at her the wrong way, and I will kill you."

Challenge glinting his eyes, Sir Lochlann stepped forward. "Dare you threaten me, Sassenach?"

He ignored the ugly slang for an Englishman. "I make no threats. A promise, the same as I made at the tavern two years past."

Surprise flared in the Scot's gaze.

"Griffin, Lochlann," Rois said, panic riding her voice.

"Heed my words, Scot, the next time you will feel not the lash of my tongue, but my blade. Now, keep a lookout for any danger." Griffin caught Rois's hand. "I need to speak with my wife—in private." He strode with her into the moon-ridden land.

She hurried to keep by his side. "Lochlann is a friend. He would never harm me."

Griffin grunted.

Frustrated, Rois glanced back, caught the outline of Lochlann against the glow of the rising moon. "And what did you mean by a promise you made two years back? Do you know him?"

"We have met."

The anger in his voice assured her the meeting was neither friendly nor welcome. "When?"

Once they'd rounded a boulder giving them privacy, far from where Lochlann could hear or see them, Griffin whirled. "Two years past, I was en route to deliver a writ. While drinking a tankard of ale at a tavern, I heard a woman scream."

Nerves edged through her. "What has that to do with Lochlann?"

"'Twas he who held the woman roughly, he who had shoved her in the corner, and he who was taking unwanted liberties."

"It must have been someone else. Sir Lochlann is a fierce warrior who intimidates some."

"It was Lochlann."

Anger filled his voice, raw with conviction, a belief that left Rois struggling to accept his words. "Why would he do such a thing?"

"Because he is an arrogant man who believes in taking what he wants."

"Lochlann has a stubborn streak," she agreed, "and a temper at times, but he does nae mistreat women or take what is nae freely offered."

"You doubt me?"

"From the time I have known you, you have proven yourself an honorable man."

"Yet," Griffin said, "you remain hesitant to believe me?"

"What happened between you two that night?" Rois asked, wondering if she truly wanted to know.

"When Lochlann refused to let the woman go, I dragged him from her. I threatened him if he ever touched the woman again."

Which explained the immense dislike between the men. On edge, she turned toward the moon, its silver beams spilling upon the land like fairy dust spilled. She swallowed hard. Over the years, she'd witnessed touches of Lochlann's anger, but she'd wanted to believe the best about him and had dismissed the incidents as rare. How could she nae, when he was her friend.

"Rois, you are not to be alone with him again."

At the fierce passion within his voice, she faced him. The sheer need in his eyes stunned her, ignited memories of his touch upon their wedding night, of how her skin tingled with awareness, how her body had burned for him.

She shuddered. Each moment she remained alone with Griffin, wanting him as she did now, 'twas dangerous. To linger where her fantasies lived and breathed their own life would leave her hurt in the end.

"We need to rest," he whispered, but his voice lacked conviction. "Our journey on the morrow will be long."

"It will," she agreed.

Wind slipped through Rois's hair, fluttering strands across her cheek in a gentle caress. Griffin caught a wayward lock and pushed it back, savoring the touch of his finger across her skin. Never had he wanted a woman as much as her.

Drawn, needing to taste her as he needed the air he breathed, he laid his mouth over hers in a soft kiss, one that ignited a yearning for more, invited images of him stripping her naked and making love to her.

Breaths coming fast, he broke the kiss. She was an innocent and had no idea of the dangers each second alone with him wrought, more so with them hidden from sight.

"Go," he whispered, each moment weakening his intent to leave her untouched.

She remained before him, her desire clear in her eyes, in the quickness of her breath, and in the way her body leaned against him.

He willed himself to step away. "I need you to know that if we had made . . ." He closed his eyes, opened them. "One day you will find the happiness you deserve. Happiness I cannot give."

"Why is happiness nae yours to give?"

The confusion and concern in her voice touched him deeply, made him want her more than was right. "My life is one of turmoil, of . . ." He could tell her nothing. "Due to the demands of my duties I am often away."

"Nobles are often away for various reasons of duty to whom they swear fealty, but they marry, have families, build dreams of more."

God's teeth, this woman could stir him as no other. "Rois, can you not see that our marriage will never last because"—he paused, saddened to introduce reality at what could be for them a defining moment—"we are enemies."

"Are we?"

That she dared look beyond what most saw shattered his every defense. "Rois," he whispered, his voice trembling from the intensity of wanting her, "do not do this."

She started to speak, but he found his patience for questions at an end, their earlier kiss a pittance compared to what he yearned for. On an exhale, Griffin claimed her lips with fierce possession. Her taste infused him, and her complete return of passion left him a man willing to drown.

He lifted his head, stared at her face framed within the moon's glow. "You are beautiful," he whispered against her lips, wanting her, wondering if ever he would tire of her taste.

With a gentle touch, he framed her face in his hands, took her mouth slowly, completely, capturing her tongue, suckling slowly, thoroughly. When she began to shake, he edged her back against the moss-covered stone, aligned his entire body against hers to show her the need she inspired.

"Griffin," she moaned.

"Feel me," he whispered, kissing the curve of her chin, tasting the silk of her throat. He drew her palm against his chest. "I want you to touch me."

For a long moment she studied him.

Throat dry, he watched her. "Please."

A nervous smile trembled on her lips, then she nodded. Trembling fingers rested on his chest, slid over him in an unsteady glide.

At her innocent exploration, his body hardened with a fierce ache.

"Do you like this?" she asked as she slid her finger beneath his tunic, touched his nipple.

Like it? 'Twas bliss itself. "Indeed," he hissed through clenched teeth.

She hesitated. "You are in pain?"

Yes, with wanting to sink deep in her slick warmth and take her until she screamed with her release. "No," he managed. "My reaction is normal."

"Truly?"

"Yes." Griffin steadied himself. "Touch me, anywhere you wish."

"You would be liking that?"

The disbelief in her voice had him groaning. "Yes, very much so."

"I . . ." She looked away.

He gently turned her face toward him. Within the silvery shafts of moonlight, he caught her blush. "What is wrong?"

"I do nae know what to do."

Alas, she was a virgin. How could he forget?

"Will you show me?"

Another groan slid from his mouth, his body so hot, 'twas as if he'd burst into flames. He would touch her, no more. "Yes, but you have to trust me."

Rois watched Griffin, his face a complex mask of desire and determination. She ached with need, need he inspired, need she yearned to understand.

With efficient movements, he removed his tunic and shirt, his body hard, sculpted against the sheen of the moon.

Awareness poured through her. He was beautiful. No, magnificent. With a hesitant gesture, she reached out; her fingers met silken steel.

His breath rushed out in a hiss. "No." He caught her hand as she started to pull away, gently lay it against his chest. "I enjoy your touch."

Mesmerized, fascinated with their differences, his defined muscles where her skin was soft, how his body shivered beneath her exploration, she lingered.

"Rois, I—" He closed his eyes and swallowed hard.

"What?"

He stared at her with pure male desire.

Though innocent, she understood his need, a burst of longing coursing through her as well.

"I want to touch you," he whispered, "but only if you want me to."

With his hot stare burning her very soul, to have a man look at her with such want, such desire, the reasons for her uncertainty faded. How had she ever considered denying what they both wanted?

"I would like that very much," she said.

"Would you?"

Wherever his gaze lingered, her skin tingled, and he hadn't even touched her. What would it be like to make love? Heat stroked her body until she wondered at her ability to stand. She realized Griffin was holding her up, intimately, against the moss-softened rock. Heaven help her, the things this man made her think, made her want.

"Aye," she whispered.

His nostrils flared as he caught her face. "I will be gentle."

"I know." This moment was perfect. 'Twas as if a magical tale whispered by the bards around an ember stoked fire deep into the night.

Without warning, she caught a tinkle of distant laughter as if truly of the fey. Nay, 'twas the muddying of her mind that invited fantasy. How did one think straight when alone with such a passionate man?

On an appreciative hum, he pressed slow kisses along the curve of her jaw, and her thoughts of the fey fled.

"I want you, all of you." He skimmed his destroying mouth lower, his fingers following in shameless display. "But first I need to see you, taste you"—his gaze riveted on her—"everywhere."

Anticipation swept her as his fingers loosened her gown, exposed her to his view. A breeze skimmed across her skin like cool hands, leaving her aware, needy, wanting. Instead of being ashamed, she found herself wanting him to look at her, to drink his fill and never stop.

"You are incredible." Griffin cupped her breasts, lifted his eyes to her. "Perfect in every way." With his eyes locked on hers, he lowered his head and caught the tip of her nipple with his mouth. He slowly encircled the sensitive skin with his tongue, each stroke slow, each movement shooting another wave of heat through her body.

She gasped. "Griffin."

"Let yourself go," he said as he licked the taut tip, "just feel."

Senses exploded as his tongue lavished her. Their bodies wrapped within the breeze, embraced beneath the moon so full, so vibrant as his hands moved over her with infinite precision, skimming, savoring, leaving her breaths coming fast, and her body shivering with delicious tremors.

Then, God help her, his mouth moved lower, his hands exposing her most private place to him bit by wondrous bit. A whisper of hesitation filled her. She should say something, stop him, but if she did, after the hints of bliss she experienced on their wedding night, forever would she regret not knowing the full wonder of this moment.

With her heart pounding fast, she watched and experienced the magic he seemed to wield at his every touch. And she wanted more.

Wanted to know it all.

"Griffin . . ." Her words ended on a moan as he exposed her fully.

Eyes hot, he looked up, pressed a kiss on her tender skin. "This, us, is right."

"I believe you," she replied in a throaty whisper.

"I need you to be sure this is what you want," he said, his mouth but a breath away from her, his eyes fierce with need, but his words fragile, as if desperate for her to understand.

Emotions welled within her until she thought she'd burst. Rois nodded.

"Watch me," Griffin whispered.

Fascinated, she watched his warrior's hands skim across her most private place with sublime grace, like poetry meant to seduce. Her each breath was infused with the scent of man, the taste of longing, and the sight of wonder.

With exquisite gentleness, he cupped her, his breath a sultry whisper upon her soft curls, the sensitive folds beneath quivering with expectation. Against the shimmers of moonlight, like a god unveiling its most precious prize, he splayed her soft folds to his view.

At the rush of cool air against her slick warmth, Rois trembled. The heat of his tongue transformed the swirl of her breath into a moan. Her body ignited, exploded with sensation.

"Griffin," she gasped as he relentlessly took, savored, his finger playing in accord to the wondrous sweeps of his tongue. He increased his pace, and her body began to convulse. She cried out.

Warm hands drew her to him, cradled her as she absorbed each shudder, amazed such intense emotion was possible.

"Did I hurt you?" he whispered.

The concern in his voice had her opening her eyes. "What?" she asked, suddenly shy—absurd when they'd been so intimate.

"You have tears on your cheeks."

"'Twas so beautiful. Griffin, can I . . ."

"What?" he asked, but she caught the satisfaction in his eyes. He was enjoying this. Curiosity interwove with her newfound bravery.

"I . . . I would like to touch you so intimately as well."

His eyes burned into hers, he stroked his hand against her cheek. "Do what it is you wish."

He was giving her free rein? Rois drew a steadying breath. "I—I may be slow."

His body tensed. "I am counting on it."

Confused, but nae dissuaded, she stood. Her entire body trembled, but she understood. Desire, nae fear guided her actions.

At the brush of cool air, she glanced down. She was all but naked. Gathering her courage, she discarded the remainder of her gown, exposing herself fully to his view.

"God's teeth."

At his strangled curse, confused, she glanced down. Shimmers seemed to dance upon her skin, a light pulse that conjured erotic images in her mind and if possible, made her want Griffin more.

Without warning, energy swept through her like a mystical presence. "You want me to touch you?" Rois asked, her voice thick, wanton, the lure of a siren. She had no experience. What was going on? The pulse of air increased, smothering her doubts, her thoughts until it was only him. Her. This moment.

"Yes, very much," he strangled out.

Against the glittering mist surrounding her, she skimmed her hands over her breasts, curled her fingers beneath the weight of each, slid her thumb back and forth across the still slick, sensitive tips. Sensation tore through her. She arched back, moaned.

His breath fell out in a rough exhale. "Rois . . . please . . . touch me."

Instead, she slid her hands over her body, down, savoring the feel of him watching her, of his body coiled, tensed for action like a predator.

She thrilled at the sensual danger, understood she played with fire, and with each breath, willingly dared to burn. "When you touched me like this"—she skimmed her finger along her breasts—"your tongue hot against my skin, it makes me want you deep inside me."

"Rois." His voice slid out a rough hiss. "Bedamned, touch me."

She splayed her sensitive flesh where he'd tasted her so intimately, her sheer audacity stunning her.

Griffin trembled. "I am but a man."

"A very desirable man." Her entire body ablaze, she knelt before him. "And one I want."

Hands shaking, he reached down.

She pushed his fingers away. "Your body is mine to discover." Her gazed lifted, met his. "To taste."

Need drove her actions, her mind sensitive to the scents, the cool air of the night. With confidence, she stroked his hard length through his garb.

How did she know how he would feel before she'd touched him? Never had she touched him so boldly before, never had she experienced this intimacy with a man before. Another tinkle of laughter sounded in her mind.

Could the fey indeed be influencing her actions?

Unsure of anything, only that her need for Griffin was desperate, she focused on him. Rois quickly loosened the ties and the last vestiges of his garb fell away.

His body, hard with need, trembled before her.

A shimmer of light from his chest caught her attention. She glanced up, frowned. "What is that?"

"What?" Griffin strangled out.

"Near your neck something is glowing."

With shaky hands, he lifted a chain, a gemstone hanging upon its end, pulsing with light. With a curse, he dropped it to his chest.

Like a spell broken, the stone's glow faded; her courage, knowledge of moments before, vanished.

An ancient legend of a fairy guiding a maiden into a man's arms crept through her thoughts. Her breathing quickened. Nay, 'twas a myth, none but her had made the decision to touch Griffin this night. But as she stared at him unsure, the magic of moments ago fading, her wanton actions became disturbingly clear.

Ashamed, Rois scrambled to her feet, grabbed her gown, and shielded her nakedness.

"Rois? What is wrong?"

Throat dry, she shook her head. "I should nae be here. What we are doing is—"

"Lord Monceaux," Lochlann called from a distance away on the opposite side of the boulder. "Englishmen approach!"

Chapter Twelve

His blood pounding hot, Griffin cursed as he donned his garb. Two steps away, Rois tugged on her gown. The last tie secured, he stepped over and framed her face between his hands.

"We are not done," he stated. Eyes wide and unsure, her face pale in the moonlight, she looked like a fairy tumbled. As if that helped a bloody whit.

"Aye. We are." Her voice trembled. "Neither of us truly knows the other. A moment's passion is but a bond of desire, nae more."

Fury ignited, spilled through him in a raw haze. "A moment's passion? Is that all you think exists between us?"

Her lower lip trembled. "It must be."

"With the English approaching," he stated, "now is not the time for a debate. But the time will come. Soon."

She pulled away; he let her.

Withdrawing his sword, he nodded to Rois. "Stay behind me."

Anger flared in her eyes. "My da taught me how to wield a blade."

Of course, Angus would have taught her. "As your husband I will protect you. Neither do you have a sword to fight."

On a hiss, she withdrew a dagger hidden within the folds of her gown. "I do nae travel unarmed."

He caught her hand, drew her with him around the rock. "We have little time to argue."

Outlined in the silver clash of moonlight, a distance across the smoothed rock, Sir Lochlann crouched before the boulders. At the soft crunch of their steps, he turned. Face taut, he motioned them down.

Griffin bent low, drawing Rois with him, and then led her forward. When they reached the Scot, he halted. "How many men did you see?"

Lochlann shook his head. "I am unsure."

Pulse racing, Griffin glanced at Rois. "Keep down." He edged up, peered over the slash of weathered rock.

Moonlight embraced the steep slopes, those that would hold the snow from winter storms, and challenge the stoutest man. Except now the shield of land held danger, that from his countrymen, knights who if they saw him, would believe he'd captured two rebel Scots. Never would Rois fall into their hands.

What man would not be drawn to a woman as proud, as fierce? A woman of passion?

He shook off the thoughts and scanned the sweep of trees. Beneath the swath of frayed light, he followed each ripple of movement below, frustrated when within the weave of darkness he could make out naught.

A lone cloud overhead moved past and unveiled the moon. Ice-grey light illuminated the land, exposed the emptiness as if a hand waved.

Long moments passed.

Nothing moved below.

It couldn't be.

A muscle worked in his jaw as he continued to scan the moonlit, battered land to find a threat. But as he scoured the weave of trees and rocks and the slash of hills, it became clear. He'd find naught but Lochlann's fury, his warning a lie.

Body taut, Griffin knelt back behind the shield of stone, his focus on the knight.

"What did you see?" Rois asked.

The waver in her voice tempted Griffin to look at her, but he kept his gaze leveled on the Scot. "Naught."

Sir Lochlann swore. "By God, I saw them."

"Did you?" Griffin demanded.

Rois lay her hand on his forearm. "What is going on?"

Griffin glared at the Scot a moment longer. "'Twould seem the threat has passed." Her body sagged with relief, and he drew her against him, his eyes piercing the Scot in warning. The bastard must have surmised what they were doing behind the stones. Not that he cared. Rois was his.

The Scot's eyes narrowed in an age-old gesture of defiance.

Pleased when outrage burned in Lochlann's eyes, Griffin stood, holding Rois tight. Mayhap in the end Rois would belong to another, but for now, for this moment, she was his. After witnessing the knight's abuse of the woman at the inn two years ago, he would die before permitting Rois to become more than the Scot's acquaintance.

However much Rois believed otherwise, Lochlann was not her friend. Whatever it took, he'd ensure Angus knew how dangerous the knight was, and ensure Rois never married the Scot.

"Where are we going?" she asked.

"Abed." Griffin caught Sir Lochlann's muttered curse. A sense of victory filled him and fell away as fast. He'd won but a moment.

In silence he walked to where a short while before Rois had stood naked before him, her eyes rich with desire, and her body welcoming. He made their pallet, determined in this emotionally battered night that they would find much needed rest. After he tugged the final corner of their bedding straight, he motioned Rois to lay down.

"I canna sleep next to you."

Griffin stared at her in disbelief. "After what we have shared?"

She glanced in the distance where Sir Lochlann made his own pallet. "'Tis unseemly."

At her nervous whisper his jaw tightened. "We are married."

"In name only."

His anger rose a notch. "Had we not been interrupted, by now 'twould be a fact." Her face paled, and Griffin damned his words. Like he needed the reminder of how close they'd come to making love, or how with the Scot's interruption he'd avoided a sheer disaster?

Bloody hell!

He would damn the time when they parted. He'd come to know and like her. How could a sane man not? Rois was everything a man could want and more.

Griffin shoved back the emotions, and focused on his vow to Angus to keep her safe. "'Twill be a long journey tomorrow. We will but rest."

She hesitated.

"Trust me." And he found he wanted her trust. Somewhere along the way it had become more than a want, but a need. Being with her unearthed emotions he never believed he would experience. He swallowed hard. His life's mission was to aid the rebels, not to be with Rois. He refused to search his feelings deeper, to understand more. He held out his hand.

For a moment she held his gaze, her own somber, and then she placed her fingers on his palm.

His throat tightened at her belief in him, and he brushed his thumb against her cheek. "If necessary, I will give my life to protect you."

Softness gentled her gaze. "I know."

Her tender words curled around him, made him want her always. A ridiculous notion. He forced a smile. "We had best watch it or we might become friends." He awaited the laughter in her eyes, instead found hurt.

"Friends, is it?" She turned away. Without a word she lay by his side as he wrapped them both within a blanket of wool. But her silence fed his mind, conjured her meaning. She wanted more than friendship. If strife didn't exist between their countries . . . but it did.

What had her father been thinking, insisting that Rois remain with Griffin? Familiar with his covert travels as *Wulfe*, Angus knew that Griffin could not keep Rois by his side. Mayhap her father had drunk one too many a whisky before they'd discussed the matter?

Rois shifted; her bottom brushed him with the lightest touch.

He hardened to a painful ache. Images of Rois naked and embraced by the shimmering light rolled through his mind. Her eyes had taken on a knowing, a woman's power at odds with her innocence. And the way she'd touched him without hesitation. Her actions as if guided by another.

Or magic.

He frowned at the memory of how his gemstone had glowed during their intimacy. Well he knew each of the halved gemstones gifted by the MacGruders' grandmother held strengths to complement the man who received the matching stone.

Except, he wasn't of MacGruder blood.

The grandmother had gifted him his halved Magnesite in thanks for his aid to the rebels. Not a talisman to guide his emotional fate. Except the MacGruder brothers wouldn't see it that way, especially not if they knew his gemstone glowed when he was with Rois.

She gave a soft sigh.

Sadness filled him as he watched her sleep. At least she hadn't questioned the stone's glowing. 'Twould seem that the depth of their intimacy had shaken her, and so he was spared any inquiry.

For now.

With an ache in his heart, Griffin wrapped Rois in his arms, and for this foolish moment, wished he and Rois were meant to be.

* * *

The thunder of a nearby waterfall boomed, and the swirl of amber-gold leaves clattered around Griffin's mount's hooves. He nudged his mount through the thick weave of pines, the boughs' fragrance rich, a fierce backdrop to the swirl of water beyond.

Rois, seated before him in the saddle, shifted as they wove amongst the thick pines.

He drew her against him and leaned close. "You need to try and sleep."

Rois exhaled. "I canna. I worry for Da."

"As I." Griffin pressed a kiss against her hair. "I pray he is healing fast."

"Aye."

With Lochlann's descriptions of Lord Brom's wounds, Griffin held doubts of how fast Angus would heal. An infected wound could take down the stoutest warrior, but the recovery of a man well into his prime could take many a sennight. But, before they learned how Angus fared, he must reach Andrew de Moray.

Sir Lochlann glanced over. "Rois can ride with me if she wishes."

Griffin met the Scot's cold glare, the man's sincerity-coated words a mockery against the hatred in his eyes. "My wife remains with me."

The Scot gave a rough snort. "Wife is it? Now you want her?"

Enough of his prodding, badgering. A fight he wanted, by God he would have it here and now! Griffin halted his steed. "Get off your horse."

A smug look carved in his face, Sir Lochlann swung down.

Griffin dismounted.

"Do nae do this," Rois gasped.

"Leave it be, Rois." With slow precision, Lochlann withdrew his claymore, set it upon the flat of a rock, and straightened with the swagger of a fight won.

Griffin removed his sword, laid it to the side, but kept a dagger hidden. He would fight fair, but held doubt about the Scot.

Rois scrambled from the mount. The lackwits. "Gr—"

"Take the horses near the trees, Rois," Griffin stated.

"I will nae—"

"Listen to him, lass." Lochlann's cocky voice filled the tense silence, a tone she'd heard over the years when her friend was confident in his game.

But this was no game. The fierce light burning in both men's eyes exposed the seriousness of their intent. To fight, not from their dislike of the other, but to claim their territory.

Her.

Except by their base actions, she was far from flattered. "Have you both forgotten that the English could be about?"

"You forget," Lochlann spat, "I have a bloody Sassenach in my sight."

Trembling, Rois tossed the reins on a limb, strode between the fools.

Griffin's eyes narrowed. "Move aside."

She shook her head. "I refuse to let you fight."

"We are nae asking your permission, lass."

Rois whirled to face her friend. "Lochlann, stop this. Now!"

Her friend gestured her away. "'Tis been a long time coming, that you know."

Frustrated, she turned to Griffin. "I will—"

"Go," Griffin said. "I will be finished with the braggart soon enough."

"Listen to the Englishman, Rois," Lochlann spat. "He is a man used to giving orders."

Eyes narrowed, Rois glared at her friend. "You are nae any better prodding him."

"'Tis nae prodding," Lochlann replied, "I will beat his bloody arse."

"A fight?" Griffin asked, a dangerous edge to his voice. "No, you want me dead."

She caught the deadly glint in her friend's eyes, and stilled. Nay. It could nae be. "Tell him 'tis nae true, Lochlann." But she knew, a fool could see the truth.

Her heart pounded with a bitter taste upon her tongue, a taste she didna want to recognize—fear. Dear God in heaven, she was afraid. Nae for Griffin, but Lochlann.

"Please," Rois whispered to her friend, "do nae fight."

Each man's breaths fell out, steady, raw with intent. And she knew. She couldn't stop them. As Lochlann had said, this moment had been a long time coming. Terrified, she turned to Griffin. His gaze remained locked on Lochlann. Wetness slipped down her cheek as she took several steps back.

Damn them both. Never did she cry!

With a battle yell, Lochlann rushed Griffin.

The impact had Griffin stumbling back. He shook his head, drove a merciless blow.

With each slam of a fist, each curse, Rois's tears flowed unchecked. Griffin had nae asked for this. From the first, Lochlann had goaded him like a stick to a badger. And Griffin was a man who walked his own path.

Lochlann lashed out again.

Griffin ducked, then caught his fist and jerked him to the ground.

Sunlight glinted off Lochlann's knife.

Rois screamed.

On an oath, Griffin sprang atop Lochlann, jerked the blade free. He held it against her friend's neck.

"Do nae kill him!" Rois yelled.

The rumbling churn of water pouring into the falls echoed in the tense silence.

Griffin's hand trembled.

"Griffin," she called, "please."

His breaths coming fast, he pressed the knife harder against Lochlann's flesh; a red line appearing across his skin. "Next time you pull a knife on me in a fight meant to be fair, you will die."

"You carry a blade," Lochlann ground out.

"I do, but 'tis secured in its sheath." Griffin stood and hurled the Scot's dagger into the rush of water beyond.

On a curse, Sir Lochlann staggered to his feet, his face battered, and his lip starting to swell. "'Twas a knife handed down to me by my father."

"Be happy I did not end your life." Griffin turned to Rois, his eyes hard with determination. "He lives, because of you." He nodded. "Come." Griffin turned, strode toward their mount.

Rois hurried to his side. "What of Lochlann?"

"We ride through a land he is familiar with," Griffin replied. "Once he crawls to his steed, he can catch up."

"Do nae leave with him," Lochlann boomed.

She turned toward her childhood friend. Did he nae understand what he asked? "I must."

Grey eyes darkened. "Nay, lass, the choice is yours."

Her mind torn with emotions, she backed away. "You dinna understand."

"Aye," he spat as he cast a damning glance toward Griffin, who retrieved his steed. "I believe I do."

"Rois," Griffin called.

Aching at the turmoil, she walked to where Griffin stood beside his mount. In silence he lifted her onto the saddle, then swung up behind her. A gust of wind spun the wash of fall-dried leaves past as he kicked his horse forward. A moment later, a thick fir erased the view of her friend with his hands upon his hips, his gaze riveted on her.

Shaken, she stared straight ahead. For now her life, by her own words, had bound her with Griffin. A tie that, however much she was starting to wish otherwise, would be severed.

"Sir Lochlann will never have you."

At Griffin's fierce claim, Rois hesitated. "Have me?"

"As his wife."

She glanced back. "If you have nae noticed, 'tis you I wed."

"Only to protect your father."

At the frustration edging his voice, she stilled. Griffin was clear that he intended their marriage to end. Had he changed his mind?

He scanned the sweep of land, the tangle of limbs void of leaves, and frowned. Eyes as bare as the weathered bark settled upon her.

"Remember what I told you about him? Sir Lochlann is a man known for his brutality."

Any hope wilted. His caution was for her safety, nay more. "You witnessed but one event two years past. Many a reason could explain his anger toward the woman at the inn."

"You think there are not more women he has abused?"

"He is nae a cruel man."

"'Tis not an answer."

Frustration built. "Once the annulment is procured, you will leave. Griffin, what is it you want of me?"

"To swear you will never go to him once you are free."

She swallowed hard. "I see."

Anger glittered in his eyes. "I am not a man who can afford the luxury of marriage."

"Luxury?"

He shrugged. "But another poor word choice."

"Is it?" Rois asked.

Griffin watched her with unnervingly intense eyes. "Marriage is not mine to offer."

Hope again ignited. "Do you nae want a family, an heir to one day bequeath your lands?"

"My wants matter little, 'tis the needs of a country at war."

A shiver crept upon her skin, and she understood. "Nay, as King Edward's advisor to the Scots, you have little time for the pleasantries of life when your work is to conquer a land nae yours."

"Is that all you see?" he demanded.

All she saw? As he was King Edward's man, how could she view his employ as any other? Confused, understanding somehow she'd insulted him, but having no idea how, she remained silent.

"It matters not," he said after a long moment. "'Tis best if you think me the enemy. 'Twill make the challenges ahead easier to bear."

"Think you the enemy? What are speaking of?"

"'Tis of no concern."

'Tis of no concern? He would confuse a sage. "Griffin—"

The slide of stone against the rocky path in their wake had her glancing back. "'Tis Lochlann."

Griffin gave a grunt of disgust, then guided his horse around a boulder. "Nor did I doubt he would come. The man is like gout and causes naught but suffering and grief."

A chill swept Rois, and she leaned back against Griffin. Whatever was between him and Lochlann was far from over. She prayed her friend would nae try again to kill Griffin. If he did, after witnessing Griffin's skill, next time Lochlann would lay dead.

Chapter Thirteen

Beneath the cloud-smeared afternoon light, the Scottish rebels' makeshift camp came into view. A steady wind casting reckless leaves about through the day now rattled branches overhead, the taste of fall steady upon the breeze.

Griffin slowed his mount, glanced at Sir Lochlann. "Where is de Moray?"

The rebel gestured toward the rear of the encampment where several guards stood beside a large tent. "In there."

With a curt nod, Griffin nudged his steed forward, Rois sitting in silence before him. Since his and Lochlann's fight a day past, the Scot had spoken little. A choice he'd honored. Ironically, he kept silent due to Rois, who, with each passing day, Griffin cared about more. Regardless, with the demands of his secret life as a spy for the Rebels, a life with Rois was one he could never have.

Over the years he'd held naught but pride for the Scots, his work as *Wulfe* offering fulfillment in helping deter the strong-arm tactics of King Edward. For the first time, however, emptiness haunted him.

Fatigued, Griffin focused on the encampment, the battle-weary men scattered about, bindings covering many a wound, and for some, a macabre frame where a leg had once stood.

War.

He damned its vulgar hand, the cost, the stench that haunted a mind forever after. This was real, not the yearnings of a lonely fool. Lonely. Yes, he was that and more. Incredibly, Rois had taught him how alone he truly was.

For a short while he'd found a woman who made him feel more than he'd ever believed possible. But, he was a warrior. If he yearned for her when he rode away, so be it. Yearnings were inspirations of the mind, thoughts he could quell.

On a curse he kicked his horse forward. The soft cadence of hooves upon the pine needles echoed around them. A solemn hush swept the men as he passed. Several rebels sent curious glances his way as they rode past, but none offered a challenge.

No doubt Wallace had spread the word of his request for Griffin's presence, but it far from answered questions the Scots would have of why a high-ranking Englishman loyal to his king would be entrusted to escort their other rebel leader to an Abbey. And him riding with Rois in tow but stirred the pot.

At the outskirt of the camp, he slowed his mount to a walk.

A laird walked nearby. Cool eyes met his.

Griffin recognized him as one of the men who had cursed him the day he'd wed Rois in the great room. Griffin nodded in acknowledgment.

The laird's brow drew into a deep frown, and he turned away.

No, he'd won no friends that day.

"Rois, your father is camped a short ride to the north of here," Sir Lochlann said.

"He is?" Hope filled Rois's voice.

Griffin shot the Scot a hard look. "We will see Andrew de Moray. 'Tis why we came."

Sir Lochlann nodded.

The Scot's silence fooled him not. No reason existed to remind Rois of her father, except to cause division between her and Griffin as well as guide her mind to thoughts of seeing Angus.

Eyes dark with worry, she turned to Griffin. "But if my father is close—"

Griffin gave her hand a gentle squeeze. "I must see Lord Andrew first."

"Lord Monceaux," a guard called at their approach. He nodded to Rois. "Lady Monceaux. Sir Lochlann. We have been awaiting your arrival."

"How fares Lord Andrew?" Griffin asked as he drew his mount to a halt.

The guard shook his head, his face grim. "He lives."

Foreboding twisting in Griffin's gut, he swung down, helped Rois dismount. "Take us to him."

"Aye, my lord." The guard started forward.

"My lord," Sir Lochlann said from behind.

Tense, Griffin turned toward the Scot. "What?"

Sir Lochlann swung to the ground. "There are tasks I must address. I will be nearby if I am needed." With a nod, he walked away.

Griffin watched the Scot depart with a wary eye. After his abrasive presence, odd he'd not remain near Rois. Whatever the Scot's reason, his absence would make the meeting with de Moray easier. On edge, Griffin took Rois's hand and followed the guard. A woman's touch was a comfort he'd never sought before. Until Rois.

The scarred earth held firm beneath their careful steps. A bite of winter edged the cool September breeze along with an ominous sensation that weighted his each breath.

A guard stood outside the tent's entry. As they neared, he nodded and lifted the flap. "My lord, my lady, Sir Andrew is expecting you."

"My thanks." Griffin ducked inside, led Rois in his wake. The stench of blood hit him first, a cloying unhealthy taint, that of rotting flesh, of herbs scalded in their brewing to aid in treating wounds. In the corner sat the rebel leader's shield, three white stars displayed amongst a field of blue. A swath of dried, mottled crimson smeared two of the stars.

Her green eyes edged with worry, Rois's hand trembled in his.

Griffin squeezed her hand, the macabre silence of the men inside intensifying his concern.

"Lord Monceaux?" De Moray's throaty whisper rattled out.

"I am here, Lord Andrew." Griffin stepped before the powerful leader, nodded. Except the man before him watched him with his face pale from weakness, agony-stricken eyes, and his each breath labored. 'Twould be a man deluded who couldn't see his dire condition.

De Moray glanced toward the guards. "Leave us."

Wind-tossed leaves scraped against the battered tarp as the men exited the tent.

Alone, de Moray looked at Rois and his taut expression softened. "Cousin."

On a soft cry, she knelt before him. "Andrew." Her hand trembled as she took his hand. "God in heaven, you look a tragic state."

His weak laughter collapsed to a fit of coughing.

Red stroked her cheeks. "I should nae have spoken so."

"Nay, lass." The smile in his eyes darkened with pain. "Everyone else swears I am the vision of health. But you"—he dragged several steadying breaths—"you tell me the truth."

Her lower lip trembled. "I— I should lie."

De Moray gave her hand a gentle squeeze. "You should always be you, a fresh breath in a sea of those vying to earn my regard." He paused, the lines of strain upon his face betraying the cost to speak. "Too often men give answers they believe others wish to hear." Grim eyes lifted to Griffin. "Keep her safe. She is a woman unlike any other, one any man would be proud to call his wife, a gift only you have been given."

Emotions storming him, Griffin silently swore. As if he didn't know how special Rois was? Still, how could the rebel leader make such a request? And he understood. De Moray loved his cousin, wanted her protected, and in his anguished haze, knew Griffin would keep her safe.

"I will protect Rois," Griffin replied, "that I swear." Until Angus recovered. Then, he would turn over her protection to her father.

She frowned up at him. "'Tis my cousin's health that needs tending, nae the rambling of men and their vows."

"So it is," Griffin replied, her passion something he would miss. Her cousin was right, Rois could always be counted on to speak her mind, even when the words evoked a hard truth. "Sir Andrew, William Wallace requested my presence with instructions to escort you to Cumbuskenneth Abbey."

De Moray scowled. "I assured him 'twas but a battle wound, one no deeper than I have suffered in the past."

"Mayhap," Griffin replied, "but given the seriousness, you must understand 'twill take a month or more to heal."

The rebel leader sighed, fatigue riding his face. "Aye. But my injury was well worth the accomplishments the rebels achieved. Our victory two days past at Stirling Bridge is the foundation to Scotland's freedom. Wallace is a man driven, but . . ."

"He holds not the expertise of strategy for war," Griffin finished.

Somber eyes met his. "Aye."

"Nor," Griffin said, "the training you experienced while living with the Swiss mercenaries." At the curiosity in Rois's eyes, he refrained from saying more. With her ignorant of his position as *Wulfe*, further discussion with de Moray would invite questions he could not answer.

"We must depart for Cumbuskenneth Abbey immediately," Griffin said, regretting that seeing Angus must wait. "'Tis best for all involved."

"Aye," de Moray agreed. "But there are a few things I need to take care of first."

Bedamned. "Lord Andrew, to delay offers naught but risks to your recovery." Griffin fought to keep emotion from his voice. "Already we must keep our pace slow. Our travel will be arduous at best."

Mouth firm, the rebel leader held his gaze. "I have stated when we will depart." The taut lines in his face eased. "Do nae worry, 'twill be before the sun sets."

Hours mayhap, but did he not realize how each could make the difference in his life saved? Griffin wanted to argue further, but from the firm gaze in the rebel leader's eyes, he would not yield.

"I will await word from you then, Lord Andrew," Griffin said.

De Moray nodded.

Rois pressed a kiss upon her cousin's brow. "I love you and will keep you in my prayers."

A smile edged the Scot's mouth. "You have always been a smart lass. Mayhap I love you as well."

Tears filled her eyes.

"Do nae cry for me, lass."

"Damn you, Andrew, I am afraid for you, for my da."

His face weary, De Moray exhaled. "We all are at times. 'Tis what assures us we are alive, and teaches us to appreciate the good when we have those precious moments within our hands."

Her lower lip quivered. "Were you with Da when he was injured? Do you know how badly he was wounded?"

Her cousin's brows dipped with concern. "He fought alongside his men to the north. After the fighting was over, when I learned of his injuries, I rode to see him. His men had treated the gash in his head and removed the arrow in his shoulder. He had a few smaller cuts, but naught that with time should nae heal."

"Do you know where he is now?" Griffin asked.

"Nay," de Moray replied.

Rois met Griffin's gaze, then faced her cousin. "We will find him."

On a sigh, he closed his eyes. "Tired I am."

"Take care, Andrew," she whispered, her voice thick with tears. "May God guide you in the journey ahead."

"That He will." He shot her a wink, and then closed his eyes.

Frustrated for the hours lost before they would begin their travel, Griffin took Rois's hand and led her from the tent to a stand of pine where they could be alone. Sheltered by the thick boughs, insulated by the hush of wind, and surrounded by the freshness of pine, he drew her against him.

"Let the tears go," he urged.

"Griffin, terrified I am to lose him." The first sob broke, then another. With tears streaking her cheeks, she looked up. "What if his injuries have become infected since Lochlann departed? What if he has become delirious? What if we do nae reach him in—"

"Rois"—he lifted her chin and pressed a soothing kiss on her mouth—"we will do the best we can. Your worry will change naught."

"I am"—she sniffed, hiccupped—"so scared. My da and Andrew . . . What if they both die?"

A worry he shared. Neither would his telling her his concerns give her calm. He smoothed his hand against the length of her chestnut hair in steady sweeps.

"'Tis not my decision to make, nor a thought I will entertain," Griffin said. "Your cousin is with us now, and I will do all within my power to deliver him safely to Cumbuskenneth Abbey. Once I return, I will take you to see your father."

"I canna wait to see him," she said, her words desperate.

"Rois," Griffin said. "'Tis a difficult time, and I need your patience. Focus on the now.

"H-how can one focus on anything when your mind is in turmoil?"

Fatigue swept him as he thought of the many battles in the past, of the many friends lost. "Regardless the cost, you learn to move forward, to make decisions against the mind's anguish in order to survive."

Her face blotched from crying, Rois looked up and frowned. "To survive?"

He wished his words back, damned that he'd said them. Never had he meant to share the strife he kept imprisoned. "It matters not."

She studied him as if seeing him in a different light, one of understanding. Perhaps if he wished deeply enough, she would see him as one who could share her fears and dreams.

"I think it matters greatly," she whispered. "Sorry I am that your life has brought you to a place where you can function through the worst tragedies. 'Tis a wish I would offer no one."

"Paint me nae a martyr, Rois. I understand war. It is naught glorious or heroic. Battles take what they will and allow none to forget." He paused, steadied himself. "The ground beneath my boots has been bloodied by many hands. Including mine."

She studied him, her gaze shrewd. "You craft your words to push me away."

"I tell you only the truth."

"God in heaven. How can you continue after witnessing such atrocities?"

"Bedamned, Rois, do you not comprehend?"

Sadness touched her face. "Mayhap better than you want me to."

The complete understanding in her simple words moved him, touched him deeper than he'd ever believed possible. The moment shifted, turned dangerous. Wrapped in the hush of pine, with naught but the wind embracing them and drowning out the world beyond, at this moment they were very alone.

Too easy it would be to expose the horrors he had witnessed, of the black emptiness crawling through his soul, a life tainted by the deception of those who coveted their greed, and the shame he carried for his parents' deaths. Forever would he be haunted by their carriage accident, as they'd traveled to free him from an English cell.

Rois stood before him, innocent of the world's brutality, proof that against the fight for gold and power, good existed. Yes, he understood why de Moray demanded his vow to keep her safe. What man with even a fragment of a soul would not ask the same?

Too easy would it be to care for her. Care? God's teeth, a pathetic word, but to look deeper held its own dangers.

Griffin exhaled. "Rois—"

"'Tis Lord Brom," a panicked voice called, followed by the snort of a horse reined too fast.

Rois spun toward the voice, trembled. "Da."

Angus! Griffin caught Rois's hand, and ran toward camp. As they broke the shield of fir, a lone rider, streaks of dirt staining his face, eyes frantic, halted his mount before the gathering men.

"What news do you bring?" Griffin asked.

The mounted knight turned, his eyes narrowing on Griffin, then softening when they found Rois. "Lady Rois, 'tis your father."

Rois jerked her hand free from Griffin and ran to the Scot. "Is he worse?"

"Aye, my lady, he has taken a serious turn." Grief played upon the Scot's face as he struggled to speak. "He calls your name."

Eyes wide with fear, Rois spun toward Griffin. "I must see him immediately."

"Rois, your father requested you to stay away." He faced the knight. "How far is Lord Brom?" Griffin asked, estimating how long it would take to travel in his mind.

"A few hours," the Scot replied.

Hours? Time he didn't have. Once he received word from de Moray he was ready to leave, they would depart for Cumbuskenneth Abbey. However much he wished, for now, he could not take her to see her father.

A murmur rose from nearby. After glancing back, men shuffled aside.

Sir Lochlann nudged his way through the crowd. "What is going on?"

Relief swept Rois. "Lochlann, 'tis Da. He is—" Her voice broke. "He calls for me."

"Christ's blood." Lochlann met Griffin's eyes. "I know you prepare to leave with de Moray. I will take her to see her father."

Anger stormed Griffin. "You will take her nowhere."

Lochlann's eyes burned with challenge. "What kind of husband allows his wife to worry while her father may lie dying? I say, 'tis one who doesna give a damn, or a man who is naught but a bastard."

Chapter Fourteen

"I owe you no explanation, Sir Lochlann," Griffin stated, concealing his anger. He refused to give the Scot the outburst he sought. But as he was surrounded by rebels who already resented his presence, to attack Lochlann could sway the others to turn on him. Already he walked a fine line, and refused in any way to endanger Rois. "Rois will stay with me. While I am gone, you will guard her. No more."

Face pale with shock, Rois stepped back. "I will see my da. Nor you, nor any other, will stop me."

The Scots gathering round eyed Griffin with malice.

"He bade you to remain with me until his return," Griffin said, damning that he could not take her and tend to Angus as well.

"He made the request when he was strong," Rois countered, emotion dredging her voice, "before the battle, before an English blade found its mark."

"I always keep my vows, Rois. A vow I will keep now, a vow given to the father of my wife."

"You would deprive the lass of seeing her father," Sir Lochlann snarled, "a man who may be dying with his last breath?"

Rois gasped, then began to shake.

Against the murmurs of dissent amongst the warriors, Griffin held the Scot's gaze, if possible despising the bastard more. Deprive her? Well he knew the torment of lives destroyed. Because of his foolishness, his parents lay dead. What he would not have given to have been there for his sister during the traumatic time, to have offered support. Support he wished to give Rois now.

"You canna keep me from seeing him," Rois stated.

Griffin hesitated, torn between Lord Brom's request to keep Rois by his side and wishing for her to see her father possibly for the last time. If Sir Lochlann spoke the truth.

"Blasted Sassenach. You have the compassion of a bog worm," Sir Lochlann spat. "I am taking Rois to see her father."

Grumbles of agreement rippled through the crowd of Scots. Faces tense, their eyes darkened with fury.

God's teeth, could this situation grow worse? Griffin crossed his arms over his chest. "She goes nowhere without me."

Eyes raw with misery met Griffin's. "I must see my da, Griffin. I have known Lochlann since he was a child. He will keep me safe."

"The way he offered protection to the woman within the tavern two years past?" Griffin demanded.

"Griffin"—her body trembled as she struggled for control—"we speak of my father."

"I know who we speak of," Griffin stated, "and to whom I offer my trust."

Sir Lochlann grunted. "Trust?"

A commotion started from behind the group. The Scots stepped back. One of de Moray's personal guards pushed forward. "Lord Monceaux, Lord Andrew wishes to depart."

Bedamned!

Rois clasped his arm. "Griffin, I will be safe with Lochlann."

Griffin met the Scot's hard gaze with a silent threat.

"Trust me to make the right decisions," Rois urged.

Green eyes as fragile as a spring morning watched. He silently cursed, furious he must leave.

"We will ride with several Scots," Sir Lochlann said, his voice hard. "Know I would never jeopardize Rois's life. Ever."

The truth, Griffin mused. The Scot wanted her. Would do anything to get her.

De Moray's man stepped forward. "Lord Monceaux?"

"Tell Lord Andrew I will be there in but a moment," Griffin replied.

"Aye, my lord." The knight turned, pushed his way through the crowd.

Griffin took Rois's hands, damned his decision. God's teeth, he was a fool. "I will be gone but days."

Relief swept her face. "You are giving your blessing to my traveling to see Da?"

"Aye." He shot the Scot a warning look. "God help you, Lochlann, if upon my return I hear you have slighted her in any manner—"

Rois stiffened. "Griffin—"

"Those are my terms, Scot."

Sir Lochlann's jaw tightened. "Rois will be well protected."

Everything in Griffin screamed for him to keep her with him, but with the battle past and the English still fleeing south to the safety of England, the threat to her from King Edward's troops was minimal. More important, if Rois rode with him as they brought her cousin to the abbey and Lord Brom died, never would she forgive him.

"Upon my return from Cumbuskenneth Abbey," Griffin said, "where shall I find you?"

"At Stirling Bridge," Sir Lochlann replied, "along the eastern boundary where the rebels have camped to tend to the wounded."

Unease built inside Griffin as he drew Rois in his arms. "I will be gone but a few days. Be safe."

"We will be fine," Rois said. "Godspeed, my husband. Know I await your return with news of my cousin."

Griffin hesitated. Did Rois realize she'd acknowledged him as her husband before the Scots? With her emotional guard shattered by her worry for her father, had she exposed her desire for their marriage to be real?

"I will return for you, Rois." Leaving no doubt to whom Rois belonged, Griffin drew her into a hard kiss. He'd made the best decision he could, but he still worried for her safety. Without another word, he strode to where knights and riders mounted their steeds in preparation for the journey.

He glanced at Rois, who watched him, her vulnerability easy to read. He'd chosen right to allow her to see her father. Not that his gut agreed, but then, how did one allow a wife to ride with a man for whom you held naught but contempt?

"Lord Monceaux," a knight called.

Griffin accepted the reins of his steed, nodded toward de Moray, who was secured on the litter ready to travel, then mounted.

Several Scots kicked their horses forward, the slow pace dictated by their leader's condition.

Branches brushed Griffin as he started through the shield of trees to move beside the rebel leader. Between the fragrant, needled limbs, he caught glimpses of Rois as she watched him go. A keening built in his chest, an emptiness he'd rarely experienced.

He would miss her.

An odd thought when he would be gone mere days. Except the days ahead seemed as if a tremendous amount of time. He shook his head. One would think he was a man in love.

Impossible.

Logic guided his emotions. How could a man come to know Rois and not care? Confident he'd solved the unsettling question, he guided his mount alongside his wounded friend and, step by slow methodical step, headed toward Cumbuskenneth Abbey.

Dark clouds churned overhead smothering the rays of the late afternoon sun. Another cold gust battered Rois as she rode across Abbey Craig next to Lochlann. She tugged her cape tighter, struggling against the emotions warring in her soul. *Please God, let Da live.* Let her every fear be for naught. When she reached Da, let him gaze upon her with a smile and a familiar twinkle in his eyes.

They rode past a body made unrecognizable by the smear of decaying blood coating his face.

Nausea crept up her throat, and her wish faded against the slap of reality. Tears threatening, she scanned the land, the trees an ominous backdrop against the whip of wind and rain-blackened clouds.

"Sorry I am, Rois, for having to ride through where we fought the English," Lochlann said. "If we had ridden around, we would have lost another day."

Throat tight, she shook her head. "There is nothing easy about war."

Lochlann grimaced. "Aye. No one truly wins."

On that they both agreed.

In the distance the battered remnants of Stirling Bridge jutted toward the sky, rugged pillars once the foundation of a formidable bridge. Now, the sturdy expanse lay in a disjointed heap. Bloated bodies floated at the river's edge. Near the banks, congealed swaths of blood smeared the frostbitten grass in a hideous display.

"How much farther until we reach Da?" she asked, fighting to ignore the bodies scattered about, their garb identifying them as English.

"A short way. If you wish," Lochlann said, "you can ride with me."

However tempted to lean on her friend, this she must do on her own. She patted her mare's neck. "My thanks, but I am fine."

"Are you?"

She ignored the brisk cut of his words. Worry culled his ire. "I didna know Stirling Bridge would be in such shambles." As horrified to learn as she was fascinated, Rois needed to know. "You explained that the English decided to cross here, but how did Stirling Bridge end up destroyed?"

Pride filled her friend's face. "'Twas a brilliant strategy."

"Strategy?"

"Indeed. With the thousands of armed knights against us, never should we have won."

"Aye."

"First," Lochlann explained, "de Warenne sent two Dominican friars to ask de Moray and Wallace if they would cede."

"Cede?" She shook her head in disbelief. "Was he mad? Never would de Moray or Wallace cede."

"Indeed." Lochlann rubbed his jaw, drooped his hand. "Regardless, Wallace told the friars to return to de Warenne and inform him that they were here nae to make peace, but to free Scotland."

A smile touched her mouth, with ease envisioning Wallace sending the Friars on their way.

"When English infantry began to cross," Lochlann continued, "they left their flank pitifully exposed. Once de Moray and Wallace determined enough English had made their way over, they sent rebels to collapse the pillars beneath the bridge, cleaving the English army in two. Many of the bastards drowned, but those stranded on the north side were cut down, their reinforcements on the southern shore helpless, to watch us reap our vengeance."

Rois closed her eyes, screams of the dying too clear in her mind. "God in heaven."

"Feel no sorrow for the bastards. Be proud of the Scots. 'Twas their wit that drove the English scum back."

Her heart filled with sadness at the death and devastation of so many, she looked at her friend. "Proud I am, but the loss on both sides is enormous."

His mouth tightened. "More so had we lost."

The condemnation in her friend's voice underscored the grief he'd suffered through the battle. "You are right."

"The bodies you see strewn about would be but a pittance if the English had been victorious," Lochlann stated. "Had they overpowered us, they would have continued northward. As with their butchery at Berwick, they would have spared nae a man, woman, or child. And in their wake, left naught but careless destruction of life, and the homes leveled beneath the blaze of fire."

The stories of the carnage at Berwick came to mind. Indeed, the greed of King Edward knew nae limits. To him, a country's boundary defined naught but the next land to concur.

For now, the English king was at war in Flanders. When he returned to England and learned of Stirling Bridge, then what? Rois made the sign of the cross. *God help us all.* However much she wished otherwise, Scotland had far from seen the last of the English monarch.

And what of her cousin? Griffin would still be en route with him to Cumbuskenneth Abbey. Had Andrew begun to fever?

Her heart pounded as they rode up the spill of land cluttered with trees, brush, and bodies. As they crested the brae, before a thick swath of fir, her father's flag came into view. Relief swept her, followed by fear. *Please let us find him well.*

Lochlann pointed toward a stand of fir. "Lord Brom is camped within the trees."

Rois kneed her steed into a canter; Lochlann rode at her side.

Several lengths from the trees, a guard stepped forward. Recognition flashed in his eyes. "Lady Rois?" Then he glanced toward Lochlann with a grimace.

Unease filtered through Rois. Why would the guard act apprehensive? He must have known Lochlann had ridden to bring her to see her father . . . Fear shoved through her. Had her father's state degraded?

Her body trembling, Rois dismounted. She ran toward the break in the trees.

"Rois," Lochlann called.

Branches whipped her face, but she didn't care. Naught mattered except seeing her da. She shoved aside the next limb, and a sturdy tent came into view. Afraid to see him, more afraid nae to, she took a deep breath and ducked inside.

Near the center of the interior, a fire blazed. Thick smoke swirled against the tent's peak where it churned out of a hole and into the murky afternoon sky. Wrapped within a blanket in the far corner, her father lay with his eyes closed and his face twisted in agony.

"Da?"

A frown wrinkled his brow, then slowly, as if in an act of immense will, he opened his eyes. The agony there almost brought her to her knees.

"Rois?"

His whisper-thin voice had her rushing to kneel beside him. "I am here."

His mouth worked, then he gave a feeble exhale.

She uncapped her pouch of water, lifted it to his lips. "Drink. Please." She helped him take several sips, and then set the cured leather sack aside.

Misery-wracked eyes darkened. "Wh-why have you come?"

Before she could answer, the tent flap slapped open. Lochlann stepped inside.

Her father began to shake as he tried to lift his head. Tired eyes narrowed. "She was to stay with her husband."

Lochlann held fast. "She is your daughter and deserves to see you."

"Enough," Rois said. "Now is nae the time to argue." She gave her father a gentle look. "Nor are you in any condition to do so."

Her father crumpled back against his makeshift bed. "You . . . You sh-should nae have come."

"'Tis too late." Rois steadied herself. "Let me see your wounds."

Her father tugged the cover snug, but his hand trembled from the effort. "They are better."

Nerves shot through her. "Has a healer tended to your wounds?"

Wizened brows narrowed. "Rois—"

"Truth," she interrupted. Damn him, she had to know!

"His wounds are infected," Lochlann stated.

Her father shot Lochlann a withering glance. "A healer has c-cleansed the wounds several times as well as bound them with a poultice of goldenseal and sage."

Lochlann crossed his arms over his chest. "You need the comfort of a bed and warmth of a hearth. Nae the chills of the cold ground."

"Aye," Rois agreed, "but 'tis too far for my father to journey to our home. The long trip could reopen wounds starting to heal and he could bleed to death."

"A crofter's hut lies but a short distance away," her friend replied.

She frowned. "Why was he nae moved there immediately?"

Angus touched her hand. "There is no need. Once I am a wee bit better, I will ride home."

Tears built in her throat at his bravado. "Oh, Da." Rois brushed the hair from his brow slick with sweat. "You need the warmth of a fire in the hearth and the comfort of a bed. Stubborn you are, but I am taking you to the cottage."

"Nay—"

"'Tis why I brought you, Rois," Lochlann stated. "Lord Brom needs proper rest, but ignores our requests to help him."

"Blast your interfering hide!" Her father began to cough.

Rois shook her head. "Do nae be angry at Lochlann. He but cares for you."

Her father grunted, his expression far from convinced.

"He does," she repeated, well aware of her father's opinion of her friend. "Sir Lochlann risked upsetting you in bringing me here, but 'twas for you, because he knows I love you." Lochlann's hand lay upon her shoulder. She reached up with her own, placed it atop his.

Her father frowned. "I didna gave the blasted upstart permission to leave or to inform you of my wounds."

"'Tis done," Rois said softly.

"Aye, behind my back." Wincing, her father started coughing again.

"Shhhh. You are doing naught but opening wounds fighting to heal." Rois nodded to her friend. "My thanks."

Her father raised his head as if to argue, than a pained look crossed his face.

"Da?"

"Rois . . . I . . ." Her father collapsed.

"Lochlann!"

Her friend knelt beside her father, leaned down, and met her gaze. "He has but passed out again."

Again? Panic filled her. "What should we do?" If only Griffin was here.

"He needs to be in a place where we can build a decent fire to keep him warm," Lochlann said.

"I agree, but Da refuses."

"And always will." Her friend took her hand. "'Tis best if we move him while he is still unconscious."

Rois stared at him unsure. "'Twould be wrong to move him without his consent."

On an oath he released her hand. "Bedamned, Rois, I have tried to talk sense into him. God's teeth, I even pleaded!"

She nodded. "When he sets his mind, he is stubborn as a badger."

"Aye." Lochlann winked. "A trait he passed to his daughter."

"Do nae flatter me," she said, but a smile tugged on her lips, one raw with memories of their youth. How easy life had been then. Through a child's innocent eyes, she'd seen naught but challenges.

"Rois, listen to me. Your father's thoughts are mulled by his pain, by his worry over you." He swallowed hard. "And of his men, who he is too ill to check on. Though he is their lord, he, too, needs time to heal. The distance to the crofter's hut is less than half a day's ride. I believe it is the best choice." He glanced toward the tent flap. "'Tis why I brought you. The guards will nae let me move him, but if you give the order, they will allow it."

She hesitated. "Da will be upset."

Lochlann reached out, lifted her chin. "Upset, aye, but alive."

Tears burned her eyes. "I am afraid."

"I know." Lochlann softly swore. "Even protected in a crofter's hut with a fire burning hot and proper treatment, I canna guarantee nothing. But, if we do nae try . . ."

He was right. Her father's anger was a small price to pay to save his life. She stood. "I will speak with the guards."

"You will nae regret your decision."

"I know." And prayed she was right. Her father would be furious, as would Griffin. "I must send word to Griffin where we are."

Lochlann nodded. "I will take care of that while you are gone."

A shiver whispered through her, and she hesitated. With the dissent between him and Griffin, would he? The guard's troubled look when they'd arrived haunted her as well.

What was she thinking? The horror of this day infused her with doubts. Throughout her life, Lochlann had always been a friend she could trust.

"My thanks," she said. "I know nae what I would have done without you."

He took her hand, pressed a kiss upon the back of her hand. "I will always be here for you, Rois. That I swear."

"I know, and for that I thank you." Her mind spinning with the events to come, she turned toward the entry, and prayed her father indeed would live.

Chapter Fifteen

Hands clenched in frustration, Griffin stared at de Moray, who slept in the bed. Flickers of yellow candlelight scraped the aged stone of Cumbuskenneth Abbey with morbid glee, the odor of beeswax melding with the stench of illness. Two days of slow, monotonous travel, and with each sunrise he found himself thankful when his friend raised his eyes to meet his.

But for how long?

With the rebel leader's face waxen, his breathing labored, 'twas a miracle he still lived. And, 'twould take another miracle to allow him to celebrate Beltane.

Terrified for the life of a great man and friend, Griffin knelt before the bed, folded his hands in prayer. A rough cough had him glancing up.

Eyes clouded by pain stared back.

"Mayhap," Griffin said as he stood and crossed his arms, refusing to dishonor this proud man with any show of weakness, "I should follow my wife's lead and tell you that you look like Hades."

A smile trembled on de Moray's mouth. "You should," he replied, his voice thick with exhaustion. "A special lass she is. And with Rois never will you be bored."

"An understatement."

"Aye, that it is. Never have I known a woman whose emotions seem to burst from within and too often guide her."

He grimaced. "That I can attest to."

De Moray smiled, this time fully, then exhaled, the moment intense, but also filled with a sense of peace. As his smile fell away, the rebel leader reached beneath the covers and withdrew a leather-bound writ.

"When you depart Cumbuskenneth Abbey," de Moray said, "deliver this to Lord Grey."

At the seriousness of his words, angst crawled within Griffin like soured ale.

Shrewd eyes studied him. "'Tis my will."

"Andrew—"

"Truth," the Scot hissed. "Do you nae think I know the seriousness of my wounds? Or, the odds that I shall live?" He closed his eyes, drew several ragged breaths. After a long moment, he struggled to force them open. "Scotland's freedom is too high a risk for me to do nae but plan for the worst. If I live, the writ shall be cast aside, forever forgotten. But"—he stared at the stream of light thick with dust shimmering within the twilight's golden rays and then faced Griffin—"if I indeed die, these are instructions for Lord Grey to stand in my stead as Wallace's advisor."

De Moray had considered every critical venue. Why would he not? He was a strategist, a man who planned for success, and 'twould seem a man who planned for his death.

With a heavy heart, Griffin accepted the leather-bound writ, Lord Andrew's seal impressed in the wax upon the rolled documents inside. His fingers shook as he secured the leather case beneath his shirt.

"Death awaits each of us," Griffin said, his words solemn, "and I pray yours will be many years from now, long after your son grows strong."

Warmth touched the rebel leader's face. "Andrew will grow to be a fine man."

"He will," Griffin agreed. "As is his father."

Mirth sparkled in his eyes. He reached over, lifted a goblet of wine, and took a long swallow. "I think your English king would deem your words traitorous."

"Indeed." Griffin lifted his own cup in a toast. "To Scotland, may she forever be free."

His friend took a deep drink. With a grimace, he set it back, his lids starting to droop. "Go now. Much remains to be done. Until I am on my feet, Lord Grey must be aware of what I request."

Griffin nodded, started for the door.

"Griffin?"

He turned. "Yes?"

"My regards to your sister."

Warmth filled him. "Nichola holds great admiration for you, you know."

"Aye," Andrew replied, his voice growing thick with fatigue. "Married a Scot. Always a smart lass."

"She is." And on this Griffin agreed. Nichola's husband, Alexander MacGruder, was a man to admire, even if their meeting had begun with his abducting Nichola. Griffin nodded. "Godspeed."

"Godspeed," de Moray returned.

Griffin exited the chamber, the slap of fresh air potent against the heavy scent of illness inside Andrew's chamber. He cursed with frustration, and then grimaced as it echoed along the abbey walls. Yes, he would deliver the missive to Seathan MacGruder after he retrieved Rois, but he prayed Andrew would live and the instructions would rot from nonuse.

Rois. The thought of her with that bastard Lochlann cut through him as if a curse. Indeed, 'twas time to go. He wanted his wife within his arms.

Dust and sweat coated Griffin as he galloped across the battlefield of Stirling Bridge. The orange-red rays of the late afternoon sun coated the browned earth and clumps of leafless trees. Though days had passed, many bodies of the English remained strewn about.

Thank God the rain had washed away much of the blood and stench. 'Twould take many more months before the last sign and smell of the battle faded. Still, the land would never truly be cleansed.

Like many others, Griffin believed the memories of the horrors suffered lay embedded within the earth, a terrible angst that would forever exist and be sensed by those who walked upon the ground in the future.

As he crested the next hill, he drew to a halt. His mount's hard breaths against the chilled air rolled out in puffs of white as he scanned the field below for Lord Brom's tent.

Naught.

Where was Lord Brom's camp? Had Angus's condition improved and he now rode to Kincardan Castle? Or, had he worsened?

With his heart in his throat, Griffin kicked his mount forward. He galloped past the blackened remnants of the campfires and the disturbed earth, evidence of where Lord Brom's tents had stood.

Griffin dismissed the Scottish noble's return to Dunadd Castle.

Lord Brom's dire condition warranted not moving him for many a sennight. But someone had.

Someone?

No, Lochlann.

With a curse, he galloped toward a stand of trees outlining the river Forth as it wound its way along the sheath of land. He followed the thicket along the marshy banks. As he broke through a line of fir, he came upon an encampment of Scottish knights. He scanned the staggered tents for Lord Brom's standard.

Naught.

And what of the bastard Scot? A quick search exposed no sign of Sir Lochlann, Rois, or their mounts. Mayhap they'd decided 'twas best to go elsewhere. No, the self-serving Scot's departure would occur only if Angus had recovered and booted Lochlann's arse out.

A fetid ball of anxiousness roiled in his gut as Griffin drew to a halt before a Scottish knight.

Recognition flashed in the man's eyes, and he stiffened. "Lord Monceaux."

Griffin nodded. "Do you know where Lord Brom is?"

The knight tensed. "Two days past Lord Brom's men passed by on their way home. They shared the news that for his health, Sir Lochlann escorted Lady Rois and Lord Brom to a crofter's hut they were told was nearby."

"Why was he not moved to Dunadd Castle?"

"He was nae strong enough to travel that far," the Scot replied.

Anger rose. "Then why was he moved at all?"

A frown dredged the Scot's brow. "'Twas upon the orders of Lady Rois, my lord."

No, upon the orders of Lochlann. Without Griffin there to watch the Scot's every move, the bastard had manipulated her into the task. "How do I find the crofter's hut?" After brief directions, Griffin whirled his mount and rode hard northwest, but leagues from Lord Grey's home where he must deliver the missive penned by de Moray.

Mayhap the knight who'd given him directions was confused, and Rois was taking her father to Lochshire Castle? No, the knight had insisted they were headed to a crofter's hut, which made no sense. With Seathan's castle so near with the ability to provide immediate care for her father, why wouldn't they travel to the powerful earl's home?

With each league he traveled, Griffin's fury grew. A man as sick as

Angus needed not to travel this far, or over such rugged terrain. If the bastard valued his life, Lochlann had best pray Griffin found Lord Brom alive.

As the dregs of night clawed across the land, the leafless trees scraped the air like bony fingers. Beneath the wash of moonlight, the vague outline of the crofter's hut came into view. Smoke chugged from the roof in a lazy swirl as if a night like any other. Except, this night he would learn the fate of a man for which he held great respect.

With his emotions caught in a dangerous roil, he sighted Sir Lochlann's mount tethered to a tree. Nearby stood Rois's horse. Beside the hut's door a rough litter, similar to the one they'd used to carry de Moray, lay askew.

His blood pounding hot, Griffin halted and swung to the ground. Even at a slow pace Angus must have suffered. By God, what was Rois thinking? No, in her distraught state she'd sought guidance from a man whom she believed she could trust, a bastard under the guise of a friend. Griffin stormed forward, jerked the door open.

At the scrape of wood, Rois turned from her seat beside the bed. Caught within the candlelight, Griffin's half-shadowed outline filled the entry. Stunned and thrilled, she scrambled to her feet.

"Griffin!" Desperation filled her voice, but she didn't care. Until this moment she'd nae realized how much she'd missed him, had yearned for him to be at her side.

Hazel eyes hard with anger met hers, then scanned the room. At her father, they stilled. Amidst the anger on his face flashed relief. "Where is Sir Lochlann?"

Rois stilled. She'd expected Griffin's anger, had struggled with the decision of bringing her father here. "Moving Da was for the best."

Griffin strode over. "Was it? Can you not see that moving Angus has worsened his condition?"

"It has," Rois agreed, "but Lochlann explained however much the move weakened my father's condition, the effects will be temporary. That the warmth of a hearth and cover of the crofter's hut will quickly nurture him back to health."

"And you believed him?"

"Never would Lochlann do anything to hurt Da."

"A fact however convinced you are, I disbelieve." His eyes narrowed. "Where is he?"

"Here, English."

Nerves wrapping around her throat like a hand squeezed, Rois turned. Lochlann stood at the entry, the gentleness of his expression earlier transformed into pure hatred.

"Quiet, the both of you," Rois said, determined to diffuse the situation. "Da needs quiet to rest."

Griffin's furious gaze held Lochlann's. "He needs a healer."

"One is en route," Rois rushed. "Lochlann sent for a healer when we departed the camp."

Griffin snorted. "Had he sent for a healer, think you he or she should not have already arrived?"

Lochlann's face shuttered to a mottled red. He stepped forward, his blade drawn. "Dare you call me a liar?"

Rois stepped between the two men, her entire body shaking. After their last brawl, this time Griffin would nae walk away and leave Lochlann alive. "Enough!"

"'Twas foolhardy to move Lord Brom," Griffin said, his words ice, "more so to a pitiful crofter's hut when Lochshire Castle is but leagues away."

Stunned, Rois faced Lochlann, nae wanting to believe it true, but against his mask of outrage, she saw a wisp of guilt. Disbelief swarmed her, crumbled against the mountain of hurt. So caught up in her worry, she'd lost her bearings, had trusted her friend to ensure her father received the best care.

"You knew Lochshire Castle was near?" she whispered.

Guilt again flickered on Lochlann's face.

Hurt couldn't describe the pain inside her. "Why did we nae go there?"

Lochlann stepped toward her.

"Do not come near my wife ever again," Griffin said as he stepped to her side.

Face drawn with anguish, Lochlann shook his head, his gaze never leaving hers. "Coming here 'twas for the best. With your father feverish and already too weak, traveling farther to Lochshire Castle might have invited death."

"Why did *you* not ride to Lord Grey's castle for a healer?" Griffin demanded.

Sir Lochlann rounded on him, the loathing in his gaze answer enough. "A healer was sent for."

Griffin held the Scot's glare, his own outrage burning hot. "Were they? I see no one."

"Bloody Sassenach!" The Scot lunged forward.

Griffin caught the hand wielding the blade as his other fisted, connecting solidly against the Scot's jaw. The dagger clattered to the floor, and Sir Lochlann stumbled back, fell to the floor.

"Go," Griffin ordered. "Your presence is no longer wanted."

The Scot's hand edged toward his dagger.

"Draw your weapon," Griffin warned, "and I will kill you."

Sir Lochlann's hand relaxed. With a glance toward Rois, he wiped his chin, and satisfaction filled Griffin as the Scot's hand came away with the smear of blood. Hatred burned in Lochlann's eyes.

Griffin nodded toward the entry. "I will not tell you to leave again." As much as he wished to end it now, Lord Brom's needs were most important. Once Angus was safe, the writ delivered, and his tasks complete, he would return to confront the Scot, alone.

For a long moment Sir Lochlann eyed him. As if he understood they would finish this in the future, he stepped back, his gaze softening as they settled on Rois. "I leave for Lord Brom's sake and yours."

Rois nodded, her face pale, her eyes unsure.

Good, Griffin wanted her to doubt the Scot. She believed him her friend, but she was wrong. He was a bastard on every level.

With one last glare at Griffin, Sir Lochlann strode into the night. The whinny of a horse sounded, then the thrum of hooves. Moments later, quiet echoed in the forest, broken by the errant hoot of an owl.

Griffin walked to the door and shoved it closed, shutting out the cold air pouring into the room, as bitter as the man who'd departed. He turned to find Rois watching him, her expression confused and hurt. Bloody hell, what a mess.

"Rois, I—"

A dull cough sounded from the bed.

On a gasp, Rois whirled. "Da." She hurried across the worn floor.

Griffin walked to her side and knelt beside Lord Brom. Against the flicker of flames, Angus's face lay pale, his cheeks hollow. 'Twas amazing he still lived.

"How fare thee?" Griffin asked.

Rois laid her palm on her father's brow, turned toward Griffin. "He has done naught but ramble since we began to travel."

Griffin silently cursed. "I wish not to move him, but given his failing condition, we must bring him to Lochshire Castle this night."

Fear flashed in her eyes, but she nodded.

He laid his hand atop hers, gave a gentle squeeze. "I will return once the horses are readied."

"The litter is outside."

Her bravery touched him deeply. She was terrified, afraid, but pushed on. "Leave it. I will carry him."

On a shaky exhale, Rois nodded.

Griffin leaned forward, pressed a kiss upon her brow. "Know this, Rois. I will do my best to ensure your father recovers." Wishing for time, aware that each moment was critical, he made preparations for them to leave.

With the full moon illuminating the cloudless sky, Griffin's breath misted in the icy air. He held Angus close, the blanket wrapped around his friend like a prayer, each league traveled passing with aching slowness.

He prayed God would allow Lord Brom to live. Or, at least spare Rois the hell of living a life of guilt, of wondering if she'd made another decision, her father may have lived. Well he knew of the crush of guilt for being responsible for your parent's death.

Heart heavy, Griffin guided his mount through the thick stand of trees, the rich scent of earth and pine far from a balm against the troubles cascading his mind.

Thank God Angus still breathed. With a fever riding him, another day in the crofter's hut without proper attention and he would have died. A fact the Scot had kept from Rois, his purpose easy to discern. With Lord Brom dead, and Rois free once the annulment became final, Sir Lochlann would court her with false words, his sole purpose to claim her father's title.

At Rois's gasp, Griffin looked around, drew his horse to a halt. Below them, the land curved in a wide arc to expose a huge lake surrounded by weathered hills. Beneath the silvery crush of moonlight, from a peninsula extending from the southern curve, a majestic fortress rose without excuse.

"Amazing," Rois whispered, as if to speak out loud would break a spell.

"'Tis," Griffin agreed, remembering his awe the first time he'd seen this immense fortress. Even years later he found himself moved. He noted the standard flying atop the tower; Lord Grey was in residence. "Welcome, my lady, to Lochshire Castle."

"Lochshire Castle," she breathed. "Built by the Normans and passed down through the MacGruders ever since."

"It is indeed." As a Scottish noble's daughter, she would be aware of the castle's heritage. Nor could they linger.

He nudged his mount forward, the steep bank demanding all his attention. Rocks clattered as they loosened beneath their mounts' hooves. With each slide and jolt, he worked to ensure Angus remained as still as possible in his arms.

As the land flattened out to field, where the roll of hills led to the causeway, he breathed a sigh of relief. He guided his steed toward the rutted tracks leading to the castle.

"How fares Da?"

At the waver in her voice, Griffin glanced over at her; the pale sheen of moonlight lent her face a fragile look. "The same."

She nodded.

Somber, Griffin focused on the castle arching toward the sky. Embraced within the silvery cast, the hewn stone fortress seemed insurmountable, yet, at the same time magical.

Magical?

God's teeth, 'twas naught but a thought conjured by the days of hard travel and by the worry overwhelming him.

"You know Lord Grey?"

He nodded. "I have visited here many times."

Rois lifted a surprised brow. "You have?"

"Indeed, my sister lives within."

"Your sister is married to Lord Grey?" she gasped.

A smile tugged at his mouth at the shock in her voice. "No, she is wed to Alexander MacGruder, Seathan's younger brother."

"You said the Scot she married abducted her for ransom. You meant Alexander MacGruder?" Disbelief filled her voice.

"Indeed." And until he'd rescued her, he'd been frantic for a sister he'd believed lost all because of a dangerous tale he'd contrived to cover his actions as *Wulfe*. "In the end, Alexander and Nichola fell in love and married."

"I have briefly met them and understand why the MacGruder brothers are well known as fierce warriors. 'Tis an incredible tale."

"Incredible, but true."

The halved gemstone at his neck shifted, and Griffin grimaced, well aware of the stories crafted about its powers by the MacGruder brothers. Regardless whether the gemstone held the ability to identify the woman meant for the man who wore the halved stone 'twas truth or fable, Rois had no reason to visit the grandmother's chamber, which allowed no opportunity for her to see his halved stone inside, resting in the bowl.

Or remove it.

God's teeth, his mind rambled with the thoughts of a lad off-kilter. He focused on the steady clop of hooves upon the causeway echoing around them, the rush of wind cold against his skin.

"There are four brothers," Griffin said, refusing to ponder further the stone and the magic believed to exist in the grandmother's chamber. "Seathan is the eldest and lord of the castle and married to a Scottish noblewoman named Linet. Alexander is married to my sister, Nichola. Patrik, a brother adopted, is married to an Englishwoman named Emma. The youngest is Duncan, who is married to a Scottish lass, Isabel."

"Two of the MacGruder brothers are married to Englishwomen?"

"Yes."

"And," she asked with disbelief, "they accept you?"

He smiled. "Being a Sassenach who has given his fealty to King Edward, you mean?"

She hesitated. "Aye."

"With Alexander married to my sister," he said with a smile, "I doubt there would be any way around me being otherwise."

She studied him a long moment. "You could join the Scots."

The hope in her voice touched him. Again he wished he could explain his secret life as *Wulfe*, and admit that his loyalties lay not with King Edward, but with the Scots—and had since his youth.

An ache built in his chest as he focused on the stone-cluttered road, the shadows and moonlight exposing a timeworn trail, one that offered a sturdy defense, one that bridged the land to a castle where men lived, dreamed, and had found love.

Love?

Bloody hell.

"The castle is imposing," Rois said with awe.

With a frown, he scoured the sturdy walls where torchlight battered the weathered stone with intangible delight.

"Riders coming!" a guard's voice rang out.

Muffled shouts rang out from the wall walk. Armed men moved atop.

Griffin focused on the reality of this moment, of saving Lord Brom, not thoughts conjured by needs, desires he must ignore.

"Who goes there?" a deep male voice boomed.

Griffin halted with Rois before the gatehouse. "The Baron of Monceaux. Pass word to Lord Grey I ride with Lord Brom and his daughter. Lord Brom is ill, and needs a healer. 'Tis urgent!"

"Aye, my lord," the guard replied.

Moments later, the creak of wood and rattle of chains sounded as the drawbridge was lowered, and then the iron gate raised. Guards with torches stood beneath the gatehouse, their faces illuminated by the wavering yellowed light.

"Enter," a guard called from above.

Griffin gave Rois a tender smile. "All will be well."

"I pray so," she replied, her gaze upon her father in Griffin's arms, her worry building with her every breath. She nudged her mount forward, into the shadows of night interwoven with flames.

As they rode into the bailey, a tall, well-muscled man walked toward them. Black, shoulder-length hair framed his face, his stride that of a man of authority, that of a warrior, that of a man confident in his decisions. Even if they'd never met, from descriptions she'd overheard, she would have recognized Seathan MacGruder, Earl of Grey.

Lord Grey halted before them, his gaze riveted on her father, his brow deep with concern, then shifted to Griffin. "A healer awaits him. Guards, take Lord Brom to the readied chamber."

Two knights hurried forward and helped Griffin lower her father into their arms.

With a weary exhale, Griffin swung down. He helped Rois dismount, clasped her hand in his, and followed the guards toward the keep.

Tears burned her eyes as she hurried at his side. At their approach, the keep doors opened wide, the burst of candlelight like a promise of hope.

The murmurs of the women who cleaned the great room whispered around her as she moved through the large expanse. Within the wash of light her father appeared frail, his face ashen. *Please, Da, do nae die.*

A curve of steps led them to the second floor. Down a corridor, they entered a chamber on the right. A fire burned bright in the hearth, and a wizened old woman, her face sagged with age, stood near the bed, a basket of herbs by her side.

With a somber nod, she gestured toward the bed. "Set him there. Gently now."

As the guards lowered Lord Brom to the awaiting crush of linens, her father began to ramble.

"Da," Rois whispered, and her body began to shake.

Griffin drew her against him, and pressed a kiss upon her brow. "He is with a healer now, 'tis calm he needs."

It was, but how did one keep at bay the terror slicing her heart?

"Griffin, Lady Rois," Lord Grey said, his voice rough with concern, "let us wait in the corridor."

Fears for her father's health left her trembling. "Do nae ask me to leave him."

The earl's piercing green eyes held hers, then softened. He nodded. "I ask you to wait outside the room only while your father is made comfortable and is tended to."

She nodded.

"I am remaining with her as well," Griffin said.

Lord Grey arched a curious brow, then nodded. "Once Lord Brom is settled, I will have food brought up for you both."

Rois fought to control the fear for her father's life. "My thanks, Lord Grey."

The hard face of the earl softened. "Seathan, please. You are my second cousin, after all."

Chapter Sixteen

"S-second cousin?" Stunned, Rois scrambled to absorb the implication, the conviction in Lord Grey's words assuring her the powerful lord of Lochshire Castle had spoken truth. "Surely you jest, my lord."

With a frown, Seathan glanced at her father sprawled on the bed, before focusing back on her. He waved her and Griffin to follow. "Come, we will discuss this outside Lord Brom's chamber." He walked to the doorway.

"Cousins?" she repeated to Griffin.

He shook his head. "Unbelievable."

To say the least. At her da's groan, a shudder swept Rois. She looked at her father while the healer cleansed his battle wounds, his sallow complexion and weak breaths at odds with his sturdy frame. Trembling, she met Griffin's gaze.

Worried eyes held hers. "'Tis difficult, I know, but your father is receiving the finest care." He took her hand. "Let the healer work." Griffin took her elbow and guided her from the chamber.

"Do you need anything, Rois?" Seathan asked as they stepped into the corridor.

With a glance at her father, she shook her head. "Naught but my father to regain his health."

"As I," Lord Grey replied, his voice somber. A long second passed as he studied her. "You were never told of our family relation?"

"Nay," she replied, overwhelmed by the revelation, and struggling from fear for her father's health. Praying her father would recover, she focused on Lord Grey. "Da never spoke of any family connection to the MacGruders. Nor my grandda." She frowned. "Which makes nae a whit of sense. I saw you on occasion at Kincardan Castle. Twice you came with your brothers." She paused. "Now that I think of it, never did you or your brothers linger."

"With your father's refusal to acknowledge our blood tie," Seathan said, "we had no reason."

"Did you ever ask your father about Seathan or his brother's presence?" Griffin asked Rois.

She nodded. "Once, when after a meeting, Da seemed tense. He dismissed their attendance to aid in the rebel cause. Never did he mention our relation. 'Tis sad to have lost the years between us."

"It is," Seathan agreed.

"But," Rois said as she studied him, "you are nae as surprised to learn I am ignorant of our family tie, are you?"

Lord Grey glanced at the fairy upon the sword hanging on the wall at his side, then slowly met her gaze. "Nay."

"And why is that?" Rois asked.

Seathan exhaled. "We are a family whose past carries a tragic story, but one you should know."

A tragic story? Is that why had her da had never told her of their family connection, or the reason for their division? Anxious, Rois nodded.

"When my grandfather, Trálin MacGruder, Earl of Grey, met my grandmother, Lady Catarine MacLaren, theirs was a love few experience." Seathan stroked his finger along the sword's hilt, paused when he touched the fairy. A faint smile lingered, then faded. "When Trálin brought her to Lochshire Castle, his brother, Faolan, Rois's grandfather, was in residence. Upon their meeting, Faolan fell in love with Catarine. Regardless of her assuring Faolan she would always love Trálin, Faolan stated his intent to win her over."

Rois tensed. "Which started the conflict."

"Aye," Seathan replied. "Furious, my grandfather warned Faolan away. They fought. My grandfather broke his brother's sword arm, and swore if he came near my grandmother again, he would kill him."

"How awful," Rois said. Griffin took her hand, gave a gentle squeeze. "Did my grandfather and yours ever try to put their troubles behind them?"

"To try and make peace," Seathan explained, "my grandfather gave Faolan their mother's lands. For Faolan, his offer mattered little. He denounced the MacGruder name. Then, my great-uncle claimed the name of their mother, Brom."

"Brothers," she said, saddened by the events. "How awful that jealousy tore our families apart."

"Aye." Seathan lowered his hand to his side. "After Faolan rode away, and with the division between the brothers so bitter, none spoke of the other. Years passed. Except for the mention of the incident within the family journals, 'twas all but forgotten that a great-uncle did exist."

"But my grandfather did remarry," Rois said. "One would believe that with a wife and children of his own, he would release his anger and rebuild a bond with his brother."

Seathan shook his head. "My grandfather learned through another lord who had drank one night with Faolan that Faolan never loved his wife, his marriage that of duty to procure an heir."

Sadness tightened Rois's throat. "How tragic he nurtured his bitterness."

"'Tis," Seathan said. "A resentment he passed to his son, Angus."

"Did you try talking with Lord Brom?" Griffin asked.

"On several occasions," Seathan replied. "Over the years, raising the topic has sparked only upset. So, I learned to leave the past be."

"It makes no sense," Griffin said. "Angus is a rational man.

Seathan nodded. "On most things, but 'twould seem being raised beneath his father's kindled anger has soured Angus's belief that our family could ever again be close."

"Still, I canna believe he kept my heritage from me over a feud so long ago," Rois said, her anger gaining foothold. "But no longer. The gift of a family is precious. Once he is recovering, I will speak with him. 'Tis time long past for our families to heal."

"It is," Seathan said, "but do nae expect a miracle. 'Twill take time for Angus to understand that the separation of our families lies in his mind, nay more. I, and my brothers, hold no grudge for his grandfather's actions. Our wish is for our families to reunite. Above all, family should be coveted."

"Aye," Rois agreed.

The familiar ache of regret filled Griffin as he recalled his own past. He understood too well the struggles Rois now dealt with. How he wished his parents still lived, that he could erase the mistakes he'd made. But, as a flicker of torchlight, naught remained the same.

Stability was but an illusion. 'Twas a person's choice to grasp the moment, to decide if one but existed or chose to truly live.

As had his sister.

With Nichola's marriage, Griffin had inherited the MacGruder brothers, men who he was honored to call family, men who he would do whatever to protect, including sacrificing his life.

"Yes," Griffin said, meeting Rois's gaze, "family should be nurtured against all." She nodded, but he caught the shimmer of tears in her eyes. "You worry for your father."

She nodded. "A-aye."

"Rois," Seathan said, his face somber, "while within my home, your father will receive the best care."

A tear spilled upon her cheek. "I know. Still, I find myself afraid. His wounds are deep, and infection has set in."

Griffin drew her against him, her tears warm against his skin, and with each that fell, he ached to quell her distress. "Quiet now," he whispered and pressed a kiss upon her brow, well aware of Seathan's curious look. He could imagine the shock when Lord Grey learned that in addition to his family connection through Alexander, they were now connected on a second front, through his marriage to Rois.

Rois withdrew from Griffin's hold. "I wish to remain with my father. I must be with him in case he . . ."

In case he dies, Griffin silently finished. He looked through the entry at Angus, relieved to find his friend's breathing had slowed to an even rate. But, his pale skin spoke of fatigue, of his struggle against the agony, and Griffin prayed that indeed his life would be spared.

He caressed the soft sweep of Rois's cheek. "Go. I will join you in a moment."

Emotion-filled eyes met his, her fear evident, her desperation clear. "I am being foolish."

"No, you are a woman who loves her father."

Tears glittered in her eyes. "Thank you for understanding."

"Along with you now." Griffin lifted her hand, pressed a kiss upon her knuckles, his eyes never leaving hers. "I will be there shortly. That I promise."

A wisp of a smile touched her lips, and then she turned toward Seathan. "Thank you, cousin." Rois hurried inside the chamber.

An ache built inside Griffin as he watched Rois kneel beside her father's bed. She was an amazing woman, one any man would be blessed to have in his life, one he found himself wanting to keep with every breath.

A glint of light drew his attention to the wall-mounted claymore near Seathan. From atop its leather-bound hilt, a finely carved fairy peered down. Embraced in the flicker of torchlight, delicate wings lay open as if she was ready to ascend into the night. An impish grin framed her face, and her eyes shimmered with pure delight.

The first time he'd seen this fierce weapon, he'd thought the fairy's presence odd and out of place against the brutal weapon. On closer study, he found that somehow, the delicate carving completed the blade in an unexpected regal union.

Fitting, as the weapon belonged to the MacGruders' grandfather. The blade, a gift from a young King Alexander III in 1257 after Trálin had saved Scotland's king from an abduction attempt by the families of Comyn. An attack where he'd met and later married Lady Catarine MacLaren.

"'Tis a fine piece," Seathan said.

"It is," Griffin agreed, finding life a curious mix. "Never would I have believed myself to become part of your family."

A smile played upon Seathan's mouth. "When Alexander was sent to abduct you, and instead abducted then fell in love with your sister, 'twas a fine twist of fate."

"Indeed. Who would have believed it possible to find love with your enemy?"

Shrewd eyes narrowed, softened. "Christ's blade, you love Rois."

"I care deeply," Griffin reasoned. He refused to acknowledge the words that would make their inevitable parting worse.

His expression far from convinced, Seathan rubbed his jaw. "From the way you held Rois, cared for the lass, you are nae bloody immune."

"Immune?" Griffin gave a rough laugh. "Far from it, but then . . . how does one properly treat a wife?"

Surprise flashed within Seathan's eyes, and then laughter. "Christ's blade, for a moment I believed you."

"'Tis no joke."

His eyes widened. "You married Rois? I didna realize you had met her before?"

"I had not."

With a grimace, Seathan glanced where Rois remained by her

father's side, then met Griffin's gaze. "How could you have married her when you do nae even know the lass?"

"An understatement," Griffin replied dryly. In short, he explained the meeting as the rebels prepared for war, and his errand to deliver the request from King Edward and de Moray's father to Lord Andrew. Finally, of how Rois, a woman who tended to act on impulse, had challenged him.

"She accused you of taking liberties before a chamber of warriors at a rebel meeting?" Seathan gasped. "Is she daft?"

The shock in his friend's voice matched Griffin's own at the bewildering event. "At the time I believed so."

"God's teeth, 'tis a miracle you escaped unscathed."

"Unscathed?" Griffin arched a brow. "Is that what you call marrying the lass?"

"Why did you nae confront Rois then and there?"

"When the room calmed," Griffin explained, "I caught a glint of fear in her eyes. Foolishly, I believed when faced with marriage she would admit the truth. I knew not Rois, her stubbornness, or her passion for those she loves."

"Why would Rois call attention to herself in such a volatile setting?" Seathan asked.

"She believed my presence was a threat to her father, that I would expose his Scottish loyalties to King Edward. So, when I apologized for my untoward behavior before the rebels, then asked her to handfast, instead of admitting 'twas all a lie, she accepted and in the mayhem that followed, escaped with her father in tow."

Seathan chuckled. "Had another told me, I would have accused them of telling a bard's tale. But, 'twould seem that however peculiar the beginning, you have found someone—"

"No," he said, wishing he could allow their marriage to remain, "we have found naught."

"Bloody hell, I saw you with her. You care for my cousin." Seathan paused, his gaze shrewd. "Nay, I have known you for many a year. You love her."

For the briefest moment, Griffin allowed himself to consider the fact. His mind braced, he awaited the panic, the soul scraping fear of truly caring for a woman. Instead, warmth filled him, that of completeness, of having someone forever in his life.

God in heaven, 'twas true.

Heavyhearted, he blew out a rough breath. "I would be a fool to not want to keep Rois in my life. But I refuse to endanger her."

"Do you think you are alone?" Seathan demanded. "That I and my brothers didna face the same questions when we found women we loved?"

Griffin cursed. "But——"

"Nay excuses. You will hear me out," Seathan stated. "Alexander married your sister, an Englishwoman. By rights they should be enemies. Now, they are wed, happy, and in love. Duncan reunited with a woman he believed a mistress to his enemy. I married an Englishwoman whose brother sentenced me to hang. And Patrik." Seathan exhaled. "If any should claim a reason for nae marrying, 'twas him. Having watched his family butchered by English troops in his youth, never would any of us, much less Patrik, have considered he would fall in love with or wed an English lass. But it happened. Blast it, Griffin, we are at war! Do you think anyone is safe? That there is logic in whom we fall in love with?"

"No," he rasped, his heart aching, "but you and your brothers do not work for the English king. My position as King Edward's advisor to the Scots exposes me to continued scrutiny. If any shred of proof could be provided of my work for the rebels, 'twould mean my death. And if I kept Rois with me, hers as well. Do you think I want her living in constant danger? When I depart on a mission under the guise of *Wulfe*, how could I leave her and not fear for her life?"

"Never did I say it would be easy," Seathan stated. "Many never find love. You have. And, with a woman who, if I judge accurately, cares deeply for you if nae loves you as well. You both need time. Once she comes to know you and you her, any doubts about your situation will fade."

"I——"

"Regardless," Seathan interrupted, "you are wed."

"We are." Griffin gave him a wry smile. "After the convoluted mess that tossed Rois and I together, I admit I entertained the prospect of stowing her away within an abbey. But, Angus bade me to keep her with me, to protect her." He grew somber. "Once he recovers, however much I care for Rois, I will procure an annulment."

"Impossible. You have traveled with her, slept——"

"No."

Seathan's mouth opened. Then closed. "You have nae . . . God's teeth."

A muscle worked in Griffin's jaw. "My decision is made."

"Decision? Aye, that you are a stubborn arse."

"A trait," Griffin drawled, "'twould seem common within the MacGruders."

Irony flashed in Seathan's eyes. "Common indeed."

Griffin refused to say more. 'Twould change naught and breed more upset. Still, he must face the remainder of the MacGruder family and his sister. For now, he and Rois would remain here until Angus healed, and prayed indeed his friend would recover. Then, he would leave Lochshire Castle.

Alone.

He shifted, and his fingers bumped against the bulky roll beneath his garb.

The writ.

Images of de Moray and his grave condition flickered to mind. White-knuckled, he withdrew de Moray's writ. "Seathan, there is another reason I have come. Lord Andrew bade me to deliver this to you." He handed his friend the writ.

Worry creased Seathan's brow as he broke the seal and unrolled, then scanned the rough-inked parchment. After a long moment, he glanced up, his face pale. "If de Moray dies, he requests I stand in his stead and act as Wallace's advisor."

Griffin nodded. "He told me of his request. Though the English have retreated, we both know 'tis but to regroup. More so once King Edward learns of the Battle at Stirling Bridge and the catastrophic loss to his forces."

Seathan's mouth thinned into a tight line, and he rerolled the writ. "Are Sir Andrew's wounds so dire?"

Emotion stormed Griffin. "I fear for his life."

Seathan swallowed hard and looked away. "God's teeth."

A low pounding began in Griffin's temple. He rubbed his brow. How could Seathan not be affected by the news? Sir Andrew was their friend.

"Where is he?" Seathan asked.

"Cumbuskenneth Abbey."

Lord Grey turned, his face composed, but his skin taut. "I will pray for a miracle."

"As I." Somber, Griffin glanced inside the chamber where Angus rested. "'Twould seem we need many as of late."

"Indeed."

Silence fell between them, the normalcy of distant voices from the great hall below at odds with their fear, as the lives of many they cared for lay in jeopardy.

"You will want to return to Rois," Seathan said.

Griffin nodded.

"Before you go, why was Angus brought to Lochshire Castle? In his condition, to move him from the battle site could easily have killed him."

Anger stormed Griffin at the reminder. "I agree. Worse, 'twas done with ill intent." He explained of how upon Griffin's return from taking de Moray to Cumbuskenneth Abbey, he'd had to track her and Sir Lochlann down, only to discover Angus near death in a crofter's hut. Then, he relayed Sir Lochlann's intervention, the knight's lies to Rois, and that the Scot wanted to wed her once she was free.

Seathan clasped his dagger. "Sir Lochlann's blood will spill beneath my blade."

"No," Griffin stated. "He is mine."

Seathan eyed him hard. "And what of Rois when she learns of your intent?"

Griffin held his hard glare. "'Twill be a blasted mess."

"Aye, 'twill be that."

"Griffin?"

At his sister's voice, Griffin turned toward the turret. A slender woman hurried toward him, the warmth of her smile inspiring his own. "Nichola." He drew her into a fierce hug. "I have missed you." He stepped back, swept her with a critical eye, and then tugged the neat plait of her auburn hair. "You look content."

She laughed.

With happiness beaming on her face, Nichola reminded Griffin of his mother, and a pang touched his heart.

"I heard you had arrived with a party." She glanced around, frowned. "Who?"

"Lord Brom and his daughter accompany your brother," Seathan explained.

"Lord Brom?" Nichola asked. "Why have I never heard mention of him?"

"He is a powerful Scottish lord who lives in Kincardan Castle," Alexander said as he strode toward them. "Remember I told you about the feud between my grandfather and Lord Brom's father?"

She nodded.

Griffin smiled at the warrior he now called brother, hair black as Seathan's and of his equal height. But the similarities ended there. A scar angled down his brother-in-law's cheek, the battle wound adding to his daunting presence.

Cobalt eyes studied him with unapologetic interest. "I was surprised to hear Lord Brom would grant his permission to be taken to Lochshire Castle," Alexander said.

"I knew not of the discord before our arrival," Griffin explained. "Had I known, I still would have brought them."

Alexander grimaced. "Mad as a badger Angus will be."

Griffin shrugged. "A worry I will tend to once he awakens."

"Griffin?"

At Rois's unsteady voice, he glanced over. She stood at the door to the chamber, her eyes wide, unsure. His heart tightened in his chest. Seathan was right. He loved Rois, which complicated everything.

Rois glanced at the gathering group, then toward Griffin. "'Tis Da. He is calling your name."

"Who is that?" Nichola whispered to Griffin, curiosity rich in her voice.

"My wife." Ignoring the shock upon both his sister and Alexander's faces, he turned to Seathan. "Rois and I will meet with you shortly in the great room." He strode past. Time for explanations would come, but at this moment Rois needed him, and by God as long as he could, he would be there for her.

Chapter Seventeen

On edge, Rois walked beside Griffin as Seathan led them down the corridor. With a discreet glance, she took in the hard angles of Lord Grey's face. He was a man well lauded for his strength, wisdom, and cool calm when a difficult situation arose. And, her cousin. At Lochshire Castle for hours now, she still struggled with the revelation of their blood tie.

Griffin wrapped her fingers within his.

Thankful for his unfailing support, she gave his hand a gentle squeeze.

"The solar." Seathan moved aside, motioned for Rois and Griffin to enter. "I thought it best to finish explaining the details of our grandparents' embattled past in private."

"Thank you." She stepped inside, the warmth of the afternoon sun welcome. "I look forward to hearing the rest of their story."

Seathan crossed to where goblets were set out along with a bottle of wine. "Would you like a drink?"

"Nay," she replied, anxious to learn more.

"Nor I," Griffin replied.

"I will start at the beginning," Seathan said. "In 1257, my grandfather, Trálin MacGruder, was wounded in an effort to halt an abduction of King Alexander III." He set the bottle down.

"I had heard of the kidnapping," Rois said, "but I didna know of my great-uncle's involvement."

Seathan swirled the wine around in the cup. "During the battle, my grandfather and the others in accompaniment fought valiantly. Due to the sheer number of Comyn's knights, their forces were overwhelmed.

My grandmother came upon the abduction. Stunned, she watched in shock as the Comyns rode off with the young king. After they'd left, she aided Trálin."

Amazed, Rois shook her head. "An incredible way to meet one's future husband."

"Indeed," Griffin agreed.

"How did your grandfather know King Alexander?" Rois asked.

"An only child, my grandfather was fostered to train with the knights in the king's service," Seathan replied, pride in his voice. "Due to his age, intelligence, and expertise with a blade, Trálin was often paired to spar with King Alexander II's son, Alexander III. Over time, they became fast friends. When Alexander II died, his son was crowned king."

"At the very young age of eight," Griffin said, his voice somber. "It must have been difficult to lose a father and gain the demands of a kingdom. More so, when he later became caught up in an embittered power play between Walter Comyn, Earl of Menteith, and Alan Durward, Justiciar of Scotia."

"Aye." Seathan took a sip of wine, swallowed. "During the turmoil, my grandfather was appointed as the king's personal guard, the reason Trálin remained by Alexander III's side."

"You said the king was abducted," Rois asked. "How was he freed? What part did your grandfather play? And what does this have to do with your grandmother?"

Her cousin smiled. "'Tis much to take in. My grandmother and her clan joined forces with him to free the king."

"Incredible," Rois said.

"It is," Griffin agreed, "but as you know, Lady Catarine was a proud, strong woman who once you met, you never forgot."

She glanced at her husband in surprise. "You knew her?"

Griffin cleared his throat. "I met her on several occasions."

"Indeed," Seathan said dryly.

Rois hesitated. From the tension between them, they spoke of something more. "How did Trálin and Lady Catarine fall in love?"

"My grandmother said that from their first meeting she felt an immediate connection with my grandfather. Trálin, intrigued by her mysterious appearance, admitted he felt the same. During their time together to save King Alexander III, the unexplainable bond grew into love." Seathan paused, smiled with remembrance. "My grandfather loved her greatly, and would do anything for her. When Lady Catarine MacLaren agreed to wed, he built the tower chamber for her, and filled it with her favorite things from her homeland for all she sacrificed to become his wife."

Rois sighed. "Their story is like a romance told."

"An interesting story," Griffin agreed dryly. "One I wonder does not grow with the telling."

Lord Grey chuckled. "Mayhap a wee bit."

"A trait," Rois said, "'twould seem carried by his grandson."

Seathan's smile grew. "A compliment indeed. My grandfather was an extraordinary man."

"'Tis sad that my grandfather's infatuation with your grandmother tore our families apart," Rois said.

"Aye, Faolan was a man as proud as stubborn," Seathan agreed. "My grandfather missed his brother, but never did his love for his wife fade. I remember standing on the wall walk with my grandfather during my youth, his eyes twinkling when he spoke of Catarine. He said theirs was a love he'd never believed possible. Eyes misty, he explained 'twas like a spell cast over him when he looked into her eyes. Fitting, as stories claim her chamber is enchanted."

Prickles slid up Rois's skin. "Enchanted?"

Seathan cleared his throat. "'Tis—"

"Naught but a tale crafted by Duncan," Griffin finished with a scowl.

"What tale?" Rois asked.

Humor flashed in Seathan's eyes. "I see Griffin has omitted an important MacGruder legend, one I will leave him to explain." He nodded to the door. "I have sent Alexander to gather the rest of our family. They will be awaiting our arrival in the great room."

"Before we go," Rois said, "I would like to check upon my father one more time before I join you."

"I will accompany her," Griffin said.

Seathan nodded. "Of course. I will see you both shortly." He turned and left.

Curious about what had passed unsaid between the men, Rois turned to Griffin. "What MacGruder legend did Seathan speak of?"

"Naught that cannot wait until after we see Lord Brom."

"Aye," she agreed, her mind immediately lost in her worries for her father. *Please let him have begun to improve.*

Still reeling from shock at news of her brother's marriage, Nichola ambled down the spiral steps of the turret. At the bottom of the stairs Alexander stood smiling up at her. Warmth burst in her heart.

Alexander took her hand and rubbed his thumb over the soft curve of her palm as he scanned her face. "Still stunned to learn your brother is married?"

"Yes," she replied, her emotions on edge. "As well as your blood tie to Lord Brom."

"Until his arrival," Alexander said, "I had forgotten of our family bond."

"'Tis sad such a division came about when family is so important," Nichola said.

"Aye, but 'twas long ago." He grazed his knuckles across her cheek. "Mayhap the time has arrived for the severed bond to heal."

"I pray so. Alexander . . ." Nichola hesitated. How did she explain she sensed something momentous had occurred with the arrival of Lord Brom, more than the possible healing of their ancestors' feud, and however crazy the thought, beyond that of Griffin being wed. "Griffin brought them here."

"With Lochshire Castle being so close, it made sense."

"Nay, 'tis not what I mean." Nichola blew out a frustrated breath. "Alexander, 'tis Rois."

"What about her?"

Nichola exhaled. "I would not have thought Griffin would marry."

"'Tis time for him to settle." Alexander winked. "And to think, Rois never entered nor stayed within our grandmother's chamber."

At his teasing reference to the tale of the halved stones in their grandmother's chamber, Nichola smiled, loving this man who had stolen her heart.

"Griffin's halved stone does still sit in the bowl in your grandmother's room." Nichola tapped her fingers against her gown. "'Twould seem Rois has proven that the chosen bride of the wearer of the matching gemstone does not need to enter the chamber, or take a gemstone."

"Mayhap," Alexander said, "but she is my cousin. Mayhap my

grandmother's magic has woven another path, one that beguiled your brother?"

Nichola laughed.

"Aye," he said with a wink. "'Twould seem that, unknown to your brother, nae only has he been charmed by my grandmother's magic, but his role is one of a greater deed. Their marriage will repair the division cast between our grandfathers so many years before."

A thought fluttered to mind. Nichola gasped. "Alexander, I know you but tease me, but 'twould indeed take magic to break Griffin's vow."

"Vow?"

She nodded. "Griffin swore off ever taking a wife."

Alexander frowned. "Why would Griffin nae desire to wed?"

An ache built in her chest at the tragic memories. "A penance of sorts. Our parents died while we were en route to free him from imprisonment. He believes himself responsible for their deaths."

"'Twas an accident during a storm."

"I agree, but Griffin dismisses fact. He is convinced that had my father, mother, and I not journeyed that night to release him from his incarceration, they would be alive today." She exhaled. "And, with his service to the Scots as *Wulfe*, he thinks his life is too dangerous to ever take a wife."

"Bloody fool. Does he nae think any of us took such a risk? That I . . ."

"What?"

A flush reddened his cheeks. "Before I met you, I believed the same."

"You mean of your father's decision in battle to take an arrow meant for you," Nichola acknowledged. She was well aware how, after his father's death, Alexander had lived a reckless life, challenging death, and not caring if it took him within its grasp.

Until he'd met her.

Until they'd fallen in love.

"Aye," he breathed.

Nichola's heart ached with love for this fierce Scot, one who had suffered overlong from guilt. "'Tis what Griffin must come to accept as well, that our parents made a choice to travel that night. But how does one convince him? My brother is foolish and stubborn."

Alexander smiled. "And wed."

Doubts about her brother's unexpected marriage increased. "I am happy for him, but I admit I am anxious to see if Rois is indeed the woman for him. A brief meeting told me little."

"Nae worry, the hard part is done." Alexander arched a playful brow. "Mayhap she already carries a nephew or niece?"

Hope bloomed. "I had not thought of that."

"Which is why you have me."

Nichola chuckled. "You are too arrogant for your own good."

Alexander claimed her mouth in a heated kiss. "Aye, that I am. Let us join the others. 'Twould seem the night holds much to discover." With their fingers entwined, he strode through the great hall toward the solar.

Rois hesitated as she and Griffin walked down the corridor. "Mayhap we should wait until tomorrow?"

He gave her hand a gentle tug, his look sure as he led her forward. "Your father sleeps. There is naught more we can do for now. 'Tis time to meet the rest of *our* family."

Our family. A tremble slid through her. Though blood tied her to the MacGruders, she wished Griffin indeed looked upon her as a woman he loved and wished to remain with forever.

"Why did you reveal to Seathan, your sister, and brother-in-law we were wed?" Rois asked.

"Are we not?"

'Twas nae so simple. "We both know our marriage is but a role played. That in time, we will part forever." She forced out the last words, damning them, wishing somehow their marriage could be real. Regardless of his touch, of his apparent desire, he'd made it clear no room existed for her in his life.

"Rois—"

"'Twould seem we are nae late, then."

At the deep male burr, Rois turned, and barely stifled a gasp as a large sandy-haired man strode toward them, his gait sure. A smile sifted through his gaze, but she caught hints of wariness. Beside him walked a slim woman who, oddly, seemed a fine match to this daunting warrior. An olive hue accented her gentle features, and the confidence in her steps radiated strength.

"Rois," Griffin said, "may I introduce my brother-in-law Sir Patrik and his wife, Emma."

Warmth gleamed in the fierce Scot's gaze a second before Patrik took Rois's hand. He pressed a kiss upon her knuckle. "Lady Rois, the pleasure is mine."

Patrik's wife nodded, her gaze lingering, then softening with welcome. "As well as mine, my lady."

Rois was humbled and overwhelmed by their genuine welcome. Tears burned her throat. Griffin's thumb caressed her finger in support, and she struggled to control her emotions. This moment with Griffin's family was a mirage, a glimpse at what never could be.

"My thanks for your warm welcome," Rois said, "and the care given my father."

"Nay thanks are necessary." Though subtle, Patrik's gaze intensified as if he detected strife between her and Griffin. "We are family."

"We are," Griffin said. "Come, Seathan and the others await us."

Rois assured herself 'twas but nerves that fed her thoughts of Patrik's insight. The formidable Scot was a warrior, a man used to sizing up those he met. She'd married his brother-in-law, which would invite scrutiny.

They walked down a long corridor, the sturdy stone hewn beneath a brilliant eye, the paintings adorning the walls unique and unexpected. After they passed an archway, she paused, taken by the fairy captured in each canvas hanging in a row before her. Cupped within each fairy's hands lay a round of stone, each different.

"You have fairies upon your walls?" Warmth crept up Rois cheeks. "Sorry, 'tis obvious."

Emma smiled. "Worry not. I said the same when Patrik brought me here after we wed."

"They are so beautiful," Rois said, stunned by the sheer magnificence. "I find it intriguing that each holds a stone—" She gasped. "Griffin, the fairy at the end is holding a stone exactly like the one you wear."

Patrik arched a brow. "Indeed?" Laughter danced in his hazel eyes, and Rois caught the look that passed between him and Griffin.

Her husband frowned.

"Is something wrong?" Rois asked.

"Nay," Patrick said, "'twould seem all is right."

"Enough of this idiocy." Griffin gave Rois's hand a tug and started down the corridor.

"Idiocy?" Rois asked as she walked at his side.

Patrik's faint chuckle echoed behind them.

Griffin cleared his throat. "'Tis nothing."

Nothing? By his withdrawal, clearly there was something of relevance, but he chose nae to share it with her. An ache built in her chest. Should she expect otherwise? Still, it hurt that he pushed her away when she wanted him, when she . . .

Loved him.

She stumbled.

Griffin caught her. "What is wrong?"

"Naught." Everything. Heaven help her, she loved him. A man determined to leave her. A man she'd once believed her enemy.

"You are here."

As they entered the solar, Lord Grey's deep burr jerked her from her thoughts. Rois forced a smile.

A stately woman stepped to his side, her amber-gold hair woven into a plait.

"Lady Rois," Seathan said, "'tis my pleasure to introduce you to my wife, Lady Linet."

"Lady Grey," Rois said, liking the woman immediately, appreciating the sincerity in her smile.

"Please, call me Linet. I am sure we will become close."

Because she and Seathan were cousins? "I would like that very much," Rois replied, and realized she yearned for the close bond of this family. Except, regardless of her relation, visiting Lochshire Castle with any frequency meant she would risk seeing Griffin.

En route to Lord Grey's home, she'd focused on the dire condition of her father. She hadn't considered Griffin's family or their acceptance of her.

"This is my brother Duncan and his wife," Seathan said.

Rois turned and found herself greeted by a man whose eyes were bright with interest, his sun-bleached hair framing a face that could easily be that of a Greek god.

Heaven help her, she'd been staring. Heat stole up Rois's face. "Oh, I—"

Laughter spilled from the woman at his side, the sheen of whisky-colored hair a warm complement to her amber eyes. "Do nae worry. Your reaction to Duncan is that of most women."

"I like her already," Duncan said, the dimples on his cheeks deepening. "Lady Rois, my wife, Lady Isabel."

"A pleasure to meet you," Rois said.

Griffin drew Rois to his side and grinned at Duncan. "She is mine. You have your own wife."

"Never mind them both." Isabel smiled at Rois. "It pleases me to welcome you into the family."

Rois smiled at Nichola, thankful to have met Alexander's wife and Griffin's sister before the family had gathered. Trying to keep everyone's name straight and who was wed to whom was overwhelming.

She took in the brothers, their similarities easy to see, except for Patrik. Of course, Griffin had explained he was adopted. Still, his mannerisms were those of the MacGruders.

Seathan motioned toward a servant waiting nearby, who brought in wine and a platter of cheese, bread, and meat. Once all were served, Seathan raised his cup. "A toast. To our cousin, Rois, and Griffin. God bless their marriage, one that will reunite our families."

At Rois's stricken look, Griffin silently cursed. Though thankful Seathan had explained their marriage to everyone before he and Rois had arrived, he'd not meant to embarrass her, or to make a mockery of their union. Yet, he had achieved both.

Rois lifted her goblet, her eyes avoiding his.

Griffin drank deep.

"I will say," Alexander said, "the news of your marriage surprised us all."

Aye, Griffin mused. It had surprised him as well. But he would not remain on this topic and add to Rois's discomfort. "Though we traveled here to seek care for Lord Brom, I have come for another reason. I bring news from Andrew de Moray."

At the mention of their rebel leader, the room quieted.

Patrik clasped his wife's hand. "How fares he?"

Well aware Patrik had worked with Sir Andrew under the guise of *Dubh Duer* while he and the MacGruder brothers had believed him dead, Griffin quietly explained Lord Andrew's condition, and of the writ he'd passed to Seathan.

Alexander shot his eldest brother a hard look. "We stand behind you, whatever the need."

"Aye," Seathan said. "Later we will retreat to the war room for further discussion. For now, we celebrate that our cousin and uncle are back in our midst." Lord Grey met Rois's gaze. "I pray your marriage to Griffin will bring our family close again."

Rois glanced at Griffin, the doubts and questions in her eyes clear. By God, he would spare her further scrutiny. "'Tis many miles we have traveled, and Rois is exhausted."

"Of course," Linet said. "I have a chamber readied for you both."

"My thanks," Griffin replied, catching the nervous glint on Rois's face. Before he said something bloody asinine, he escorted Rois from the room. Once they'd checked on her father, he prayed his fatigue would allow him to rest. But, cloistered with Rois over the next several hours, doubts weighed heavy he would find naught but fragments of sleep.

As Griffin and Rois exited the chamber, Alexander smiled.

Duncan frowned. "With de Moray's wounds, I find little to smile about."

"Aye, 'tis of grave concern." Alexander drummed his fingers upon the table. "However," he glanced up the stairs. "The lad is in love."

Patrik shrugged. "A bloody fool could see that."

Alexander raised his goblet, drank a deep draught. "Aye, all except Griffin."

"What?" Duncan's brow dipped. "Does he deny it, then?"

"I would like to know as well," Patrick said, his gaze shifting from Duncan to Alexander.

Seathan remained silent.

Alexander shot his older brother a grimace, then faced the others. "Griffin wants an annulment."

"What?" everyone said in unison.

"'Tis true," Nichola said, then explained Griffin's guilt at wishing never to marry in fear of endangering a woman's life.

"It matters not," Patrik said, "Griffin and Rois are wed."

"Aye," several agreed.

With a rough sigh, Seathan shook his head. "Handfasted, but in name only."

Stunned silence fell about the chamber.

"Bloody fool," Patrik said. "Stubborn as well. Well we know that danger is a foolish thing to toss in the way of love, and I believe from the covert looks Rois gives Griffin that she cares deeply for him as well."

"Aye, from watching her with Griffin, I agree she does," Seathan replied.

Eyes bright with mischief, Duncan folded his arms. "And what are we going to do about it?"

"Naught." Seathan's brow drew into a stern frown. "However much I disagree with Griffin's decision to nae seal their marriage, 'tis nae for us to interfere."

"Mayhap nae yours," Alexander replied, "but I say we get Rois alone, then find out her true feelings for Griffin. If she loves him as well, we give them a push. Let them decide if indeed they will sacrifice a marriage a bloody lackwit can see should be real."

"Push?" Isabel said with a laugh. "A saint's curse, you are as bad as my husband."

Duncan winked at his wife. "Nay, lass, I am worse."

"Listen." Nichola leaned forward. "I have a plan."

Alexander chuckled, admiring his wife's spirit. "Well, Griffin is your brother, after all. 'Twould be fitting you led to his marital demise—I mean, to ensure he lived happily ever after."

"I still disagree with interfering," Seathan stated. "Nor shall I partake in such."

"Husband," Linet said, "did any here ask you?"

Their brother's shocked look prompted a round of laughter.

"So, Nichola," Alexander said with a wide smile. "What do you have in mind?"

Nichola smiled. "Seathan, you said Rois tended to act on impulse?"

Lord Grey grimaced. "Aye."

"Does she know of the room's magic?" Nichola asked.

Seathan hesitated, shook his head. "Griffin said he would explain it to her later."

"Which I doubt he did." Nichola's smile widened. "I say we encourage Rois to drink a wee bit too much, and if during our conversation we decide Rois indeed cares about my brother as we believe, then we tell her about the myth surrounding the stones, and how Griffin's half still resides in the chamber. If she decides to stay there for the night in hopes to consummate their marriage, the decision is hers."

"'Twould aid the cause if Griffin found her there naked," Duncan added.

"How Rois is clad once alone in the chamber is her decision," Nichola said, "but mayhap us women will encourage her to disrobe once alone and before Griffin arrives."

Patrik chuckled. "And what of Griffin? How will he find Rois?"

"I will let it slip," Alexander replied with pride.

"However much I disagree with your tactics," Seathan said, "neither will I allow it while her father struggles for his life."

Alexander grew somber. "Aye, the lass has enough worry for now. Until Angus is on the mend we will leave Griffin and Rois alone."

Everyone nodded.

"With the way they looked at each other tonight," Nichola said, "our plotting may be for naught. Mayhap time together will ignite what already exists."

"I did leave wine in their chamber," Linet said with a delighted smile.

"And they intend to do naught but sleep," Alexander said, his mind working with ease. "When he finds Rois naked, after nights of sharing her bed . . ."

"How will you convince him to go to her if he suspects a trap?" Seathan's wife asked.

"We tell him where Rois is—in our grandmother's chamber," Alexander explained. "Except, we do nay tell him she is naked. 'Twill be his to discover."

Chapter Eighteen

The scent of roasted venison, herbs, and bread from the evening meal lingered as Griffin departed Angus's chamber. He rubbed his brow, thankful that over the past two days his friend's condition continued to improve.

In but a sennight, Lord Brom would be well enough to return to his castle, but not alone. However much Angus wished his and Rois's marriage real, Griffin refused to endanger Rois's life by bringing her with him to Westminster Palace. News he would break to her father in the morning. News Rois had taken hard.

Sadness weighed on Griffin as he neared his chamber. He took in the simple oak door behind which held life's most precious gift—Rois. The ache at the thought of leaving her forever intensified.

'Twas absurd that he'd allowed himself to fall in love with her. An act for which he would dearly pay. Not that his leaving wasn't hurting Rois as well. Over the past few days, he'd caught her looking at him when she believed him unaware. Her distrust toward him at their first meeting had transformed into intrigue. Or, had it built into something more?

Griffin dampened the flare of hope. Regardless of how much they cared for the other, the time had come for him to leave. He laid his hand upon the door, took a deep inhale. This night would be their last.

Forever.

Heart aching, he shoved open the latch.

On a soft creak, the door swung wide. He stepped inside.

Empty.

Griffin leaned back, glanced down the corridor, and frowned. Earlier this evening when he'd departed their room to go and speak with

Seathan, Rois had said naught. With her upset, he'd believed she would remain in the chamber for the night. She must have wandered downstairs and become caught up in talking with one of the brothers' wives.

Or his sister.

Nichola's pleas earlier this day to reconsider his staying wed to Rois replayed in his mind. His sister had ignored his reasons, but neither had he expected her to have discerned that he loved Rois.

Unease slid through him. Nichola wouldn't interfere with his and Rois's marriage, would she? Indeed she would, if she believed her actions would aid Griffin, as she'd done so many years before when she'd kept creditors away from their home when she'd believed them destitute.

Determined to find out, Griffin hurried to the turret and down the curved steps. The rumble of voices from below increased. Anxious, he stepped into the great room.

Alexander sat at a trencher table nearby the hearth. Duncan and his wife, Isabel, sat beside him, and Duncan's arms moved with animated gestures.

Laughter sounded from the trio.

Where was Rois?

Nichola glanced up. Hesitation flickered in her eyes, then her expression softened into a smile.

Unease filtered through Griffin as he strode toward her.

"I thought you had *retired* for the night," his sister said.

Griffin ignored her emphasis on the word *retired* and its intimate implications.

Alexander lifted his goblet of wine, drank a sip. "Sit and join us. Since your arrival at Lochshire Castle, we have had little time to talk. 'Tis time to relax."

Griffin shook his head. "I must sleep. I have a long ride on the morrow."

Duncan turned his goblet in his hands. "Do you nae think it best to wait one more day before you leave?"

One more day with Rois. No, too much of a temptation. "I have much to tend to at Westminster Palace."

"With King Edward in Flanders, his troops scattered about licking their wounds from Stirling Bridge," Alexander said, "I doubt your remaining here another day or two would incite royal dissent."

True, but loving Rois, each day he remained by her side tempted fate. He cleared his throat. "'Tis time I depart."

Sadness darkened Nichola's eyes. "Alexander's words hold wisdom. Griffin, please consider his request. Your each visit is wrapped in affairs for the rebels and your duty. You now have a wife. Can you not stay one more day?"

His jaw tightened. "I explained everything to you this morn."

"All you explained," Nichola replied, her voice cool, "is that you bury your life in demands that allow you not to live, but merely exist."

"What I choose to do, or not, is my decision." Tired of her interference, aching at leaving Rois, Griffin scanned the great room. "Have you seen Rois?"

Amusement touched Alexander's face. "My cousin?"

As if his brother-in-law didn't know whom he meant? "Yes," Griffin replied, barely concealing his frustration.

Nichola's gaze slid to the abandoned goblet near the edge of the table. She cleared her throat. "She was here some time ago."

Some time ago? Rois must have left their room right after he'd gone to speak with her father. "I just came from our chamber and she was not there. Have you any idea where she could be?"

His sister chewed on her bottom lip. "Well, she did mention something about needing to be abed."

"Aye. Indeed those were her words." Duncan shot Nichola a wink. "However slurred."

"Slurred?" Griffin repeated, a sinking in his gut. Well he knew his family's love of a prank. God's teeth, he didn't need their interference.

Duncan's face grew smug, and Isabel's cheeks flushed a delicate pink. Mirth sparked in Alexander's eyes.

Dread crawled through Griffin. "Rois is drunk?"

"Drunk is a harsh word," Nichola hurried out. "Your wife had a meager amount. Though we were unaware she rarely imbibed, or how much a few drinks would affect her."

Griffin clenched his teeth, envisioning Rois tipsy, and in her inebriated condition, telling his family God knew what. "How many is a few?"

"I believe," Isabel scraped her teeth across her lower lip, "'twas four."

Griffin stared at Duncan's wife. "Four?" He would not panic. Rois might be drunk, but she was safe. Alexander laughed, and Griffin's hard-won control shattered. "Why in bloody hell would she drink four glasses of wine?"

"'Twas a celebration," Duncan said, his dimples digging deep. "Rois told us of your halved gemstone and how one evening when you were together it glowed."

Griffin muttered a curse. "As if what my gemstone did or didn't do bloody matters. We are handfasted."

"You are," Nichola agreed, her voice somber with challenge. "With a woman you love and a woman you seek to sever from your life."

Rebuttals flew through his mind, those laced with frustration and dredged in anger. To engage his sister now would open a topic Griffin refused to discuss. A subject he'd pondered, foolishly, with naught but one end.

He must set Rois free.

Weary, Griffin narrowed his gaze on the youngest MacGruder. "Duncan, you know where she is."

Green eyes widening in mock surprise, Duncan laughed. "I do?"

Griffin eyed those he loved. "By God, you will tell me where Rois has gone."

"Afraid of our grandmother's magic then, are you?" Alexander challenged.

"There is no magic," Griffin replied, recalling how he'd enjoyed the brothers' torment as they'd struggled with the same question in the past. 'Twould seem now 'twas his conflict to bear.

"No?"

At Linet's voice, Griffin glanced back to find Seathan and his wife walking toward them.

"Is it nae true your halved Magnesite glowed when you were with Rois?" Linet asked, a mischievous smile upon her face.

Griffin grimaced. 'Twas conspiracy.

"Did it?" Isabel pressed.

The image of Rois naked and his all but making love to her filled his mind. Neither could he forget how his halved gemstone had glowed. He shrugged. "'Tis vague."

"It indeed glowed," his sister said with a wide smile. "A fact we all heard Rois reveal." She hesitated. "Well, mumble."

Laughter echoed around the table.

Far from amused, Griffin glared at his family.

Patrik's wife, Emma, poured herself a goblet of wine. "Would you like a drink, Griffin? You seem tense."

"No," he replied, his calm comparable to that of a saint, "I seek naught but my wife."

"I may have seen her," Linet said.

Nichola chuckled.

Griffin clenched his hands at his sides. "Where is she?"

His sister arched an amused brow. "Abed."

"I told you, I came from our chamber, and Rois was not there."

Nichola's smile grew. "Did I say your wife was in *your* chamber?"

He stilled. Their questions about his halved gemstone glowing. Their mirth on the topic. Had they somehow convinced her to go to the MacGruders' grandmother's chamber? After four drinks Rois would be pliable to his relatives' guidance.

Uneasy, he scanned the group. "Where, pray tell," Griffin drawled, "is she?"

Alexander lifted his goblet in a toast, then downed the cup. "After our tales of the fey and explaining the magic in our grandmother's chamber, I believe Rois mentioned she wished to go exploring before she went to sleep."

Griffin fought for calm. All the stories of magic in the chamber mattered not. They were already wed.

But Rois was still a virgin.

A smile widened Patrik's mouth. "You look a touch pale."

Griffin shot a cool glare at the adopted MacGruder brother, then scanned the remainder of his family seated around the table. "Rois did not *decide* to explore your grandmother's chamber," he ground out, "but was prodded with drink and stories to stir her interest. She may be inside your grandmother's room, but by God, she will not stay." Laughter on his heels, Griffin strode toward the turret.

Inside the carved stone tower, he bolted up the steps as if chased by the hounds of Hades. The second-floor corridor flashed past, then he rounded the final turn.

The entry to the third floor tower chamber came into view. The sturdy door stood edged open, the flicker of torchlight exposing naught but normality.

Fatigue washing over him, Griffin slowed. He rubbed his brow. What was he doing? Alexander, Nichola, and the others had teased him for this exact reaction. Even if Rois was drunk and passed out in their grandmother's chamber, there was naught challenging about the situation. He'd simply carry her to their room below.

Calmer, he continued up the steps. "Rois?"

Silence.

Of course she didn't answer. Rois was not here. Wherever his sister and the others had put her in her inebriated state, 'twas to make him fear the worst. A ploy he'd fallen for. On a chuckle, he started to turn.

Griffin glanced back. What if Rois was in their grandmother's chamber? She would have answered his call, wouldn't she?

Not if she was drunk and had passed out.

He grimaced. Well, he was here. A few steps and he could see for himself.

With a frustrated sigh, Griffin ran up the remaining steps. At the entry of the MacGruder brothers' grandmother's chamber he halted.

Moonlight poured through the arched window in a pale swath, melding with the flicker of flames in the hearth, illuminating Rois lying on the bed.

Naked.

Not a stitch of clothing. Her luxurious body exposed for anyone to see.

Not anyone.

Him.

Blood pounding hot, his body hardened. Fighting the desire coursing through him, he damned Nichola and his in-laws for their meddling. Did they think his seeing Rois naked and vulnerable would break his willpower? That caught up in the heat of the moment, he'd claim her as his wife?

Indeed.

They'd assumed once his and Rois's marriage was consummated, he'd abandon his decision to send her with her father, and keep her at his side when he returned to England.

But they were wrong.

On a rough swallow, he focused on the dance of flames from a nearby wall sconce. Regardless of how much he desired her, he'd made up his mind. In the morn, he would ride to Westminster Palace.

Alone.

With a steadying breath, Griffin stepped inside the chamber. He tried not to stare at how the fire in the hearth illuminated her silken curves, or how the spill of her chestnut hair framed her breasts.

Laughter flitted through the chamber.

He spun on his heel and searched for the origin of the sound.

In the corner sat a small table, simple in its design, elegant in the craftsmanship. He glanced at the bowl and the other items atop, then skimmed past the woven tapestry upon the wall.

No one.

A gust of wind rattled against the glass, then softened to a moan.

He rubbed his temple. Laughter? 'Twas naught but the wind. Griffin studied the tapestry on the far wall woven with an intricate pattern of fairies amidst the leaves.

The tales of the fey and the magic within this room came to mind. He shook his head. Magic? No, none existed. Duncan had crafted the stories over a year ago, after Alexander had abducted Nichola and brought her to Lochshire Castle as a prisoner.

Duncan's far-fetched tale—that if Nichola stayed within their grandmother's chamber, then she and Alexander would fall in love—was intended to trouble his sibling. Nichola's having taken Alexander's halved stone before her escape 'twas a fluke.

The story of the chamber and the magic inside had grown with each telling. More so as the prospective wife of each MacGruder brother had taken from this bowl the respective matching stone, the other half which hung around her future husband's neck. That the brothers now believed the tale true was laughable.

Magic didn't exist. Naught was real except for the struggles of men, determination, and in the end, death.

Another burst of wind buffeted the handcrafted glass.

With a frown, he walked to the window. Outlined by the moonlight, a bank of clouds lay to the west. A storm was moving in. If he departed at first light, he should be hours south before the rain began, hours away from Rois, and hours into his life.

A life alone.

On a curse, he turned toward Rois. A very naked Rois. His body hardened further. Bloody hell!

He strode to the bed, caught the hand-stitched quilt, and pulled it up to her neck. Except the image of her naked remained etched in his mind. Nor could he dismiss that if he lifted the covers, he could see her every curve.

Griffin smothered the erotic thoughts that could well lead to disaster. Hours remained before dawn. These past few nights in Lochshire

Castle with her but a hand's length away, he'd not touched her. He would not break his resolve now. He nudged her shoulder.

"Rois?"

Her nose wrinkled in a dainty slant.

Blast it. Griffin sat on the edge of the bed. His weight against the lush coverings tilted her body, and she slumped against him, her breasts pressed against his thigh.

He burned for her. "Rois, wake up."

Thick lashes swept open. Within the cast of firelight and moonbeams, vivid green eyes studied him. Her lips curved in a wide smile, one that spilled over into tipsy wobble.

"Griffin," she hiccupped.

God give him strength.

She laughed, the sound rich of drink and seduction. "'Twas a secret wish of mine that you would come."

He would not think of her naked, nor of making love with her. "Rois, I am going to carry you back to our chamber."

Eyes confused, she frowned. "You do nae want me?"

Griffin took several deep breaths. She wasn't going to make this simple. Neither was he foolish enough to answer. Already he wanted her too much.

Her lids drooped closed.

He shook his head, grimaced. He reached down.

At his touch, her eyes flew open. "What are you do-doing?"

Patience, by God he would have it. "I am taking you back to our bed."

Desire darkened her gaze. "You didna answer my question. Do you want me?"

"Rois . . ." Blast it. "'Twould be unwise."

"Unwise?" A frown deepened on her brow. "To have such a memory of us would be a grand wish." On a tired exhale, she rolled to her other side, and the coverlet inched up, exposing an incredible view of her tempting bottom.

On a curse, Griffin jerked the finely woven material lower, his hand skimming across her skin.

"Mmmmm," she sighed. Her hand moved atop his, her thumb gliding across his skin with a silken stroke.

He froze.

"Griffin?"

The wanton purr of her voice had him looking up.

Eyes wide with questions and need, she watched him.

His heart pounded. God he loved her, wanted her more than his next breath. Except, war cared naught whom you loved.

"You have changed your mind?" she asked.

The situation was hopeless.

At his silence, her brow rose. "Good."

"Good?"

"Aye." Rois brushed her finger across his hand in an erotic slide. "So, husband, will you join me?"

"What?" he replied, his voice strangled.

Rois tugged the sheet off, sat up and began dusting kisses along the soft hollow of his neck, her breasts sliding against his skin.

His breathing coming fast, Griffin caught her shoulders and drew her away. "'Tis not a good idea." He struggled to keep his focus on her face, not her lips, or the soft curve of her throat, or the way her naked body would tempt the will of the strongest man.

Her fingers crept up his chest, her eyes closed as if savoring a treat.

Griffin caught her hand, and her body slumped flush against his. Bedamned! "Rois."

Her lips grazed his neck. "You taste wonderful."

He pushed her back, and his skin tingled where her tongue had trailed. "Rois."

Slumber-laden eyes met his. "Do you nae want me?"

"Too much."

Confusion illuminated her face with awkward appeal. "Then why do we nae make love?"

His throat worked. "'Tis a long story." One he wished not to discuss now. "'Tis time we return to our chamber." With enormous will, Griffin disengaged himself from her and stood. "I am going to help you stand." He reached out for her.

Rois fell back upon the daisy coverlet with a laugh, her breasts like tempting mounds of gold illuminated in the brush of firelight. "Why would we leave? We have a bed here."

He gulped another deep breath. "Rois, our chamber is below."

"Then why am I here?"

Why indeed. A question his family would find amusing. "I will tell you in the morn." Griffin clasped her hand, fighting to ignore her breasts swaying with bold appeal, and the soft curve of skin leading to her alluring bottom.

"Wait!"

He cursed. "What is wrong now?"

"The bed, 'tis spinning." On a gasp, she pressed the back of her hand upon her forehead, closed her eyes. "Pl-please make it stop."

A tinkle of laugher drifted through the chamber.

Griffin scoured the richly adorned room with a critical eye. A shift of movement had him glancing up.

A fairy wearing a dark green gown stared down at him. Mirth twinkled in her eyes.

He rubbed his eyes, then glared up at the vibrant colors crafted by a brush. The fairies on the ceiling were paintings, far from real. Any shimmer of light he'd seen was reflected from the hearth.

"Griffin?" Rois said, her voice thick with sleep and wine, "are you coming to bed?"

Bed, where they both needed to be. But not in the grandmother's chamber. Regardless if he believed the brothers' stories, their grandmother's chamber left him on edge. But, if he moved her now with her head spinning, 'twould make her retch.

As if a man sentenced, he leaned closer. "I am going to tuck you in."

"Griffin, are you leaving?"

"No, I will stay beside you this night." If she became ill, he needed to be there to tend her.

A pleased sigh fell from her lips. "My thanks . . . husband." She closed her eyes, and a soft snore escaped.

Asleep. His throat strangled on a frustrated laugh. How fitting. Griffin's body burned with need as he gently tucked the coverlet around her, surprised to find a sense of peace in the mundane task.

For long moments, he watched Rois lost to her slumber, and found himself wishing he could be with her every night.

Unsettled by his thoughts, he stood, ambled about the room. Over the years, never had the luxury to linger existed. Before, he'd ridden to Lochshire Castle to complete a mission, his visits with his sister enjoyed, however short. Neither would he be here now if not for Lord Brom's injuries.

On a sigh, Griffin paused before the small table. He ran his finger around the ivory-framed mirror, and then followed the outline of the simple gold ring. Intrigued, he lifted the circle of gold and laid it on his palm.

Odd how the MacGruder brothers had left their grandmother's

chamber untouched since she'd died, as if one day she would return. He shrugged, returned the ring. Their decision held little consequence for him.

He focused on the bowl. A lone halved stone sat inside, infused with a mix of grays and stark yellows. With a smile he lifted the Magnesite. Until the day the brothers' grandmother had presented him the pendant crafted with the matching half for his service to Scotland, never had he seen such an unusual mix.

Griffin lifted the gemstone from around his neck, and pressed it flush against its mate.

A long sigh whispered behind him.

His body tightened. Rois. Somber, he donned his pendant, then returned the halved stone to where it would forever rest. Unlike the MacGruder brothers, whose wives wore the respective mate of each stone around their necks, Rois would not remain in his life and wear his.

With a heavy heart, he returned to the bed, lay atop the blanket, and drew Rois against him, the coverlet her only defense. Given his resolve to leave her untouched, it may as well have been a stone wall.

Determined to cull a few hours of sleep this night, Griffin closed his eyes. Rois's soft breaths whispered against his cheek, lulling him to dream, to wish that she loved him, and that somehow against every obstacle they could find a way to be together.

Whimsical thoughts indeed. On the morrow and with the rise of the sun, he would leave.

Without Rois.

Chapter Nineteen

The distant clatter of hooves from the bailey rattled through Rois's mind. Her thoughts sleep-laden, she shifted, and the scenes of hard travel, the worry for her father, and the longing for a mysterious man who made her want his touch faded.

A dream, naught more.

On an exhale, she tugged the covers up. Her hand bumped against a very solid form, and her eyes flew open.

Griffin.

Her husband.

And this morn he would depart. Last eve he'd assured her that once her father had recovered enough to travel, she would return with Lord Brom to Kincardan Castle.

She should be thankful the madness incited by challenging Griffin in the war chamber of Dunadd Castle would end. Now, she could return to her home, to her life. With her country victorious at Stirling Bridge, until the English regrouped in the future, she could find peace.

Rois awaited the relief of imagining Griffin out of her life.

And found naught but emptiness.

Frustrated, she shifted on the bed.

A soft throbbing pulsed in her mind, bordering on the edge of pain. She lifted her hand to her brow, frowned. Why would her head ache so?

The events of last eve came to mind. Of drinking wine with the MacGruders. Nay, 'twas more than a simple gathering. Last eve she'd shared the night with her family, savored their complete acceptance of her and her father within their fold.

Caught up in enjoying everyone, 'twould seem she'd drank a wee too much. A small price to pay for a family gained.

She blinked against the flicker of flames, thankful for the blackness filling the sky. But hints of dawn trickled through the arched window with the promise of day, a day when Griffin would depart for England. Rois frowned.

An arched window?

Pain seared her head as Rois sat up too fast. She winced. With care, she examined the richly adorned chamber exposed by the gentle flicker of flames.

Against the far wall hung a finely crafted tapestry, an intricate forest scene woven within. Where had she seen that before?

In the turret below.

As with the other woven scene, fairies peeked through the breaks within the leaves. They must be related.

Why would a fierce warrior such as her cousin adorn his home with such touches of whimsy? Nay, with the extremes within this chamber, more than whimsy lay behind the decisions. Whoever selected the items within this room and the remainder of Lochshire Castle did so with love.

As Rois took in the luxurious setting, contentment sifted through her, a sense of peace so complete, 'twas as if she'd lived here forever. Ridiculous, never before had she stepped foot inside this room.

Where was she?

'Twas nae the chamber Seathan had given her and Griffin for their stay. She vaguely recalled departing the MacGruders around the table last eve and heading for the turret. After, she remembered naught.

Had Griffin brought her here in her inebriated state? That made little sense. Why would they have retired to the wrong room?

A shimmer of light glinted from a hand-carved table.

After one last glance to ensure Griffin still slept, curious, she pushed away the covers and rose. With cautious steps, she walked over to the table. Atop its sturdy frame laid a mix of intricately carved jewelry, a simple gold band, a bone comb, and an ivory framed mirror. Amidst the clutter sat a bowl, inside which rested a halved stone. The unusual mix of stark yellows and a swirl of grays was identical to the pendant Griffin wore around his neck.

Intrigued, Rois lifted the halved gemstone. Warmth shimmered from the stone, and images of her and Griffin appeared in her mind, of them laughing, making love, and embracing their child.

She gasped. Fingers trembling, she returned the halved gemstone to the bowl. They were naught but the wishes of a brokenhearted woman.

Light pulsed from the gemstone, the same as when she and Griffin had almost made love.

Trembling, Rois stumbled back. 'Twas a dream. She was inside her room at Kincardan Castle and would awaken any moment.

A soft snore resonated behind her.

She spun.

Griffin remained sound asleep upon the bed. Spears of the breaking dawn severed the sky, its brittle purple fingers like claws of dread.

The reality of the moment, of what this day's arrival indicated, shattered her musings. Never again would she see Griffin, feel his warmth against her skin. More devastating, never would he know how much she loved him.

Until this moment she'd accepted his intent to procure an annulment. With the day having arrived, the thought of a life without him left her shattered.

"Destiny is yours to choose."

At the soft, lyrical voice, Rois peered toward the fireplace.

In the chair near the hearth, an elderly woman sat, her wizened eyes regarding Rois with keen interest. She clasped in her hands the near complete embroidery of a fairy. Flames surged in the hearth as the woman watched her, the soft yellows of light caressing her skin.

Rois shook her head. She was still dreaming. On a steadying breath, she closed her eyes, opened them.

The age-softened mouth widened to a smile. "Lass, I am far from a dream."

"Wh-who are you?"

The woman secured the needle and thread into the side of the embroidery. "Someone who cares about you, and who holds regrets."

"Regrets?"

Her smile wavered, tumbled into a frown. "Aye. Regret to be the cause in separating our families. Never would I have wished that."

"Our families? We are related?"

The elder watched her in silence.

Rois shook her head. She must be asleep.

"A part of me wishes indeed 'twas a dream," the elder said, "but I came across the Earl of Grey due to circumstance." A wistful smile touched her face. "Or, mayhap 'twas our destiny."

"The Earl of Grey? You know Seathan?" she asked, latching onto any fiber of normality.

Warmth etched her time-wrinkled face. "Aye," she replied, her rich burr thick.

Heat rose up her cheeks. "Of course you would, you are in his home."

Laughter twinkled within her eyes. "Rather, he now lives in mine."

Rois touched her brow, the low throbbing growing as she struggled to understand.

"It matters naught. Now, 'tis Seathan's hand that guides Lochshire Castle and the MacGruder lands."

"But you said you know the Earl of Grey?"

Mischief creased her face. "Indeed, but Trálin."

"Trálin?" Why was this woman speaking of Seathan's grandfather, of her great grandfather? Regardless of what the woman said, Rois was either asleep or had gone mad. No other explanation existed. She closed her eyes tight, took three deep breaths, and opened them.

The woman remained.

Surprised by her lack of fear, of the comfort this woman's presence wrought, Rois shook her head. "My apologies, none of this is making any sense."

"I know . . . but it will." She picked up the embroidery of the fairy, withdrew the needle, and made one stitch, then another, before looking up. "Remember, Rois, destiny is yours to choose."

"But I—"

The flames within the hearth flared and then receded to sway upon glowing embers. In the bleakness of the morning, the chair sat empty.

Rois rubbed her hands over her trembling arms. 'Twas a dream. Naught more.

A tinkle of laugher had her looking up.

Fairies shimmered above her.

They were nae real, but paintings, the artist having a clever hand. Again she scoured the images.

None moved.

With the last dregs of sleep mulling her mind, she'd imagined the fairies as real. Whoever the artist of the fey on the ceiling, they had matched those woven within the tapestry with a master's hand. Unlike the wall hanging, which crafted but eyes and a hint of wings, on the ceiling the artist had exposed the entire fairy.

Shimmers of light pulsed from the left.

Rois looked over.

A fairy wearing a dark green gown watched her.

Nay, 'twas the recklessness of her dream that invented such a crazed thought. Unsure of anything, Rois turned. Outside the window, sunlight peeked over the ridge, the richness basking the curve of land.

Griffin's exhale had her glancing at the bed, and her heart ached. Soon, he would awaken.

And leave.

Without her.

Destiny is yours to choose.

She whirled toward the hearth. The flicker of flames remained unchanged, but the woman's whisper echoed in the chamber. Rois touched her brow, found the earlier headache gone. Heaven help her, she had lost her wits.

Linen shifted.

Griffin.

On a deep breath, she faced him. Dream or nae, the elder was right. Destiny was hers to choose. If she and Griffin made love, their marriage would be real. But if they made love, would he accept her into his life?

Over the years she'd acted on her passions, followed her heart, but now was different. Love guided her, that of knowing a woman's yearnings, of wanting forever with the man she loved.

A man who wanted her.

Determined, Rois stepped forward. A sheen of golden light grew, filled the chamber. With her mind emboldened, she released the finely spun sheet, and it puddled into a heap upon the floor.

On a nervous exhale, she sat next to Griffin. How was she to seduce him? However much she wanted him, the choice must be his. But she would surely try and make refusing impossible.

With one last glance up at the fairies on the ceiling, she leaned over and slowly kissed his neck. Savoring his taste, she caressed his face as she moved up, and with her each kiss, her body warmed, ached with the need of him.

"Griffin," she whispered as she lay her body flush over his and feathered kisses upon his neck, along the soft curve of his mouth.

His eyes slowly opened, clouded with pleasure. On a groan he drew her against him and was kissing her back, hot, hard, taking her every demand, giving until she was wonderfully breathless.

"I want to make love with you," she whispered between heated kisses as his hands found her naked flesh, stroked her with a knowing touch until her entire body ached.

His mouth demanding on hers, he turned her over until she lay beneath him, his hands skimming along her skin with mastery, his every touch igniting her desire more than she could have believed.

Rois gasped as he cupped her breast, slid his thumb along the hard tip, then again, sending her mind into a blistering spin.

At her unsteady breaths, through the haze of pleasure, Griffin smiled, savoring her gasps of pleasure, her trembles of need—for him. He closed his eyes and sank deeper into the dream. He was making love to Rois. It was so real he could taste her, feel her move against him with a wanton slide.

"Griffin!"

He stilled, and his entire body screamed at his hesitation, but 'twas as if she'd spoken. It could not be. "Rois?" He waited, prayed he was wrong.

Her body slick and hot trembled against his. "A-aye?"

God's teeth! He opened his eyes, met her gaze burning with need. "I—"

"Make love with me."

At her sultry request, heat surged through him, blurring the lines of sanity, of why it was important to leave her untouched.

Her slender hand slid down his chest, freed him.

Cool air slid over his fullness, and he groaned against the pleasurable ache. "I—"

"I need you, Griffin."

His breaths coming fast, he caught her hand. "Rois, we cannot do this. We both agreed." And he damned his every word.

Rois's body trembled as she pressed her face against his neck.

Griffin drew a ragged breath, then another. Warmth slid down his skin.

She was crying.

Shaken to the core, he caught her face within his hands, staggered by the rush of emotion pouring through him. He wanted her, desperately, always. Bedamned his blasted position with King Edward!

"I never wanted to hurt you," Griffin rasped.

A fat tear rolled down her cheek, then another. "'Tis too late. I love you."

His heart slammed. Words he'd longed to hear, words he wished to return. "You cannot."

She wiped away the next tear with the back of her hand. "As if what we feel is up to either of us to choose?" Hurt wrapped her voice. "Think you I wanted this? Wanted you?" Anger creased her face, then utter hopelessness crushed her expression. "Damn you, Griffin, you are my enemy!"

The passion in her words tore him apart, her vulnerability more so. "No, I am not."

Unsure eyes stared at him, the edge of hope tearing him apart. Should he tell her of his secret life as *Wulfe*? Dare he? And God help him if she knew he loved her as well.

On a shaky breath, he swept his thumb across the velvet of her cheek. "You are an amazing woman, Rois."

"Do you want me?"

The doubt within her words shook him. He held her gaze, needing her to understand that he struggled to hold himself back. "Very much so."

"Never before did I understand loving someone so much that I ache with it."

"Do not," he breathed, savoring her every word.

Another tear wobbled upon her lid, then rolled down the curve of her cheek. "Too late. I—"

"Rois—"

"Nay," she whispered, her words raw in their passion, "let me finish. I want you, more than I ever believed I would want a man. But I willna beg. If you leave this bed, 'tis your choosing, nae mine." Eyes as green as Scotland's fields blurred with the rush of more tears.

Griffin drew her against him, her each shudder like an arrow to his soul. "I want you as well," he whispered, his lips tasting her skin, the essence that would always be Rois, the only woman who'd ever drawn him. "Never will anyone fill my heart as you do."

"Your heart?"

Her stunned words had him pulling back. "Rois, I—"

"You love me?"

Regret poured through him at the hopefulness in her voice. He could not tell her of what she made him feel, but by God he could show her. Neither would he leave her with her body aching. At this moment it was about Rois, the only woman he would ever love.

With deft movements, Griffin stripped off the last of his clothing. His heart pounding fast, and her taste infused in his every breath, he claimed her mouth. As his hands stroked against the lush velvet of her skin, he pressed her back, rested his hard length intimately against her, her slick heat proof of her desire.

As he drew out each kiss, he skimmed his fingers over the curve of her neck. He lingered at the base and then slid lower, his each movement rewarded by her moan of pleasure.

"I am going to make love to you," he whispered, "Show you what you make me feel."

Her lips swollen from his kisses curved with satisfaction. "I would be liking that."

"Aye," he said, mimicking the Scottish burr, pleased by her laugh.

"'Tis a pathetic burr, Sassenach."

"Ouch, lass, you wound me."

Rois caught his hand, drew it to the curve of her breast, her eyes dark with need. "You, my husband, are wasting time."

His body tightened, savoring if only for these few moments her words. "A task I will take care of." He cupped her breasts with his hands, lowered his mouth to taste, suckle each with reverence.

She arched against him, her body responding to his every touch, her passionate responses those any man would dream of. "I want to touch you, taste you everywhere."

Her eyes met his, widened in understanding, then she smiled a warm welcome, and his heart filled. He sprinkled kisses across the flat of her stomach.

"What is it you want me to do?"

"I . . ."

Red slashed her cheeks, her innocence to him a precious gift.

"I want to please you," she whispered.

His mind conjured images of her taking him, touching him, using her hands and mouth. His body jolted. "It pleases me to make you smile, to watch you as I touch you."

She shivered at his confession. "Then take as you want."

Griffin swallowed hard. Slow, he must take it slow.

"Watch me," he whispered, holding her gaze he kissed the silken skin of her stomach, slid his hands in wondrous exploration of each curve, every slant of her body. His tongue feathered across the downy triangle of curly hair.

On a soft moan, she arched against him.

Her woman's scent lured him, driving him wild as he tasted her, savored how her eyes glazed with passion. He caught her slick nub with his mouth, and slid his finger deep within her heat.

"Griffin!"

At her gasp, he set a slow pace as he flicked his tongue over her swollen, sensitized skin.

On a moan, she arched to meet his every drive, her body's trembles growing, and her gasps fragmenting to moans.

He increased his pace, understanding what she needed, what for this moment only he could give.

Her body shuddered. "I— I need you."

"You have me." Always, he silently finished. He drove his tongue against her slick sheath, loving her taste.

Lost to her need, her frantic movements assured Griffin she'd succumbed to the building of heat, to a moment so perfect a man lived and breathed to find it.

With frantic movements, her hands came down, slid across his shoulders, and urged him up.

"Rois, I—"

"I need to feel you inside me," she breathed.

He swallowed hard, wishing he could fulfill her request. He stilled. In a sense he could, but he must be careful. With his finger stroking her, Griffin slid up, covered her swollen folds with his hardness.

Her warm slickness welcomed him.

Immense peace surrounded him, enveloped him until he immersed himself in the near experience of making love with her.

She moved against him, her full breasts making him groan. He rubbed his thumb over her slick, swollen nub, gritting his teeth as his length slid across the entrance of her swollen sheath.

Her body arced in a chaotic dance.

Griffin shifted again, careful to not slip and sink deep inside her slick warmth, her pleasure worth the moment's risk. To ensure her innocence remained intact, he laid his hand over his sensitive tip, pressed his remaining length against her slick length, pressed harder.

She groaned.

Headiness enveloped him, her frantic movements threatening to shatter his hard-won control.

"Griffin, I—" Her body bucked. "I . . . Help me!"

As her body jolted against him striving toward release, he pulled back and drove again.

A creak sounded.

Wood shuddered.

Gave way.

The bed was collapsing! Griffin thrust his hands out to cushion her fall as his body surged forward. Unprotected, he sank deep.

And her barrier of innocence shattered.

Chapter Twenty

Hands gripping the slats of the fallen bed, Griffin stared at the stunned expression shattering Rois's face, assured with their bodies intimately connected, his expression held the same shock. On a gasp, she turned away, but he caught her wince of pain.

"Rois."

"I— I . . ." Her voice wavered.

"Look at me." He struggled to keep his words gentle as his entire body raged to drive into her over and again. And if he did so, he would be a bastard. She was a virgin, or had been until moments ago. She needed tenderness, to understand the beauty and pleasure of their bodies joined. He took another steadying breath.

Encased by the fragile morning light, her chestnut hair fell aside and wary green eyes met his. Her lower lip trembled. "Our marriage is now real, is it nae?"

"Yes," he replied, humbled by the enormity of the fact. Worries overwhelmed him that between the complications of his serving King Edward and often being away, in the end he would hurt her. Griffin stared at the burst of sunlight streaming into the chamber, the rich rays welcoming the newborn day.

The day he was to leave.

Alone.

Except the collapsed bed aiding in the consummation of their marriage had changed everything.

"Griffin?"

Her unsure whisper refocused him on her shattered innocence. He stroked her cheek. "I never meant to take you so roughly." Or to take her at all. Now, Rois was his in every way.

She studied his face, hers void of condemnation. "'Twas an accident."

Anger rumbled through him that she would offer understanding when he deserved none. In an attempt to pleasure her, he'd courted the chance of her losing her virginity.

And lost.

Griffin ran his thumb across the sweep of her lower lip. "Do not excuse me."

Shadows of laughter filtered through the chamber.

He caught the sparkle of light above and looked up.

Fairies glanced down at him.

No, not fairies, paintings. For a moment he swore one moved.

"Griffin, what are you looking at?"

He tore his gaze from the ceiling. He'd witnessed naught but the exhaustion of his mind. "It is—"

Light glinted from across the room.

He looked over. Inside the bowl on the table, the mate to the halved stone he wore around his neck glowed.

"It is what?" Rois asked.

The shimmer of light faded.

On a rough exhale, Griffin faced her. "Did you see naught odd about the gemstone on the table?"

Her brows drew together in confusion, then she glanced at the bowl. Shaking her head, she turned. "Nay. Why are you asking me if—"

"Never mind." He'd seen naught. Nor would he give further thought to the images induced by the MacGruders' talk of their grandmother's chamber holding magic. This moment was about Rois, her first time making love, precious moments he would give his wife to cherish.

His wife.

Moved by the gift of her in his life, he cupped her face in his hands. With exquisite slowness, he drew her into a searing kiss, seduced her with expertise to make her forget the chaos of the moments before. Feather-lightly, he slid his hands over her naked body, savoring each curve, her every tremble.

Slowly, her body began to relax, her lips responding to his, and her soft writhing shifting to exciting demands.

Griffin lifted his head. "'Twill not hurt again." Eyes locked with hers, he skimmed his mouth against the slender column of her neck.

Her body stiffened against his, but he understood her nerves. She'd experienced the pain. "Trust me."

The depth of sincerity in Griffin's request moved Rois, and tears burned in her eyes. "I do."

He pressed a kiss against the sensitive hollow of her neck. "I wish to show you naught but pleasure."

With complete faith, Rois lay back and enjoyed the wanton luxury of his nakedness against hers, of how his fullness tight inside her made her feel complete.

"You taste amazing," Griffin whispered, his tongue sliding down her skin to encircle her nipple. The warm heat of his mouth against the coolness of the air had her gasping. Then his lips covered and suckled.

Her sensations built as he continued. Inside her, his hardness lengthened.

Deepening the kiss, Griffin began an easy rhythm within her, his strokes soft like a summer rain.

Spasms tore through Rois, each one stealing her breath, increasing her body's tremors.

On her moan, he slid his thumb down to her sensitive nub to tease her further.

Her mind blurred, and her body grew desperate. Loving the feel of him, his complete passion of her body, she rose up to meet him.

With his next drive, her body began to convulse. His pace increased, heightening her sensation. Brilliant bursts of reds, blues, and yellows exploded around her, and she cried out.

Griffin's body tightened. "Rois!"

Warmth spilled into her, and another round of waves took her up again. As her body's shudders slowed, he drew her into his arms and cradled her against his chest.

Emotion swamped her. She wished they could lay here forever. Then doubts crept through her mind. He'd agreed she was his wife and had seemed sincere, but did he intend to keep her with him when he traveled to England? Or, would he keep to his original plan and send her with her father to Kincardan Castle?

Griffin pressed a kiss upon her cheek. "You are thinking."

His lighthearted words teased a brief smile. As quickly it fled. She searched his face for a sign of his intent, his answer able to destroy her.

"What?" he urged.

"Now that we have . . ." She took a deep breath and pushed past her nerves. The topic was too important to avoid. "As I am now your wife in every way, will you take me along when you ride to Westminster Palace?" Hesitation flashed across his face, and she swallowed hard. "I see."

He rubbed the back of his neck, sighed. "You cannot understand the breadth of what you ask."

The turmoil-roughed reply gave her hope. "That you serve King Edward?"

"Yes. That I have pledged fealty to your enemy." Griffin damned the peril he would expose Rois to. Firsthand he'd witnessed what happened to traitors of England. The lucky ones were strung up before their wives and children. Those who caught King Edward's attention were drawn and quartered, their bodies displayed on pikes at town entries.

She laid her hand on his shoulder. "Loyalties are easily changed."

At Rois's hopeful voice, he cupped her hand within his, thankful for her belief in him. "I will take you with me."

A smile widened her mouth. "Truly?"

"You are my wife, whom I adore. Never could I leave you behind." She threw her arms around him, her fervent kiss making his body harden and his mind frenzied until he wanted to drive into her over and over again as she cried out from release.

From below a man's voice called out for knights to pair up to spar.

On a shaky breath, Griffin broke the kiss. He held her tight, his body ferocious with need. "Rois, if we remain here any longer, I will make love to you again. For now, we should not. Your body is tender and needs rest."

Rois pushed up to face him. Red slid up her cheeks. "We could be careful."

Her shy smile lured him to forget the day, or her newly taken innocence, and make love with her again. The haphazard spray of the fallen bed around them tamped his yearnings. The splintered wood was a potent reminder of his family's meddling. They meant well, but did not understand the full danger he exposed Rois to by living with him in England.

He shoved aside several strands of chestnut hair from her cheek. "We have many miles to travel. Already I worry you will be uncomfortable with the long ride ahead."

"I will be fine." Rois drew the hand-stitched coverlet around her body, paused, then ran her hand over the fabric. "Never have I seen such a blend of yellow and silver. 'Tis unusual."

"It is." Like the woman who once lived within the tower chamber.

She hesitated. "Do you think anyone will mind me borrowing the sheet?"

"No. Worry not, I will return it before we leave."

"But—"

Griffin scooped her into his arms.

"What are you doing?"

He winked. "Carrying my wife to our chamber." He strode to the door, the pleasure of holding her weighing against the challenges ahead.

At the entry, Rois's face paled. "G-Griffin, the bed."

He sighed. "I know," he said as he stepped onto the top step of the turret. "I will inform the MacGruders of its fate." And what a laugh they would have.

"Nay," she whispered. "'Tis in one piece."

It could not be. On a hard swallow, he turned. Inside the grandmother's chamber, the bed stood intact. The sheet spread over the top without a wrinkle. 'Twas as if the heap of timbers and the tumble of bed linens they'd made love on moments ago was naught but a tale.

She trembled in his arms. "H-how can this be?"

Angst wound in Griffin's gut as he stared at the bed, and then toward fairies woven within the tapestry. From across the chamber, one seemed to smile. He swallowed hard. God's teeth, 'twould seem the stories of the MacGruders' grandmother's chamber and the magic inside were true.

"'Tis a long explanation." Mind racing, he battled the impossible truth in the stories of the fey. Yet, how else could he account for the righting of the bed?

"But Griffin," she said, "We both felt the bed crash to the floor."

"It collapsed beneath us," he conceded. Had destiny planned for him to break her maidenhood?

Destiny?

On edge, he glanced toward the table where his halved Magnesite lay inside the bowl. On a muttered curse, and with Rois in his arms, he strode inside and halted before the sturdy table.

"I thought we were leaving."

"We are, but"—Griffin scooped up the halved stone, laid it within her palm—"this belongs to you."

Surprise widened her eyes. She tried to return it to the bowl, but he wrapped her fingers around the halved gem. "'Tis nae mine. You must return it."

Another tinkle of laughter echoed in the chamber, and he shot the fairy on the ceiling whose smile broadened, a cool look.

"Trust me, 'tis yours," he said, his voice edged with sarcasm. "Of that I am very sure." Before something else beyond his earthly control happened inside this chamber, he carried Rois from the room.

Laughter sparkled in Alexander's eyes as he leaned against the wooden gate inside the stable. "So, you are taking your wife with you?"

Duncan arched a curious brow, and Seathan and Patrik glanced at each other before turning to face Griffin.

At his mount's side, Griffin gave the cinch one last tug. "I am."

"I take it you found Rois last night after you left us," Duncan said, his dimples deep, and a smug smile plastered on his face.

Griffin lifted the reins, then shot the youngest MacGruder a hard glance. "'Twas it not your intent?"

"Aye," Seathan agreed. "The lot of them plotted to ensure you and Rois were alone in our grandmother's chamber. I told them to leave the both of you be. Your private affairs are just that."

Alexander shoved away from the wooden gate. "Left alone last eve, he would have ridden halfway to Westminster Palace by now, and missing the lass fierce."

"What I feel for Rois matters not," Griffin said through clenched teeth.

"It does when you would have made a fool's choice and left her behind," Patrik charged.

Seathan raised his hand. "Enough. The deed is done."

"Aye, it is." Duncan winked at Alexander. "So proven since he is taking our cousin to England."

"You have told Rois you work for the Scottish rebels?" Seathan asked.

Griffin patted his mount's neck, shot the eldest MacGruder brother a cool look. "No."

Alexander frowned. "Why nae? You must know you can trust her with the secret."

"I do," Griffin replied, finding comfort in the fact. "But 'tis not so simple. If Rois was ever questioned by the English about my association with the rebels, if she knows about my work as *Wulfe*, her reaction to their inquiries may expose the truth." He shook his head. "As much as I wish to tell her, 'tis best she remains ignorant."

"Do you think it wise to withhold something so important from the woman who loves you?" Patrik asked.

Of all men before him, Patrik, with his secret life of *Dubh Duer*, knew well the risks involved. More so, since Patrik's wife was once a highly paid English mercenary.

"I do," Griffin replied. "Rois's emotions are often too easily read."

"I think it is her right to know," Duncan said, "but I see the wisdom of your decision as well."

Seathan and Alexander nodded.

"There is one more thing," Griffin said, aware his words would receive no welcome. "Once I return to Westminster Palace and finish this mission, Rois and I are moving to Scotland."

Shock, pure and simple, paled each MacGruder face.

Alexander recovered first. "By God's eyes, you are needed by the rebels. Your insights of King Edward's plans have saved of our countrymen's lives many times over."

Griffin straightened the stirrup. "I will continue to serve as King Edward's advisor to the Scots, but I refuse to allow Rois to live in a country where her every move could be suspect."

"What of Rothfield Castle?" Duncan asked.

"I will continue to maintain my home and lands in England," Griffin replied.

Seathan crossed his arms over his chest. "And how will you convince King Edward that such a move is prudent to his service?"

A smile edged Griffin's mouth. "King Edward will believe the loss of his men at Stirling Bridge but a minor setback. Building on that assumption, I will inform him my residing in Scotland will be a sign to the rebels that England's future is here."

Patrik grunted. "I can see Longshanks arrogant enough to agree with your reasoning. Except, he and his troops will learn that Stirling Bridge is but the beginning of our reclaiming Scotland's freedom."

"Mayhap," Seathan replied, his expression far from convinced.

"Ah," Duncan said with a smile, "your wife."

Griffin glanced toward the keep. His heart swelled as he watched Rois walk down the steps surrounded by the brothers' wives. At her side, Nichola carried her and Alexander's son, Hughe.

A vision of Rois cradling their babe came to mind, and pride filled his chest. Never had he thought of her pregnant. What if, after this morn, she carried his babe? Images of a son, with brown hair and hazel eyes, riding fearless across the glen warmed his heart. Or, a daughter, her laughing eyes as green as her mother's, telling bold tales as they broke their fast. Mayhap over time, Rois would bless him with several children.

"How long will you be away?" Seathan asked.

Griffin set aside thoughts of children. "I am unsure." Rois within enemy lines meant risk, but she was safer with him than allowing her to return with her father and be in the presence of Sir Lochlann. Never would the bastard Scot be near her again. "Know that I shall not depart Westminster Palace for any length of time without her."

"Wise," Alexander agreed. "With King Edward away, the tension inside the palace should be a touch easier."

"Aye," Duncan agreed. "Thankful I am his attention is on Flanders."

At Nichola's laughter, Griffin smiled at the approaching party. Who would have believed their families would end up entwined? Or, his marriage to Rois would begin to repair a family torn? Fate, some would say. He glanced at the arched window of the grandmother's tower, grimaced. Formerly a nonbeliever, well he'd learned this day that indeed magic existed.

Rois stepped inside the stable, and happiness filled her eyes when they met Griffin's.

He walked to her, lifted her hand, and pressed a gentle kiss upon her palm. "We must depart."

She nodded, her face pale; he suspected she thought of their crossing into England.

He gave her hand a gentle squeeze. "All will be well."

A brief smile touched Rois's mouth. "It will be."

"You said farewell to your father?"

Rois nodded. "I told him we would see him upon our return to Scotland."

Neither would Griffin reveal he would travel to Scotland before then for brief communications with her father—under the guise of *Wulfe*.

Rois gave each MacGruder a hug, a few quick words of good-bye, and then she walked to Griffin.

Wrapping his hands around her waist, he lifted her upon his mount. Griffin nodded to Lord Grey. "My thanks for everything."

Seathan nodded. "My home is yours, as it has been since your sister wed Alexander. With your marriage to our cousin, our bond is twice as strong."

"Indeed." Griffin turned to his sister, gave her a hug. "Take care."

"I will." A happy glow upon her face, Nichola stepped back to stand beside her husband.

Griffin swung up behind Rois. With a wave, he guided his horse from the stable. In the bailey, he kicked his steed toward the exit. Hooves clattered upon stone as he rode through the gatehouse. A burst of cool September air hit them as they cantered away from the formidable defenses of Lochshire Castle and rode toward the uncertainty awaiting them in England.

Rois strolled along the cobbled path in the courtyard of Westminster Palace. The numerous arched windows provided a magnificent backdrop to the countless, and priceless, statues, paintings, and pieces of art positioned inside. Across the neatly groomed lawns, the brown turf lay solemn against the late afternoon sun. Streams of sunlight pierced the cloud-ridden sky offering little warmth.

'Twas amazing to think that although she and Griffin had resided here a fortnight, she had explored but a fraction of the luxurious sights the royal palace offered.

"Lady Monceaux?"

At the deep male Scottish burr, Rois turned. A stately man boasting a groomed grey beard and a dignified face strode toward her. It was the Earl of Arthyan, a longtime family friend she'd come across the first night she and Griffin had dined in the palace.

A smile touched her lips at the memories of how in her youth she'd sat by the hearth and listened as the earl and her father spoke of Scotland's affairs, and the mundane issues of daily life. A time that, when compared to Scotland's current fight for freedom, seemed so long ago. She gave thanks for the earl's presence as she worked to find a customary routine on English soil. His familiar face helped temper the adjustment.

She scanned her surroundings. Since her arrival at Westminster Palace, she'd met Lord Arthyan several times at formal events, but always in the presence of Griffin. Although a maid walked a short distance away and he was a family friend, she refused to invite any speculation of impropriety. Rois nodded to the earl, and started to turn.

"Please do nae leave, Lady Rois," the earl said. "I saw you out enjoying the day, and found myself drawn to the fresh air as well." Kind brown eyes warmed. "After the stuffiness of the chamber, I pray you do nae mind my joining you." He cleared his throat. "My lady, if you think my presence is improper in any manner, regardless if you have your maid alongside, I shall depart." At her hesitation, he stepped back.

She was being rash. He was a family friend and, since they'd come in contact at Westminster Palace, he'd offered her naught but kindness. "Wait."

Lord Arthyan nodded. "My lady, I do nae wish you any discomfort."

"I am being foolish. 'Tis nae as if we are alone, or are strangers." In addition to her maid, several people strolled nearby.

His smile widened. "I found our conversation the last few nights engaging and refreshing. Long has it been since I spoke with someone from my homeland. I am sorry I missed visiting with your father during my last return visit to Scotland, but I had pressing matters needing my attention."

Rois nodded. "I admit when I saw you outside Kincardan Castle almost a moon ago, I was surprised you didna visit Da before you left."

The earl hesitated. "I didna realize you saw me? Where exactly?"

Confused by his question, she hesitated. "You were with Sir Lochlann. Near the forest where the river forks."

"So you did see me," Lord Arthyan said with a quick smile. "Aye. Sir Lochlann was pointing out the best spot to snare a few fish. Did you know he has mentioned you numerous times over the years? I admit, knowing how deeply he cared for you, I thought 'twould be him you would one day wed."

She interlaced her hands before her and cleared her throat. "My lord, ours was never more than friendship."

He arched a distinguished brow. "A belief 'twould seem only you held, but enough of such matters. You have made your choice and appear happy."

"My thanks, I am." She hesitated. "I will admit I was surprised to find you at Westminster Palace." Rois shook her head. "Forgive me, my lord, if you think I pry."

Mirth twinkled in his eyes. "Do nae worry. I understand. Are we nae both Scots whose lives have taken paths neither of us expected?"

Rois relaxed a degree. "We are."

"We have a link, a connection between us the English will never understand. Their greed for soil nae their own blinds them to realize the people of Scotland will one day reclaim their land," he stated, his last words lowering to a whisper. A flush stole across his face. "My lady, I should nae have spoken words so openly that could be interpreted as traitorous."

Sadness for his struggles for a country they both loved, as well as her own worry, weighed on her. "You have sworn fealty to King Edward. Many a Scot has been forced to bend a knee and re-swear their fealty to King Edward to preserve the safety of their family and home."

"Indeed," he replied, his voice somber. "I, Sir Robert Bruce, and many Scots have been coerced to accept England's dictate."

Her initial distrust of Griffin flickered in her thoughts. "'Tis a complicated time."

"My lady, you have great knowledge of our country and wisdom about those who swallow their pride and step in the shadows until time exposes an opportunity." His smile erased the concern in his eyes. "I regret this talk of fealty and war. A topic you no doubt find boring."

"I find the discussion far from boring. You caught me off guard, speaking of your passion for Scotland within King Edward's walls."

He nodded. "Our longtime friendship as well as your having grown into a beautiful woman loosens my tongue. I ramble like a common lad."

"I—"

The earl chuckled. "'Twould seem I again overstep my bounds. Please, forgive me. I pray you do nae think me forward, but I and many others at the palace were surprised to learn of Lord Monceaux's marriage. With your beauty, 'tis easy to see why he was smitten."

Uneasy with his praise, Rois remained silent, unsure how to reply.

He shook his head. "God's steed, I am forward. Forgive me, but when I heard Lord Monceaux had wed a Scottish lass, I found myself intrigued."

"Intrigued?"

"As one of King Edward's favorites, we expected your husband's marriage to an English noblewoman approved by our sovereign. The baron's actions are bold. However, when the king meets you, he will easily understand why his advisor to the Scots chose you as his wife."

Nae wanting to discuss her future meeting with the king further, Rois stepped back. "If you will excuse me, I must return to several tasks that await me."

The earl nodded. "Of course, my lady. 'Twas a pleasure to speak with you again. I have no doubt our paths will cross in the future. Fare thee well."

She gave him a quick smile and hurried toward her awaiting maid. In silence they made their way inside. At her chamber, Rois turned to the younger woman. "I wish to be alone. I need naught for the rest of this night."

"Yes, my lady." With a curtsy, her maid left.

Alone, Rois closed her chamber door. She missed the simplicity of her life in Scotland, and yearned for her freedom to go about without inciting speculation from her peers. An adjustment she would weather.

With a weary sigh, she washed her face in the basin, then walked to the window where the reds entwined with yellows of sunset illuminated the sky with whimsical ease. However appealing the surrounding countryside, England held but a shadow of the rough beauty of Scotland.

"You look astonishing."

Rois spun and found her husband closing the door, his eyes hungry. Her troubled thoughts of moments before fled, and she ran into Griffin's arms.

"I love you," he said, his gaze burning across her flesh. "I find myself starving, but not for food."

Heat stroked her. "As I."

Griffin arched a playful brow. "Let me not keep my fair maiden waiting."

Rois laughed as he whisked her into his arms.

Claiming her lips in a heated kiss, he lowered her to the bed. With nimble fingers, he removed her gown. Griffin broke the kiss, and with reverence, ran his hands over her naked body.

"Do you know how much I want you?" he asked as his mouth carved a searing path across her skin.

Her body on fire, her every fiber craving the intimacy they'd shared over and over again, she gave him a sultry smile. "Aye, very much so."

"My lady, 'twould seem your days of innocence are long lost."

Enjoying the game of lovers, she nodded. "Because of you. Because of the amazing way you make me feel. Because of how boldly you touch me."

He shed his clothes. "'Tis wanton you are, a fact that pleases me much." He caught her mouth in a fierce kiss and entered her with one thrust.

Loving him with all her heart, Rois lost herself to the passion that only Griffin could bring.

Chapter Twenty-one

Two days later, Rois stood upon the wall walk and stared through the crenulations at the sweep of the manicured lawns prepared for the upcoming winter storms that would ravage the lands. Against the cold air, her breath misted in a rolling cloud.

"We meet again?"

At the familiar welcome in Lord Arthyan's voice, she turned and smiled. "'Tis a beautiful night." She glanced about. "Your wife didna join you?"

He bowed. "She insisted I come up here alone. She knows I amble along the wall walk when I find myself heavy in thought."

"Sorry I am that you are troubled, my lord." Rois stepped back. "I shall leave you."

He shook his head. "Westminster is large. I will find another place."

Her curiosity piqued, she glanced toward her maid a short distance away. None would think their meeting untoward. "If I am nae intruding, I have been known to be a good listener."

His expression grew somber. "The topic is one I wish nae to ponder aloud."

At the graveness of his tone, she nodded. "I shall leave you to your contemplations."

"Wait." He darted a look around, then exhaled. "'Tis about your husband."

A chill swept her. Had her presence here somehow jeopardized Griffin? "My lord, you are making little sense."

"Forgive me." He rubbed his brow. "I have debated speaking with you these past two days. I thought my mind made up, but I struggle now. It wouldna be difficult if I didna know you so well, or think of you as a daughter."

"My lord, you are scaring me."

"My regrets, 'tis nae my intent. My lady, I am doing this poorly."

"Doing what poorly?"

"Warning you."

She fought for calm. "Warning me? I know naught of how you could warn me in regards to Griffin. His actions are above reproach. Surely you err."

"I pray 'tis true," the earl whispered, torment edging his voice. "'Tis but rumor and speculation. However, I regret to say it is quickly gaining ground." He paused. "I fear if this viciousness reaches King Edward's ear, 'twill be too late to salvage Lord Monceaux's reputation, or his life. Or"—sadness sagged on his face—"yours."

Her body trembling, Rois laid her hand upon her chest, aware of the lethal damage wrought by poisonous gossip unchecked. "If the news is so dire, why have you nae spoken to my husband?"

"My lady, I have tried. As of late, Lord Monceaux has been out of Westminster Castle or ensconced in numerous meetings."

Indeed. The last few nights Griffin had entered their chamber well after Compline, and their lovemaking gave way to his need for sleep.

"Please share with me this rumor, and I shall ensure it reaches his ears."

The distant flicker of torchlight outlined the relief upon his face. "My thanks for accepting this caution. Again, I do nae know if it is true, but I have known you since you were a child. With my deep respect for Lord Brom, I could do no other than to alert you."

Throat dry, she nodded.

He cleared his throat. "'Tis alleged that your husband delivers English battle plans and other critical information to the Scots."

"Impossible!" Rois stared at him in disbelief. But, beneath his regretful stare, she hesitated. Was it true? Regardless, she must proceed with caution. "Griffin is loyal to King Edward. His holdings are in England. He has no reason to betray his king."

"I agree, but to some, 'twould seem his marriage to you has raised questions of his loyalty."

Now she understood: Gossip spawned by jealousy. "Speculation like that is pure folly. Our marriage has naught to do with his loyalty."

And everything to do with Griffin being tricked into the act by her.

"I regret to have shared such news." The earl worried his hands. "Rois, I have one more request, which I ask only due to my having known your family over the years. Please nae say a word of where you heard the gossip to anyone, including to your husband."

Stunned by his request, she stiffened. "Do nae ask me to betray my husband by withholding secrets. I willna."

Lord Arthyan nodded. "Aye, I am wrong to ask you to keep secrets from your husband. Hence my hesitation to ask you to keep how you learned this to yourself. I make the entreaty only because my life is at risk if it is discovered I told you. But"—he paused, a touch of fear in his eyes—"I will respect your right to inform your husband what you feel is prudent. For old time's sake, I pray you keep your source hidden."

Torn by his request, Rois shook her head. She would never keep a secret from Griffin. "I make no promises."

The earl nodded. He glanced around as if ensuring none could hear, and then focused on Rois. "Rest assured, I am a man who supports your husband's actions. Please know I maintain secret ties to Scotland, which, I confess, still holds my first loyalty. If King Edward learns of my allegiance, charges of treason would befall me in a trice."

She'd suspected as much, but along with relief, the weight of his words left her shaken. "I would never betray you."

"Aye, that I believe." Lord Arthyan withdrew a document from beneath his cape. "Mayhap this will convince you."

God in heaven, what else could he share?

He unrolled it. "Here, see for yourself."

In silence she scanned the neatly penned document, noted within the content Griffin's name, and several meeting places in Scotland along with their dates.

Confused, she glanced up. "'Tis but missions assigned to him by the English king."

"Nay, look closer. Note the initial G by each meeting with William Wallace, Andrew de Moray, and other rebels of import. King Edward did nae send him. The engagements were of his choosing. My lady," he said, his words solemn, "this document was given to me by a traitor who does nae know of my loyalty to Scotland."

"The document must be fake," she whispered. "With Griffin's attention to detail, if indeed he was working with the Scots, he wouldna be so careless."

"A fact of which I agree. When I challenged the Scot, he explained he had stolen the document from Griffin's horse during a recent trip, and that the document was very real."

Fear tore through her. "'Tis treachery the Scot would act in such a brazen manner."

"Treachery or nae," the earl said, his voice grave, "the fact is a man loyal to King Edward is aware of Griffin's exploits for the Scottish cause."

Heart pounding, she shook her head. "This canna be." And prayed it was true.

The earl looked at her with shrewd eyes. "'Tis truth." He paused. "Apparently your husband has kept you ignorant of his exploits."

Torn between excitement of such a possibility and fear for Griffin's life, she hesitated. "Lord Arthyan, I still find this charge hard to accept. Except for his duties, I have been with Griffin day and night since we wed. He speaks constantly of his fidelity to England. He owns Rothfield Castle, which sits on English lands!"

The earl gave her a slight bow. "I will leave you to decide your own belief. But for your own caution, I bid you to beware. Lord Monceaux is in league with the Scots."

Excitement rushed through Rois as she again assessed the document revealed to her by Lord Arthyan.

Griffin was loyal to Scotland.

With astonishing clarity, the questions raised since Rois had met Griffin fell into place. How he had dared to enter Dunadd Castle before the Battle at Stirling Bridge. Why Wallace had requested Lord Monceaux bring de Moray to Cumbuskenneth Abbey to recover. And why her father trusted Griffin with her life.

Her father.

Da must have known of Griffin's true loyalty from the first.

Humbled by the risks Griffin had taken, ashamed she'd believed ill of him when all along he'd endangered his life to help Scotland, she found it incredible he could have fallen in love with her when she'd believed him her enemy.

"Mother of God, Griffin is in league with the rebels," she whispered, needing to say the words, their taste wonderfully real.

"Aye." Lord Arthyan pointed to the signature at the bottom of the penned document. "As you can clearly see, 'tis written by your husband's hand."

Hands trembling, Rois rerolled the writ, thankful the man she'd fallen in love with was indeed loyal to Scotland alone. She handed the document back to the earl.

"My apologies, my lord, for my outburst moments ago. It was, and still is, shocking news."

"Rest assured, I will keep this hidden. God forbid if it falls into the wrong hands." He laid his hand upon hers. "Please, my lady, all I ask is that you tell your husband his actions are being watched."

On a hard swallow, she nodded. Lives lay at stake in a very real, very deadly game. "My thanks, I will warn Griffin immediately." Heart pounding, she started to bid the earl farewell, then a new worry arose. "What of my father?"

"Lord Brom?"

"Aye," she rushed out, fear for her father growing every moment. "If this gossip reaches King Edward's ears, will my father be charged with treason?"

The earl frowned. "Why should your husband's loyalties, such as they are, affect Lord Brom?"

Did he nae understand? "Because," she explained, "my father sanctioned my marriage. He would never do so unless he believed my husband is a man he could trust. Or, he knew and has been meeting with Griffin in secret. And as I am sure you are aware, like you, his loyalties remain with Scotland."

The earl rubbed his chin. "Aye, I understand your concern. Do nae worry, your father should be safe. Once Lord Monceaux is aware of the rumors concerning his loyalties, he will quash them."

On an exhale, she wrung her hands. "Thank you, sincerely, for everything."

"'Tis my pleasure, my lady, to be of your service." He bowed. "Be off with you now, the sooner you alert your husband to the dangers the better."

"Indeed." With nerves frayed, Rois hurried away.

At the panicked look on Rois's face as she entered their chamber, Griffin shoved aside his frustrations from his recent meeting.

"Rois—"

"Thank God you are here." She hurried over, threw herself against him.

He drew back. "What is wrong?"

"Griffin," she rushed out, her voice filled with relief, "I— I know."

Unease swept him. "Know what?"

"That you are loyal to Scotland."

Astonished, he stared at her. "Rois," he said, his voice brusque, but the stakes were too high to misspeak. "What are you talking about?"

"I kn-know you aid the rebels."

Griffin stilled. She couldn't. Except by the conviction of her words, she believed she spoke the truth—which she did.

"Rois—"

"It is the reason why Da allowed you to stay married to me. And why Wallace trusted you to take my cousin Andrew to Cumbuskenneth Abbey, is it nae?"

He'd struggled to find a way to explain the truth of his loyalty, and doubted he ever would. Now, God help him, she knew, but it left a dangerous question unanswered. Who had told her?

"Is it true?" she pressed.

He would explain, but he needed answers as well. "Yes, my loyalty lies with the rebels," he replied with caution. "I joined the Scottish cause in my youth. Many rebels know of me, but nae who I am."

"Nae who you are? What do you mean?"

Pulse racing, he watched the mix of pride and fear on her face. Fear was healthy. It would keep her words and actions guarded. And keep her alive.

"I work beneath the name *Wulfe*."

Her mouth dropped open. "You are *Wulfe*?"

He nodded. "My father before me was loyal to the Scots. He worked covertly for them against England's tyranny. As a youth, I witnessed the injustice to the people of Scotland, so I joined the rebel cause as well." He paused. "Over time, my title and connections allowed me to secure a place as King Edward's advisor to the Scots, a position that has saved numerous rebel lives."

Rois scraped her teeth across her bottom lip. "Why did you nae tell me before?"

"To protect you." He caressed the soft curve of her cheek. "I wanted you innocent of the fact in case you were ever questioned, or I . . ."

"Died."

He nodded. "Yes."

"Y-you should have told me."

"Rois, you were never to know."

Shrewd eyes studied him. "Which is why you sought an annulment. Nae because you didna love me, but because you wanted me safe."

God, he loved her. "I never should have touched you."

A hint of a smile touched her mouth. "I am glad you did."

"As I." Neither could he ignore a more serious issue. "Rois, who told you of my loyalty to the Scots?"

"'Twas a trusted family friend," she explained. "He showed me a document listing your name, and the dates of your meeting with your rebel contacts."

Dread crept through him. "A trusted friend showed you this document?" God's teeth. Rois considered only one man in residence her friend—a very powerful lord with dangerous connections.

"Aye," she rushed on, "a document written by your hand. He explained they were given to him by a traitorous Scot who stole the document from your horse during a recent trip." At his silence, panic filled her eyes. "What is wrong?"

"You are speaking of Lord Arthyan?"

She gave a jerky nod.

He muttered a curse, his mind racing at what he must do, of who he must warn. First, though, he must explain to Rois. "Listen to me," he said with care, aware from their talks how she admired the earl. "No such document exists."

"But I saw—"

"Rois," he said, his voice grave, "Lord Arthyan is a man who seeks King Edward's praise regardless of the foul play used."

"Nay, you are wrong. I have known him for many years, and trust him with my life. I saw the document," she said, her voice growing panicked. "Griffin, he risked his life to warn you."

Fury slammed him. "The only life he risked is yours."

"It canna be. I have known Lord Arthyan all of my life. He would nae lie to me."

The desperation in her voice drove his anger deeper. Never was Rois to be involved in any of this. "Think you if I had such a document, I would not notice its disappearance?

Her face paled.

"Lord Arthyan is loyal to King Edward," he continued. "For his own gain, he is using you to try and set me up."

"But—"

"Only a handful of people know my loyalties are for Scotland. And, none, *none* are in Westminster Palace."

Her pallor whitened. "You are wrong."

"I wish, with all of my heart," he said, his voice strained, "but 'tis so."

She stilled, and began to shake. "Oh, God, Da!"

Fear tore through him. "What about Lord Brom?"

Desperate eyes held his. "I believed Lord Arthyan was my friend."

Griffin cupped her shoulders, his blood pounding hot. "Rois, tell me what you told the earl."

Tears filled her eyes. "I asked Lord Arthyan if because my father sanctioned our marriage, he would come under suspicion by King Edward. I— I should have stopped there, but I admitted to the earl that I believed my da would never approve our marriage unless he knew you and has been meeting with you in secret. I also assured him that my da's loyalties remain with Scotland."

A muscle worked in Griffin's jaw. "What did he say?"

"Lord Arthyan assured me nae to worry, but I have placed my father's life in danger!"

Bedamned. "Have you told anyone else?"

"Nay," she whispered. "I hurried to find you after he showed me the document."

"Full of falsehoods. No such document exists. 'Twas concocted to support the earl's lie."

"W-we have to warn Da!"

Griffin drew her against him, stroked her hair. "I will send a runner this night."

Eyes hot with anger, she met his gaze. "Lord Arthyan lied to me. I will—"

"Do naught."

Rois shook her head, frantic to find a way to repair this. "How can you expect me to do nothing when 'twas my impulsiveness that has endangered you *and* my father, and may thwart any future information the rebels desperately need?"

"Listen to me," Griffin said, keeping his voice even. "We need to stop and think this through. First, if the document was real, the earl would have delivered it without delay to King Edward's guard and ordered my arrest."

"True," she conceded. "So what do we do now?"

"You will go into hiding until I have dealt with Lord Arthyan."

Rois stepped back. "I will go nowhere! Throughout my life I have allowed my emotions to guide me, one such decision which led to our marriage. However thankful I am for that twist of fate, too many other times my actions brought about regret. But," she said, her voice rough with emotion, "this day I have learned my lesson. The danger to my family is because of me and, by God, I will have a hand in repairing it."

"Rois, I will not place you in danger."

She angled her jaw. "'Tis too late."

Griffin cursed. "I want you safe."

Her heart ached. "I know."

With a grimace, he rubbed his brow and shot her a hard look.

Rois remained silent. He hadn't said nay. But then, she was still learning to read Griffin's behavior. "What are you thinking?"

He shook his head. "An idea came to mind, but 'tis too dangerous."

She laid her hand on his forearm. "Griffin, tell me."

For a long moment he stared at her, his worry clear. "Do you think you can convince Lord Arthyan to repeat his claim of loyalty to Scotland?"

Her mind worked to discern his reason he'd want her to, but fell short. "Aye."

A grudging look crossed his handsome face. "Then, I believe we will beat him at his own game."

Nerves fluttered through Rois as she stood within the garden, the moonlight above severed by the thickening clouds as the cold breeze bit her skin. She tugged her cape tighter and scanned the walking path. Where was Lord Arthyan? She'd sent a missive for him to meet her here at the bells of Compline.

Bushes rustled to her left.

Rois glanced toward the outline of shrubs in the darkness where Griffin hid with the king's men. She must convince the earl to repeat his words of loyalty to Scotland in front of the castle guards.

If Lord Arthyan showed.

"Lady Rois?"

At the earl's soft call, she glanced down the stone path. Beneath the muted glow of moonlight, he hurried toward her, glancing about with a nervous twitch.

Let him suspect naught!

Three paces away, Lord Arthyan halted. He again scanned the

area with a slow sweep, then exhaled as if satisfied. "I received your message. What has happened?"

Rois hid her shaking hands beneath her cloak. "I— I am afraid." The truth. She was terrified for the lives of Griffin and Da if she should fail.

"Of what?"

The dark urgency in his voice put Rois further on edge. "Of the dangers to you if it is learned you are loyal to Scotland."

His body relaxed. "Lady Rois, do nae fear for my sake."

"How can I nae, when I have known you since I was a child?" she replied. "With each day you work to aid the rebels, you put yourself in danger."

"Indeed, but 'tis a risk those loyal to Scotland take, a risk," he said with confidence, "that I believe you are brave enough to be a part of as well."

Stunned, she stared at him. Please let Griffin and the guards have heard. "You wish me to spy on King Edward for the rebels?"

"Aye," Lord Arthyan replied. "Lady Rois, as you said, we have known each other for many years. You know me, can trust me. I hesitated to ask, to allow you to endanger your life, but with Lord Grey as your husband, 'twould be easy for you to learn of the king's plans. Except, you could *never* reveal this to your husband."

"I . . . I know not what to say?"

"'Tis an enormous request," he stated, "one I understand you wish to ponder."

She gave a shaky nod, then began to pace as Griffin had directed.

Keep calm, Griffin silently willed as he watched Rois from behind the brush. He turned to King Edward's knight at his side. Against the wisps of moonlight slipping through the dense foliage, Griffin caught the taut lines of anger pulsing on the man's face.

"Are you now convinced the earl is a traitor and trying to convince my wife to betray England?" Griffin whispered.

"Indeed," the head of the royal guard returned in a furious hiss. He glanced toward his men hidden within the garden awaiting the order to rush in and arrest Lord Arthyan.

Griffin focused on where Rois stood in the shadows, pleased she allowed her body to slowly relax as he'd instructed, but he caught her furtive glance toward where they hid. Stay calm, he willed. 'Tis but moments now.

Rois exhaled, took another step back. "My lord—"

"Arrest him!" a deep, authoritative voice bellowed.

Brush scraped. Steps pounded against stone as several guards jumped into the clearing and ran toward the earl.

Lord Arthyan whirled, cursed.

"Run!" Griffin yelled.

Rois bolted toward the guards.

The men allowed her room to pass, then surrounded the earl and seized him.

"Release me!" Lord Arthyan demanded. "You have no right to hold me."

The senior knight stepped forward, his face taut. "My lord, you are charged with treason against the crown!"

"Lies!" the earl spat.

"I heard your confession. The only lie told is yours." The knight nodded toward his men. "Take him to the dungeon."

The earl glared at Rois, then Griffin. Outlined in the moonlight, his expression transformed from outrage to a malicious smile.

"You have achieved naught," Lord Arthyan spat. "These charges are ludicrous."

"Are they?" Griffin asked, his words deadly quiet. "Did you not confess that your fealty to England is a lie of your own free will, then try to convince my wife to aid you in your traitorous cause?"

The earl tried to twist free. Failed. "'Tis you who is the traitor. You, who is in league with the Scottish rebels. I but wanted Rois to confess her true loyalties are to Scotland."

Griffin laughed, aware his reaction was watched, measured by the royal knight with a critical eye. "Do not think to cast your guilt away, Lord Arthyan. 'Tis not I who admitted being a traitor within the cloak of night to enlist the aid of another. But, 'twill be I who stands before King Edward upon his return from Flanders and swears I witnessed you trying to ensnare my wife in your treachery."

Lord Arthyan's vicious glare pinned Rois. "You lured me here for your foul purpose. I trusted you. And you betrayed me."

"I did naught, my lord. You approached me. 'Twas your own falseness that betrayed England. Now, I wonder how many others you have tried to enlist in your foul plans."

The earl cast a scathing glance toward Griffin, and then to Rois. "You will regret your duplicity, my lady. I may die, but your father's life is already forfeit. As we speak, a runner is en route to deliver a missive of great importance to Lord Brom. And when he is allowed entry, your father will die."

"You lie," Rois stated. "An untruth to convince others your loyalty belongs to England."

"You believe my threat false?" Lord Arthyan's cruel laughter fragmented the chill of the night. "Do you nae think your father will allow your trusted friend, Sir Lochlann, inside Kincardan Castle?"

Chapter Twenty-two

Griffin urged his lathered mount on as the light of the fading sunset trickled through the barren limbs of the familiar terrain. Each moment passed meant the loss of much needed light. Against the cool breeze thick with the promise of snow, the steady pound of hooves upon the ground was like a death knell.

"Thank God, we are almost there," Rois yelled, riding at his side.

At the exhaustion and fear in her voice, Griffin nodded. What could he say? Until they arrived at Kincardan Castle, neither would know Lord Brom's fate.

He damned the missive just days before notifying him that Lord Brom had departed Lochshire Castle for his home, but more, he wished he had killed Sir Lochlann when the man had drawn his dagger on him during their fight.

Why hadn't he suspected the bastard was a traitor? So caught up in the Scot's feelings for Rois, he'd attributed Lochlann's anger to his infatuation for her. Now, due to his inattention, her father may be dead.

In full health, Angus would drive his blade with skill into the traitor's heart. But his friend was recovering from near death, and Griffin held doubts Lord Brom could hold off the formidable Scot.

As they rounded a hillock, Kincardan Castle rose into view, the crenellations shadowed against the ominous, cloud-laden sky.

"A rider approaches!" a guard atop the wall walk called. "'Tis Lord and Lady Monceaux. Allow them entry!"

Chains rattled. The portcullis jerked up, the forged iron grinning like fangs against the darkened entry. Hooves clattered against stone as they rode beneath the gatehouse.

Painted against the waning light, several knights strode toward them as they entered the bailey.

His horse whinnied as Griffin drew his steed to a halt; Rois reined in her mount at his side. "Where is Lord Brom?"

Worry creased the guard's brow. "In his chamber, abed."

"Thank God," Rois said.

A sentiment he shared. Griffin dismounted, and lifted Rois to the ground. "Sir Lochlann, have you seen him?"

Another guard nodded. "Aye, my lord. He returned moments ago, said he carried an urgent missive for Lord Brom and departed for our lord's chamber."

"Bedamned!" Griffin dropped his mount's reins, faced Rois. "Stay here." He turned to the guards. "Alert the guards! Lord Brom is in serious danger." He bolted for the keep.

Rois's panicked steps pounded in his wake, but he pushed harder, needing to intercept the bastard before it was too late.

A knight walked out of the door to the keep as Griffin ran up the steps. Griffin shoved the man aside, and sprinted through the entry. Across the great hall he caught sight of Sir Lochlann striding toward the turret.

"Sir Lochlann, halt!" Griffin demanded.

The Scot turned. Surprise, then fury clouded his gaze. On a curse, he ran up the steps.

Griffin bolted after him.

At the first landing, sword drawn, Lochlann whirled. Yellowed torchlight outlined the violence carved on his face. "Stay back."

"Why?" Griffin demanded as he halted five steps below. "So you can murder Lord Brom?"

"Kill a man whom I back with my blade? Nay, Sassenach, unlike you who swear their fealty to the English king, I am a loyal Scot."

The slide of steel against leather whispered as Griffin drew his sword. "Is that why you plot treason against your country?"

"Treason against my country?" He scoffed. "Naught but lies you invented to impress Rois."

"Nay," Rois said as she stepped around the curve of the turret, and beyond Griffin, her friend came into view. "Claims I heard from Lord Arthyan in Westminster Palace as he was hauled away for treason by the king's guards."

Outraged flashed in Lochlann's eyes. "You should nae be here."

Furious her childhood friend would deceive her, she took a step closer. "Why?" she asked, her voice rough with emotion. "So I can nae acknowledge that a man I have known since childhood, a man who I shared many sorrows and smiles with, is a liar and a traitor? That, like Lord Arthyan, he does everything for his own gain?"

Lochlann shook his head. "Rois, you do nae understand."

"Aye," she said, aching at his deviousness. "I understand too well. You never loved me, nor truly were my friend. Instead, you saw me as a path to gain the title and wealth upon my father's passing. My father whom you now seek to kill."

"Rois, leave us," Griffin said, his words quiet.

"Order her about, do you?" Lochlann spat. "And how do you like being an English subject, lass?"

"You know naught," Rois replied. "And 'tis I who was a fool to believe you ever truly cared."

"What in bloody hell is going on?" Lord Brom's voice boomed from down the hall.

A smile of pure evil curved Lochlann's mouth. "Mayhap I will never leave here alive," he hissed to Rois, "but you will lose your father, a man who did naught but stand in my way throughout life." He whirled. "Lord Brom, I have a missive to deliver," he called and sprinted down the corridor.

Panic swept her. "Da, he lies! He means to kill you!"

Sword raised, Griffin bolted after Lochlann. "Halt!"

Heart pounding, Rois fled up the steps.

Steel scraped in the distance.

Nay! She rounded the corner, stilled. Halfway down, her father wielded his sword against Lochlann's attack. "Stop!"

Blades scraped, shuddered as they met with force.

"Be gone with ye, lass," her father yelled.

"Go, Rois," Griffin added as he halted several paces from where the men battled.

Shaking, she willed herself back, to nae be a distraction to her father as he lifted his sword to meet Lochlann's next swing.

Steel clashed.

Her father's legs wobbled. Gave. He caught himself barely.

A satisfied smile was upon Lochlann's face as he raised his sword for the mortal blow.

Griffin started forward. Before he took the first step, her father angled his sword and drove it forward, any show of weakness before gone.

On a gasp, Lochlann staggered back. Disbelief on his face shattered to pain as he stared at the sword shoved deep in his chest.

"'Twill teach you to threaten my daughter and my son-in-law, or dare threaten me," her da boomed.

The Scot collapsed to his knees, his gasps decaying to gurgles.

Rois trembled uncontrollably as she stumbled forward.

Griffin caught her, tried to move before her.

"Nay," she rasped. "'Twas his own treachery that brought him this fate."

Lochlann lay upon the floor, struggling to breathe.

Lord Brom withdrew his sword with an angry pull, the forged steel smeared with a Scot's blood. "You would betray your own?"

"Betray?" Sir Lochlann struggled out. "The rebels are fools. Scotland has no chance of winning against King Edward."

"The Scots are your people," Lord Brom stated.

"They are stupid and weak. They canna see beyond the tankard they lift. Th-their claims of freedom are naught more than sputters of fools." Sir Lochlann gasped. "They c-canna see the wisdom of King Edward's guidance—Scotland's true leader." With a shudder, he collapsed to the floor, and his eyes stared straight ahead.

Griffin drew Rois against his chest. "'Tis over."

Emotion filling her, she shook her head and looked up at him. "Nay, for us 'tis but the beginning."

Several weeks later, Rois stood wrapped in Griffin's arms on the wall walk at Lochshire Castle. She gave a sigh.

"You are heavy in thought."

At Griffin's whisper against her cheek, she turned. Her heart warmed as she looked upon the man she loved. "I was thinking of Lochlann."

He brushed a wisp of hair from her cheek. "Sorry I am at the loss of your friend."

"Friend, nay. The only person he was true to was himself. Wanting to believe him a friend, I never looked for more. Evidence that was clear to others, I refused to see."

Silence fell between them, broken by the rush of the cool fall wind, the swirl of an errant thick flake. "My father has recovered. For that I am thankful."

"As am I." Griffin pressed a kiss upon her brow. "I pray Lord Andrew does as well."

Rois nodded. "With how slowly his injuries are healing, I fear for his life."

"Your cousin is a man of courage, and a friend. I pray he recovers. The rebels need de Moray's skill, and his instinct to lead."

Concern hovered in her mind, but Rois refused to give birth to her fears, or to contemplate Scotland without the leadership of her cousin. Nay, she would think only positive thoughts.

She smiled at Griffin. "The embroidery of the fairy was a special gift for our marriage."

"Indeed," Griffin replied. "I find it no surprise that the MacGruder brothers' gift matches one of the fairies in the tapestry hanging inside their grandmother's chamber."

Memories of speaking with the elderly woman warmed her heart. "The gift is nae from my cousins, but from their grandmother."

He laughed. "Rois, their grandmother has long since passed."

"The morning after we spent the night together in the grand-mother's chamber, while you were still asleep, I spoke with her."

"What?"

In detail, Rois described her unexpected meeting with the woman, of how she was working on an embroidered piece matching the one they'd received as a gift.

"At the time," Rois explained, "I was unsure sure what she meant. Now I understand 'twas Catarine I spoke with. She regrets the wedge her coming to Lochshire Castle put between my grandfather and his brother." Completeness filled her with the blessing of the MacGruders' grandmother. "With our marriage, the rift between our families was mended. Her finished embroidery is proof."

Griffin smiled, a smile of pure happiness, of a man deeply in love. "If asked before I met the MacGruder brothers, I would have denied your words as but a tale. Now, incredibly, I believe you."

She snuggled next to him, the grandmother's story of how she fell in love with the MacGruders' grandfather, Trálin, clearly a remark-able truth.

Distant hooves sounded.

"A rider approaches," a guard yelled from the gatehouse.

Thoughts of the grandmother faded, and Rois squinted at the approaching rider. Panic swept her. "'Tis a rebel messenger."

Worry creased his brow as Griffin took her hand. "Come." He led her to where Seathan and the MacGruder brothers stood below.

The rider cantered into the bailey and drew his steed up before Griffin. He nodded to Seathan, then faced Griffin. "Lord Monceaux, Lord Brom forwards a missive to you delivered by a royal English messenger two nights past."

"Do you think," Rois whispered to Griffin, "Lord Arthyan has somehow convinced the nobles that you are a spy for Scotland?"

"We will soon find out," he quietly replied. With a worried glance toward the MacGruder brothers, Griffin prayed she was wrong. If so, he would be a wanted man, and Rois's life at immense risk.

He broke open the seal.

Hands steady, Griffin unrolled the parchment, scanned the neatly penned lines. "'Twould seem," he said with a smile, "that after King Edward received word of my uncovering Lord Arthyan's betrayal, he sends lauds for my quick intervention to expose the traitor. In addition, he has awarded me Lord Arthyan's title and estates."

Rois wrapped her arms around his neck, leaned her mouth close to his ear. "'Twould seem that *Wulfe*'s destiny to aid Scotland and fight for its independence lives on."

"Indeed," Griffin said, "but only if he knows that he has the love of an amazing woman at his side."

Laughter sparkled in her eyes. She leaned back, arched her brow. "And who would that be?"

Griffin swept her into his arms and strode past the MacGruder brothers, ignoring their amusement.

"Griffin," she gasped, "what are you doing?"

"I believe I am going to make love with my wife." He savored the slide of red up her cheeks, but more the love brimming from her eyes. Rois's antics may have ensnared him into an unwanted marriage, but in a wonderful magical twist of fate, their handfasting rejoined her family with the MacGruders. Best, he'd received the greatest of gifts—her love.

Keep reading for
an excerpt from Diana Cosby's

HIS ENCHANTMENT

The next stunning novel in her
MacGruder series
Available Fall 2013

Scotland, 1257

Beneath the October dawn, Lady Catarine McLaren scoured the hard sheer line of mountains, then the roll of field that fell away to the magnificent loch shrouded by a thin veil of fog. "I see naught."

"Nor I."

Catarine glanced at Atair, her senior fey warrior, his fierce scowl framed by coal-black hair secured with a leather strip behind his head. "We saw the English knights but moments ago. Their trail shouldna just disappear."

"Indeed," Atair replied, his deep voice rich with concern. He scanned where the remainder of the fey warriors moved through the knee-deep grass, searching for any indication of a small band of men having passed through. "The English knights are human. We trailed them with ease through the Otherworld. Yet, since we entered Scotland through the stone circle, with each step away from the magical portal, any sign of their presence is fading."

"Aye, something is greatly amiss." She frowned at the ring of stones enfolded within the blanket of fog, the daunting presence of the strategic pillars majestic against the bands of dawn severing the sapphire sky. "How did the Englishmen know to use the stone circle to travel to the Otherworld? More troubling, how were they able to pass through? Only the fey can travel from the Otherworld to Scotland."

Atair rubbed his brow. "I am unsure." He glanced toward her. "Mayhap our losing track of them is for the best."

Anger slammed her. "The best? How can you say that when English knights attacked the royal palace and murdered my uncle?"

His mouth tightened. "This is the reason your father requested that you and your sisters separate and go into hiding. Until he confirms whether Prince Johan's murderer is a threat to the entire royal family, King Leod wished to nae expose you or anyone within the royal family to danger."

Catarine angled her jaw. "Nor would my father expect me to ignore that en route to safety, we caught a glimpse of the English knights fleeing the Otherworld."

"'Twas nae King Lauchlan's request that his daughter endanger her life," Atair stated, his words tight.

"Nay, the decision to follow the English knights in hopes they will lead us to whoever planned the attack was mine." Catarine understood Atair's frustration, but being of age, and with a small contingent of the fey guard beneath her command, 'twas her choice to make.

He crossed his arms, frowned. "It does nae mean I have to like it."

Far from intimidated by the gruffness in Atair's voice—for he was a man who was more her friend than a guard—she arched a brow. "And when was the last time I made a decision you approved of?"

Atair dropped his arms at his side. "'Tis naught to joke of. I am worried about your safety."

The last of her anger faded. "I know, but 'tis not as if I am either naïve or helpless. Once my sisters and I turned five summers, we were trained with a blade by the finest tutors."

"Princess Ca—"

"Catarine," she interrupted. "We have known each other since our youth."

Somber eyes held hers. "And we are no longer children."

"Nay, that we are not." Tiredness weighed on her as she noted the roll of clouds moving in. "And I worry that my father will indeed confirm that the attack was but the first toward the royal family."

"Why do you say that?"

With a sigh she brushed back several strands of hair from her braid, loosened from the last couple hours of hard travel. "Early this morning my uncle sent runners beseeching the royal family to meet him in the royal garden posthaste. In his missive he stated the reason 'twas of the greatest urgency that concerned us all. Before I or anyone else arrived, English knights attacked, and their arrows found their mark."

"Prince Johan's warrior instinct saved your family." Atair's frown deepened to a hard edge. "Still, human arrows killing your uncle, one of the fey, should be impossible."

"It should be," Catarine agreed, "leaving one terrifying explanation—the arrows were spell-tipped."

"'Tis the only explanation," Atair agreed with disgust. "But who would cast a spell upon a human's weapon to enable them to kill the fey?"

Fear rippled through her. "Someone who dared allow humans into our realm for such a nefarious deed. It could be any of the fey nobility who have challenged the royal family's claim to the throne over the years. Or," she said, her mind mulling the terrifying possibilities, "if 'twas due to the lust for power, the traitor could be unknown. And the reason we must trail the Englishmen."

Atair grimaced. "Do you know if your father found any written notes stating Prince Johan's concerns?"

The gruesome image of her stumbling upon her uncle sprawled on the floor in the royal garden, the stench of blood, and the arrows embedded in his chest clawed through her mind.

"Catarine?"

She swallowed hard. "When my father arrived, he searched his brother's chamber in hopes of finding a clue. Whatever the threat to our family, my uncle refused to share it except to our face."

"Thank the heavens a royal guard caught sight of the men as they escaped and were able to give a description."

"Aye. 'Twas easy to recognize the English knights. I still canna believe humans were brought into the Otherworld for such evil intent." Catarine rubbed her finger over the hilt of her dagger as she glanced to where the fey warriors continued their search, then sighed. "There is little use in us continuing. The trail of the English knights is lost. We must return to the stone circle and try to track them from there again. There must be some sign of their passing that we missed."

Embraced by the mist of dawn, Atair gave a soft whistle.

The fey warriors looked over, then hurried toward them through the thin veil of fog.

Once everyone had returned, Catarine nodded to each man. "We are—"

A man's shout echoed in the distance.

"Get down!" Atair warned.

Catarine dropped to the ground and flattened herself alongside the fey warriors. The rich scent of earth mixed with the grass as a steady breeze rustled through the thick blades, shielding them from view.

"Look near the water's edge," Sionn, one of the fey warriors she felt close to, said in a low voice.

Catarine peered between the mist-laden grass. In the distance, through the smear of thinning fog, she made out a fairly large group of warriors.

"I count over twenty men," Sionn whispered.

"Look behind them," Atair whispered in return, concern edging his voice. "Several more men are leading two people from the water's edge. From their garb, they are nobility."

Nobility? Catarine frowned as she noted a man and a woman walking through the slide of water with the group, the luxuriousness of their garb indeed confirming Atair's observation of their royalty.

"Halt!" Another shout, distinctly male, echoed from a distance behind them.

Stunned, Catarine met her senior fey warrior's worried gaze. "We are caught between the two groups!"

"The tall grass and brush should keep us hidden," Atair replied.

She prayed so.

Heavy footsteps pounded nearby.

As the men ran closer, heart pounding, she withdrew her dagger.

"Halt in the name of King Alexander III!" a deep male voice ordered from the group closing in on the knights with royalty.

Stunned, she glanced toward the knights hurrying away with the royal pair. King Alexander III—Scotland's king?

Orders rang out from the knights near the water. Several men broke from their ranks and rushed up the hill toward the attackers.

Atair glanced over. "If they come closer, we will have to fight."

Her body taut, Catarine nodded.

Several feet away, blades scraped.

A cry of pain echoed.

Outlined by the fog, an armed man staggered toward them, crumpled to the earth but paces away.

"The battle 'tis nae yours, Lord Grey," a Scot warned a towering man with rust hair and a beard who struggled to his feet. "Go back."

"Like bloody hell," the rust haired man boomed. "'Tis my king you are abducting!" Arms trembling, Lord Grey raised his blade, swung.

The men clashed. Amidst the fray, grunts and curses filled the air, the slide of steel as common as the fall of men and the gasps of their last breaths.

Hands fisted, Catarine watched horrified as the battle for life and death played out before her. Without warning, an urge swept over her to jump into the fray, to stand alongside Lord Grey and protect Scotland's king. She sheathed her dagger, clasped the hilt of her sword, and started to rise.

With a fierce scowl, Atair caught her wrist. "What are you doing?"

Heat warming her cheeks, she flattened herself against the ground. "I . . ." She wasna sure, which made nae a bit of sense. She was fey, nae human, nor held any ties to King Alexander. Scotland's king and his people were nae her concern. Still, the draw to aid the man fighting to save his king remained. Uneasy, she studied the mix of men engaged in battle, her gaze returning to one—the rust-haired Scot.

Like a defiant god, Lord Grey forged ahead, his each slash at the man before him making Catarine hold a nervous breath. Why? 'Twas not as if she knew him. Never had she seen the man in her life.

Muscles bulged as Lord Grey lifted his blade, swung.

The Scottish knight before him screamed out. Fell.

Another Scot charged the rust-haired Scot from behind.

Catarine covered her mouth to stifle a gasp. Heart pounding, she watched in horror as the man swung, then his blade came up stained with a slash of red.

On a cry of pain, Lord Grey crumpled to the ground.

She must help him!

Atair's hand on her wrist tightened, keeping her there. He gave a hard shake of his head.

What was she thinking? She couldna expose their presence. But for an unexplainable reason, an urgency filled her to reach Lord Grey.

Long moments passed. Slowly, the cacophony of blades stilled to an errant shudder.

Silence.

Their movements weighed by fatigue, several warriors from the knights who'd challenged the attackers backed away from the litter of bodies.

"What of the dead?" a man with a deep Scottish burr several paces away asked.

"Leave them," a gruff voice farther away ordered. "We must reach Stirling Castle."

"And what if the king doesna comply with our lord's request?" the Scot with the deep burr asked.

"Then he will die," the gruff voice replied. "Let us go." He waved the men forward.

The slide of metal against leather hissed as knights shoved swords into their sheaths and started toward the west.

Sunlight pierced the wisps of fog as Catarine watched them catch up with the distant group leading the royal couple away. "King Alexander and his queen are in danger!"

Atair released her wrist and eyed her perplexed. "Their fate is nae our concern. We must find the trail of the English knights who entered the Otherworld and give chase."

She blinked her eyes. So caught up in the battle, of her concern for Lord Grey, for a moment she'd forgotten her purpose. Chagrined, she focused on the stone circle in the distance, then back toward the departing men.

"If the English knights we are trailing passed this way," Sionn said with a grimace, "with the battle, I fear any trace is destroyed."

A sinking feeling in her gut, Catarine nodded. "We will soon see." She pushed herself into a kneeling position, kept her body below the tips of the tall grass.

"The Scots should be far enough away," Atair said as he stood in a crouched position, "but I want to take nae chance of being seen." He faced the other warriors. "Move toward the stone circle, but keep low." He started back.

Sionn moved beside Catarine. "I will keep beside you."

His tenderness touched her. Her friend worried about her. She gave him a warm smile. "I believe I am able to defend myself."

"Aye," Sionn replied, "but I am staying still the same."

"Let us go then." Catarine started moving through the thick, dew-laden grass.

A man's pain-filled moan echoed from several paces away.

She whirled toward the sound.

Between the blades of sturdy grass, shafts of fragile sunlight illuminated a lone figure staggering to his feet.

Lord Grey!

Waves of emotion swamped her, that of pain, of anger so deep 'twas as if it lived. Catarine dug her fingers deep into her palms as she fought to steady herself against the onslaught.

Sionn halted beside her. "What is wrong?"

"I . . ." How did one explain these raw emotions? In disbelief,

Catarine stared at the lone figure, then understood. Somehow, incredibly, she was sensing what this Scot was feeling. She stepped toward him.

"Catarine," Sionn demanded, "what are you doing?"

"I must help him."

At her voice, the rust-haired Scot's head snapped toward her.

The impact of his green eyes held hers, pinned her as if a sword to flesh. Sensation roared through her, a feeling so deep, so complete, it entwined her.

"Who are you?" Lord Grey's deep burr demanded.

Sword raised, Atair ran back and moved beside her as the other fey warriors formed a protective circle. "Nay answer."

Sensation tearing through her, Catarine shook her head. "He is nae a threat."

"You know him naught," Sionn said, his voice rich with suspicion.

Atair nodded to the daunting man. "Who are you?"

The Scot straightened. "Trálin MacGruder, Earl of Grey, guard to King Alexander," he stated, his each breath rattling with agony. His body began to waver. "Who be"—on a muttered curse, he collapsed.

"Nay!" She broke through her guard's protective circle, and rushed toward Lord Grey.

"Catarine!" Atair called.

Panic slid through her as she whirled to face her senior fey warrior. "I . . . I must help him."

Atair shook his head. "There is no time. We must go. Now."

She should agree. 'Twas imperative to find where they'd lost the trail of the English knights—if it still existed. More, to remain here with a stranger, a human, went against everything she must do.

Aching inside, she shook her head. "I canna leave him."

"Canna?" Atair strode to her. "What are you talking about?"

Unsure looks passed between Sionn and the other fey warriors.

Emotion swamped Catarine, urged her to where Trálin MacGruder lay moaning in pain. "I canna explain more." She ran toward the noble.

Atair's footsteps echoed behind her. "Catarine!"

Sunlight broke through the clouds above as she knelt beside the injured earl.

Atair caught her forearm, drew her to her feet. "What in Hades do you think you are doing? Do you want to get yourself killed?"

Lord Grey moaned.

Stiffening at the pain he was enduring, at his each breath labored, she shook her head. "The Scot is far from a threat."

Atair's gaze narrowed. "He is human."

"I know," she replied, her words somber. "But here," she said touching her finger against her brow, "I know I must help him."

"To aid a human is forbidden," Sionn argued as he and the other warriors halted beside her. "We are granted the ability to leave a thought in their mind, naught more."

"I know," she whispered.

"What of the trail of the English knights?" Atair asked, his voice exasperated. "Is it now unimportant?"

Guilt swept her. Her warriors were right. To help this Scot in any mortal manner went against the laws of the Otherworld. She started to turn away.

"Do n-nae go," Lord Grey whispered as he lay upon the ground. He coughed, and his entire body rattled. "I must save my king and queen."

The soft plea of his voice struck her as if it were an arrow shot. Emotion tangled inside her as she stared at the man. Rays of sunlight illuminated Trálin MacGruder's hard-boned face, that of a warrior, of a man determined. But it also highlighted a firm mouth that would make a woman dream, and his green eyes, those which, underneath his pain, shone with kindness.

"You speak of King Alexander and his queen," she stated, pulling herself from her wanton thoughts.

Shrewd, pain-filled eyes studied her. "Aye," Lord Grey replied. "They were abducted."

Catarine glanced toward where the two people she'd seen being escorted by a group had hurried off. "By whom?"

"I do nae know, but I must fi-find out." On a curse, he tried to sit up.

"Do nae move. You are wounded," Catarine said as she knelt, placed her palm against his shoulder and held him down.

His body trembled. "My men?"

She took in the bodies strewn about, the scent of blood strong against the fresh Highland morning, exhaled. "I am sorry, they are dead."

"God in heaven," the earl hissed.

Atair stepped toward her. "Catarine, we must go."

With a frown, she met her friend's gaze. "With his wounds, if I leave him he will die."

"And the tracks of the English knights we must follow?" her senior warrior asked again, his voice impatient.

Throughout her life she had been confident in her decisions, a trait the fey guards appreciated, but for the first time, she felt unsure. Neither could she forget Sionn's mention of the Otherworld law forbidding her to aid Lord Grey. 'Twas her choice, one filled with ramifications once her father learned of her actions—if she decided to remain and offer the earl aid.

On an unsteady breath she exhaled. "Atair, take Kuircc, Magnus, Ranulf, and Drax to the stone circle and spread out. If you find any trace of the English knights' passing, return to me."

Atair nodded, his mouth grim. "And when we return, if we have found a trail, you will leave with us?"

She stiffened. "Your question is unseemly."

"Aye," Atair agreed, "as is your request to remain and aid a huma—"

"Enough," she said with a covert gesture toward Lord Grey. They knew not this human, nor could trust him enough to speak freely of any mention in regards to the Otherworld.

With a frown, Atair motioned the four men to follow him. Their steps soft upon the earth, they hurried toward the towers of time-worn stone.

Sionn nodded. "I will be nearby." He moved several steps away.

"En-English knights?" Lord Grey asked, his confusion evident.

Catarine focused on the injured man. "Do nay talk or move about," she said, settling at his side. "I need to tend to your wounds."

"No time," he gasped, his face strained as he tried to sit up. "M-must save my king."

Irritated, she held his shoulders to prevent him from moving further. "If you attempt to follow your king now, you will die."

Die, mayhap, Trálin mused, but if he did not try to follow whoever had abducted King Alexander III and his queen, the royal couple's life could be in danger.

Still, if whoever had stormed Lock Leven Castle this night sought to claim the crown, why had they not killed the king and queen in their bed? Naught made sense, but by God he would learn the truth, and free them.

He shifted and pain slammed in his head. Trálin fought for consciousness. Bedamned, he must leave.

"Lord Grey?" the soft, lyrical voice called.

Through the murky haze of agony, Trálin focused on the woman who held him down. As if a spell cast, beneath the sheen of the fragile morning sunlight, he stared, transfixed by her beauty. The intensity of her gaze drew him, made him yearn to hold her against him and trust her with his secrets.

Shaken to consider what she made him feel, he dismissed the unwanted thoughts, owing them to his injuries. "I— I must discover where the men who took the king and queen are headed."

"Stirling Castle," she replied. "Now lay back and let me tend you."

Suspicion crawled through him. "How do you know where they are going?"

She hesitated. "I overheard the knights as they led King Alexander and Queen Margaret away."

"Overheard them? What else did they say?"

"Lord Grey," she said, her frustration clear. "If you lay back and allow me to care for you, you can ask all of the questions you wish."

"Will you answer them?" he asked, finding himself intrigued by this woman who looked as if a fairy, but held herself with the confident grace of a warrior. Neither did he miss her unusual garb. Her gown, a sturdy yet silky material, adorned with a belt holding several gemstones of striking quality. He hesitated. Who was she? From her garb, a person of wealth, or the daughter of a powerful noble. Regardless, with his vow to protect the king, she was a stranger whom he could not trust. At her silence, he eyed her hard. "You said if I allowed you to tend me, I may ask all of the questions I wish, but will you answer them?"

A smile touched her mouth. Fled. "Mayhap."

"Fine then." Gritting his teeth, he lay back, the cool, damp earth a welcoming balm.

"Now, do nae move." With efficient movements, she removed his mail and exposed his wounds. "I will be back in a trice." She started to rise.

"Lady Catarine."

The beautiful woman hesitated, her look wary.

"I heard one of the men address you as such. 'Tis your name, is it not?"

"Aye." Any warmth in her eyes faded. Her expression cautious, she stepped back.

"'Tis a name befitting your beauty, a name a man savors as it rolls across his tongue."

She raised a doubtful brow. "Methinks you have had much practice in wooing a woman. Save your strength, as you are far from what I seek in a man."

Her cool dismissal left him intrigued. Regardless of what she believed, never had he spoken to a woman in such regard. "Do you n-nae feel it?"

She shot a nervous look toward a lean warrior standing nearby with blond hair. At his comment, the warrior's eyes narrowed.

The beautiful woman met Trálin's gaze, hers wary. "I feel naught."

She lied. Of that he had no doubt. And what of her quick dismissal? She seemed dubious of his compliment. Why? As if with his king and queen abducted he had time to ponder such?

"I will be but a moment," she said. "I am fetching some water to cleanse your wounds."

Curious, Trálin watched for her reaction. "I practice naught but the truth."

"Do you?"

Her skeptical reply intrigued him further, and he watched her, wished for the full light of day to catch every nuance. "Aye."

She studied him a long moment, then left. A short while later she returned with a bowl crudely made from woven grass. She knelt beside him, tore a strip of cloth from the bottom of her garb, and gently began to rinse his wounds.

The scent of the grass and the soft shimmer of lilac filled his every breath. "What clan are you from?"

She flushed the injury with water, then pressed a damp cloth over his wound.

At the whip of pain he hissed. "Was that my answer?"

A slender brow arched. "Mayhap."

'Twould seem the lass was a mite more stubborn than most. Then, as the daughter of a noble, he shouldn't be surprised. Exhausted, Trálin laid his head back. "The men with you, who are they?"

Gentle fingers cleansed the exterior of another wound. "My guard."

Though quiet, he heard authority in her words. "You are nobility."

At his statement Catarine stilled. "Aye."

With his having traveled with the king since his youth, and now as King Alexander's personal guard, how had he missed seeing this stunning woman before? "Who is your father?"

She hesitated, then cleared her throat. "You would nae know him."

Blackness threatened. Trálin MacGruder kept consciousness. Barely. "Lady Catarine, as a Scottish noble in high standing, I have met all nobility in Scotland and most in England and France as well as several other countries. No doubt during my travels, at the very least, I have heard of your father."

Her full lips tightened.

"Is it such a mystery?" he asked, curious at what incited her reserve. By her burr she was Scottish, and by her words, learned.

Her mouth tightened. "How did you come to serve the Scottish king?"

Scottish king? Why would she refer to King Alexander III as the Scottish king and nae our king? God's teeth, mayhap her loyalties lay to another sovereign?

With the abduction of his king and queen this day, dare he answer her? More worrisome, he was the only person left from the king's personal guard that had seen King Alexander III and his queen abducted from Loch Leven Castle. And what of her hesitation before when he'd begun to ask questions of the king? Something was amiss here, and he bloody would find out.

"Lady Catarine," he said, his words cautious, "you stated you overheard the men who abducted King Alexander say they were taking him to Stirling Castle."

She stilled. "Aye."

"What else did you hear?"

"That . . ." She looked away.

By God he would know. "Tell me!"

Anger darkened her gaze as she whirled and faced him. "That if King Alexander doesna comply with their lord's request, he will die."

A retired Navy Chief, AGC(AW), DIANA COSBY is an international bestselling author of Scottish medieval romantic suspense. Diana has spoken at the Library of Congress, appeared at Lady Jane's Salon in New York City, in *Woman's Day*, on *Texoma Living Magazine*, on *USA Today*'s romance blog, "Happily Ever After," and on MSN.com.

After retiring from the Navy, Diana dove into her passion—writing romance novels. With thirty-four moves behind her, she was anxious to create characters who reflected the amazing cultures and people she's met throughout the world. In August 2012, she released her story "Highland Vampire" in the anthology *Born to Bite*, with stories by Hannah Howell and Erica Ridley. At the moment, she is working on the sixth book in the award-winning MacGruder Brothers series. Diana looks forward to the years of writing ahead and to meeting the amazing people who will share this journey.

Please visit her at www.dianacosby.com.

"Diana Cosby is superbly talented."
—Cathy Maxwell,
New York Times Bestselling Author

HIS CAPTIVE

Divided by loyalty,
drawn together
by desire...

DIANA COSBY

"Diana Cosby
is superbly talented."
—Cathy Maxwell,
New York Times
Bestselling Author

His
WOMAN

Some passions are too powerful to forget...

DIANA COSBY

His
CONQUEST

DIANA COSBY

DIANA
COSBY

His
DESTINY

CPSIA information can be obtained
at www.ICGtesting.com
Printed in the USA
BVOW11s1518230218
508708BV00001B/54/P